Candy Cane CHALLENGE

MELODY TYDEN

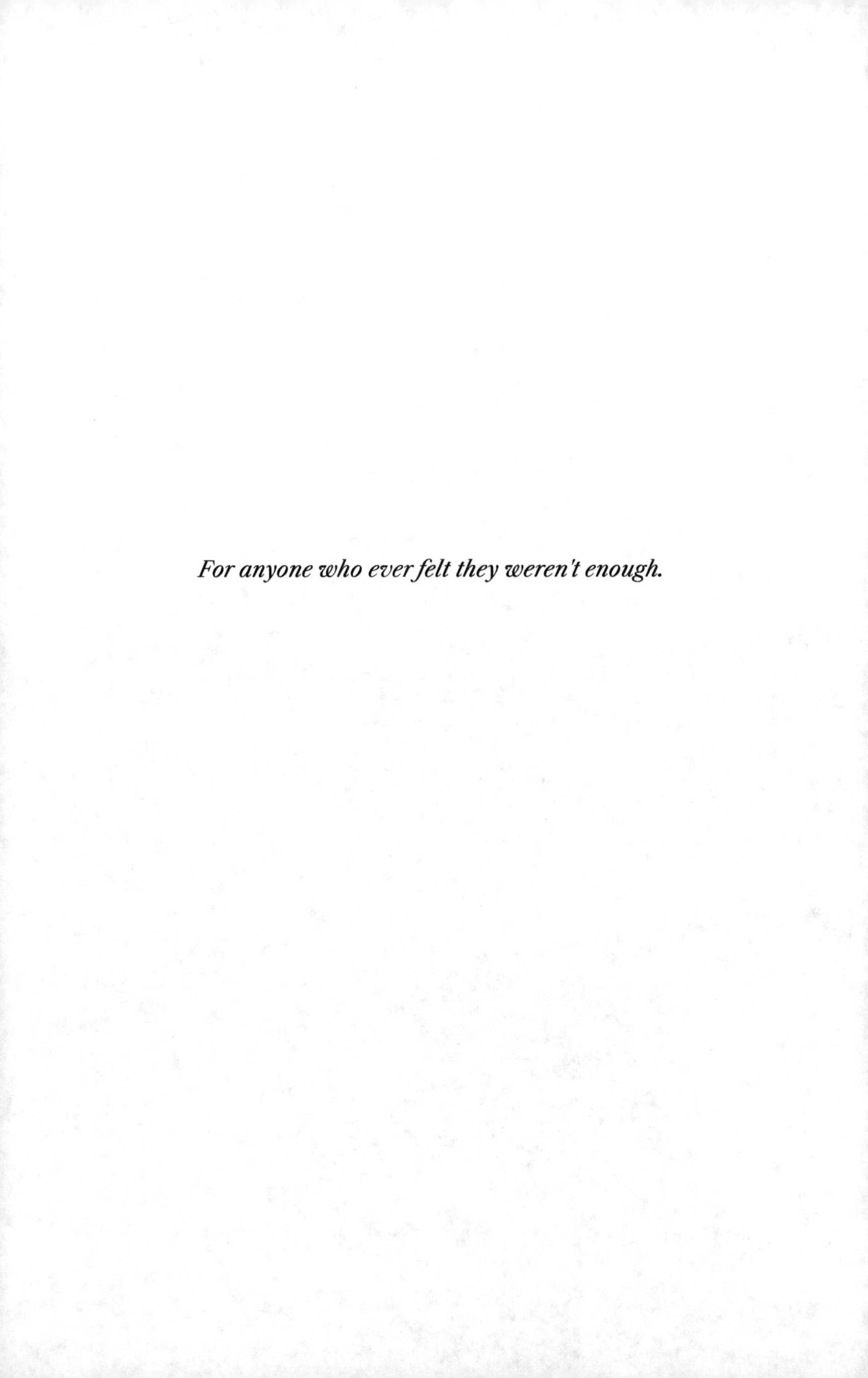

For anyone who ever felt they weren't enough.

Chapter One

A WEDDING

~Jackson~

People always said that love found you when you weren't looking for it, and I had to admit that couldn't be truer of my best friend, Cole, as I watched him tying the bow tie of his tuxedo. He met Gemma, the woman he was about to marry, when he least expected it, and they both did their best to deny the depth of their feelings for each other as long as possible. It had been incredibly frustrating to watch from the outside, but incredibly satisfying in the end when they finally admitted what I had known right from the beginning: they were absolutely made for each other.

Maybe there was a lesson in there for me, a reason why I hadn't had any luck finding the right woman yet. Maybe I tried too hard, but to stop looking would be easier said than done. I wanted to find my partner, the love of my life, and I didn't hide it. One-night stands and casual flings were not for me. When I went in, I went all in, and I wanted to find the woman who felt the same way about me. It didn't seem like too much to ask for.

"Does this look alright?" Cole asked me, giving himself a critical look in the mirror.

I couldn't help laughing. He never cared what anyone thought of anything he did, except when it came to Gemma. He wanted the day to be absolutely perfect for her, still not seeming to understand that all she really wanted was him.

"You know she'd be happy no matter how you looked, right? She probably wouldn't mind if you turned up naked."

"Don't tempt me," Cole muttered, straightening his tie again even though it had been perfectly straight to begin with. "Then we'd really give people something to talk about."

Despite Cole's efforts to keep the wedding relatively quiet, word had somehow leaked out and the paparazzi had gathered outside to take pictures of all the guests as they arrived. After all, it wasn't every day one of the richest men in the country got married, and to the daughter of a British earl, no less. That would be enough on its own, even before throwing in Gemma's previous engagement and the British media interest in it.

It frustrated Cole anyway. He preferred to have more control.

"People are happy for you," I pointed out. No one could say anything negative about two people so obviously in love with each other. "Let them take a picture or two. Don't let it ruin your day."

He sighed, closing his eyes briefly. "I've told you that I hate it when you're right, haven't I?"

"A few times," I replied drily, giving him a smug smile. "Now, what do you need me to do? We've still got about twenty minutes before the ceremony. Any last-minute best man duties?"

"I'm fine, but could you go make sure Gemma's got everything she needs? She left her phone back at the apartment so I can't call her."

I would bet anything that Gemma's maid of honour had everything under control, but I also knew that Cole would feel better if I went to take a look, so I didn't argue. Stepping out into the hall, I made my way down the corridor and across the church foyer to the room set aside for the bridal party to get ready.

My knock on the door was followed by a call of "just a minute" in a crisp, British accent. A moment later, the door opened just a crack, revealing a face I hadn't seen in almost a year.

"Well, well, well. Someone cleans up very nicely. I'm impressed, Jackson," she teased, opening the door wider as she looked me up and down. Holly Chapman was Gemma's best friend and colleague, as well as her maid of honour. She'd flown over from London for the wedding, but had only arrived late the day before so we hadn't had a chance to catch up yet. I was laying eyes on her for the first time since the previous December.

"No one will be looking at me when you look like that," I replied, returning the compliment sincerely. "You're a vision, Holly. It's wonderful to see you."

One year on, Holly was just as beautiful as I remembered. Her blond hair had been swept up into an elegant twist, her cheeks and lips perfectly pink to match the pale pink dress that hugged her curves in all the right places. Her skin was somehow still tanned and glowing in the middle of winter, and her blue eyes stood out against her slightly bronzed face, drawing me in just as quickly as they always had.

Holly and I had spent a fair bit of time together in London on the same business trip where Cole met Gemma. I had been attracted to her right from the start and she assured me the attraction was mutual, but to my disappointment, she wasn't interested in a relationship, especially not with an American only in town for a couple of weeks.

She suggested that we simply enjoy each other's company instead, including in bed, but that had never been my style. I declined her offer to get more physical and we spent time together seeing the city and getting to know one another, as well as spending time with Cole and Gemma. I loved every minute we spent together, and since returning home, she had crossed my mind far more often than I would ever admit. Even so, I had never reached out to her and she hadn't contacted me either. There didn't seem to be any point. I had plenty of friends I could call up when I needed a pleasant conversation. What I had wanted from her was something more, something that wouldn't happen if she didn't want it too.

"So, what brings you over to our side of the church?" Holly asked with a laugh. "Shouldn't you be keeping the groom from getting cold feet?"

"That's the least of my worries," I scoffed light-heartedly. "When Cole decides he's doing something, he doesn't look back. Nothing is stopping this wedding from taking place today."

That answer seemed to satisfy Holly as she gave me an approving nod. She wanted Gemma to be happy, and we both knew how happy Gemma and Cole made each other, so we had nothing to worry about on that end.

"What can I do for you, then?" she asked, reminding me that I still hadn't got to the point about what had brought me to her door.

"Cole just sent me to make sure everything's under control. Is there anything you need?"

"I think we're okay," she said before turning back into the room. "Gem? Jackson wants to know if you need anything?"

Gemma came around the corner of the door with a smile on her face, and the sight of her in her wedding dress nearly knocked me over. I put my hand to my heart, taking a staggered step back. Both women laughed at my dramatics, but I was only half-faking. She looked truly stunning.

Since Gemma moved to New York to live with Cole at the beginning of that year, she had become one of my best friends. The three of us often hung out together, and during the later stages of her pregnancy, whenever Cole had to travel for business, I stayed behind to take her to her doctor's appointments or get her whatever she needed.

Sometimes, it felt like I lived vicariously through their relationship, but seeing just how devoted they were to each other gave me hope. True love really did exist, and eventually, I would find it for myself. But not right at that second. Not until after I watched my best friend marry the love of his life.

"Cole's not going to know what hit him," I told Gemma sincerely, taking another moment to admire the sheer perfection of her dress and the way the whiteness of it brought out her flaming red hair and sparkling green eyes. No one would ever guess by looking at her in that dress that she gave birth less than three months ago to the most adorable little boy I had ever seen.

Cole was a damn lucky man.

"Alright, well, you better stop distracting us and let us get back to work," Holly instructed, shooing me back out into the hall. "We only have about ten minutes left. I guess I'll see you at the altar, Jackson."

She gave me a wink, and I grinned back, even though her words gave my heart a little twinge at just how close to my own secret desires they hit. "See you at the altar, Holly."

~Holly~

As soon as I closed the door behind Jackson, I let out a long breath, letting the tension in my shoulders release. Ever since Gemma asked me to be her maid of honour, I had been simultaneously dreading and anticipating that exact moment, the moment I came face-to-face with Jackson again.

I'd lost count of how many times over the last year he'd crossed my mind, usually late at night when I went home to my flat all alone. Lying in the dark, I remembered his warm smile, the way the corners of his eyes crinkled and his adorable dimples came out when he laughed, which happened often, and the way his lips felt when they brushed against mine the last time I saw him, the night we said goodbye.

Over and over again, I questioned whether I had been wrong to push him away as I had. He seemed so sincere when he said he felt a connection between us, that he wanted something deeper than just a casual fling, and I could still see the look of sadness in his deep blue eyes when I said I wasn't interested.

However, I'd heard promises that sounded sincere before. They always sounded sincere in the beginning, but sooner or later, it would all fall apart. I had been through that pain too many times and I had learned my lesson. I wouldn't get my hopes up again.

Undying love was all well and good for someone like Gemma, and I couldn't be happier that she'd found it, even if I still found her whole relationship with Cole a little mystifying. But I also knew that kind of happy-ever-after wasn't in the cards for me, at least not with a guy like Jackson, so I cut it off before it even had a chance to start. I had to protect my heart.

"Alright, Hols?" Gemma asked me with a look of concern on her face. She'd always been far too tuned in to my mood. Even though we hadn't spent much time together in person since she moved to New York, she still knew me better than anyone.

"Of course," I lied, putting on my best cheeky smile. My sad love life had no place in her wedding day. "Just trying to decide how it's even possible that that man is better looking than he was a year ago."

Gemma's worry dissolved and she laughed, convinced by my joking that I only had Jackson's appearance on my mind. And I wasn't lying about that part: since I saw him last, Jackson had cut his hair shorter and grown a short beard and it really suited him. Combined with the tux he wore for his role as best man, it made him look almost impossibly suave. My only concern was that the beard made it harder to see his sexy dimples when he smiled, and that was a real shame. I had been hoping to get a few more memories of those to keep me company when I went home to London in a few weeks' time.

At that moment, though, all I needed to focus on was ensuring everything was perfect for my best friend's big day. I double-checked Gemma's dress, hair and make-up, but I didn't need to do a thing; there couldn't be a more beautiful bride. Just a few minutes later, one of the ushers knocked on the door to let us know that they were ready for us.

"This is it!" I exclaimed, giving her one last squeeze. "Last chance to bail and head back to London with me."

Gemma laughed without a hint of hesitation. "I think it's a bit too late for that. Besides, my two favourite men in the world are out there waiting for me."

For a second, I thought she was talking about Jackson, until I realized that of course she meant Cole and their son, Noah. I really needed to stop thinking about Jackson.

Gemma and I headed to the back of the church to wait for our cue. She only had me as a bridesmaid since they were keeping the wedding fairly low-key, or at least as low-key as possible for two people of their status. Gemma had chosen the beautiful and historic Trinity Church in lower Manhattan for their ceremony because, of all the churches they'd visited in New York, it felt most like the churches we'd grown up attending at home in England.

The opening strains of their beautiful wedding song began to play over the church's audio system and I gave Gemma a big smile. "Ready?"

"Ready," she agreed, her eyes shining with excitement.

Turning around, I took a deep breath as I stepped into the church, all eyes in the room on me. Gemma and I had talked about walking in together since she didn't have anyone to give her away. Neither her father nor her brother was attending the wedding, and neither of them deserved to be a part of her day anyway. She hadn't heard a word from either of them since she left the UK.

So, she had considered the two of us walking in side-by-side, but in the end, I insisted on coming in separately. This was her day; all the attention should be on her when she walked in.

Wearing a sincere, happy smile, I walked slowly down the aisle, past all the beautiful fresh white and red flowers decorating the end of each pew. Of course Gemma had gone with red and white Christmas colours for her theme, but she let me choose a pink dress since pink went far better with my colouring than red did. As a combination of red and white, it worked.

The lyrics of the wedding song filled the air of the beautiful stone church as I walked, reminding me once again just how perfect Gemma and Cole were for each other. They had chosen the song In Whatever Time We Have, and the words highlighted that although life could be navigated alone, it would be better to have your partner at your side. Who would want to be alone?

Tears unexpectedly pricked at my eyes as the words hit home. That was exactly what I had decided for myself: I *did* want to be alone. From my point of view, it seemed preferable to the alternative of getting my heart broken over and over again. Reminding myself firmly that this day was *not* about me, I quickly blinked the tears away and turned up the brightness of my smile instead.

As I approached the altar, my gaze landed on Cole standing there, looking as serious and brooding as always. Gemma assured me he was capable of laughter, and I figured she must be telling me the truth, but I hadn't seen any proof of that. I wasn't looking for him anyway; the person I really sought was the man next to him, the one standing there watching me with an appreciative smile on his face, as if I were the only woman in the room.

What would it be like to be the one walking down the aisle with Jackson waiting for me at the end? For just a second, I let myself dream before filing the memory away as just another one in the list of my beautiful but impossible dreams.

When I reached the front, I took my place on the opposite side of the altar from Jackson and Cole, leaving a space for the person everyone was waiting for. The whole congregation got to their feet and a hushed gasp spread through the crowd as Gemma appeared. I could hardly blame them. She looked absolutely stunning. Though everyone in the whole building gaped at her, she only had eyes for one man, the one next to me who stared right back at her, his mouth hanging open in awe.

I caught Jackson's eye and he nodded his head towards Cole and raised his eyebrows, making me giggle. He saw the same thing I did: Cole was completely smitten.

The ceremony sped by, each part of it beautiful and emotional. Gemma and Cole wrote their own vows and there wasn't a dry eye in the place as they described what they meant to each other. I had come prepared with a few tissues tucked into my cleavage, so I pulled one out as discreetly as I could to dab at my eyes. As I tucked it away again, I felt someone's eyes on me, and glanced over to see Jackson watching me, his own eyes looking a little watery. We shared a quick smile before I looked away again.

Noah slept almost all the way through the ceremony, but then, with perfect timing, when the minister asked if there were any objections, his loud wail filled the church, making everyone laugh. Cole's sister, Isabel, who'd been watching him, quickly excused herself, taking him to the back of the church to calm him while the minister carried on with the ceremony.

Almost before I knew it, they were pronounced man and wife and with one hand on her waist and the other around her neck, Cole gave Gemma a passionate, dominating kiss that nearly took *my* breath away even though I only watched it happen.

They walked together back down the aisle to the cheers and applause of everyone gathered, and Jackson walked over to me and offered his arm with a warm smile.

"Looks like it's our turn now. Shall we?"

~Jackson~

I could hardly believe they'd actually done it. Not that I ever had any doubt that Gemma and Cole were meant to be together, but with everything they'd both been through with their past engagements, to see them officially married and looking so happy together as they shared their first dance at the wedding reception seemed almost like a miracle.

We were in the Rainbow Room on the 65th floor of Rockefeller Centre, and Cole had rented the whole place out for the night. No cameras were allowed besides the official photographers; everyone had to surrender their phones at the door. The New York skyline twinkled in the distance, the Empire State Building lit up in red and white as if it were part of their wedding decorations. Maybe it was, who could say? I wouldn't put it past Cole to have arranged for those colours to be shown that evening. There didn't seem to be anything he couldn't do if he really wanted to.

My eyes drifted around the room before landing on Holly standing across from me on the other side of the small dance floor that had been created, watching the happy couple with a soft smile on her face. Seeing that smile pulled me back to the first night we met, just over a year earlier.

Cole and I ran into Gemma in the hallway outside a Christmas party, and she looked just as gorgeous then as she did at her wedding, even if her dress was completely different. I told Cole that night that Gemma was my dream girl, but that didn't stop him from going up to his hotel room with her that night. It had happened before that Cole caught the interest of a girl I would have killed for a chance with, but I never held it against him. He didn't do it on purpose. People were just drawn to him, they always had been. Hell, even I was. Something about being around him made anyone in his presence feel special. It felt invigorating in a completely indefinable way.

But the following night, we went out to an industry event and ran into Gemma again, and that was when I met Holly.

Although I said just the night before that Gemma was my ideal woman, I had to make an immediate mental retraction of that statement when I laid eyes on Holly. With her sleek blonde hair and bright blue eyes, and the way her elegant dress wrapped around her body, showing off every perfect curve, she looked like something straight out of a dream.

I greeted her warmly and she returned my smile with one of her own that nearly made me weak in the knees.

Something special lingered in her smile and the way her eyes twinkled, looking somehow fearless and vulnerable at the same time. I could see in that look the promise of all I'd ever wanted.

If only she'd felt the same.

As she caught me staring at her across the wedding dance floor, she flashed me that same smile, a hint of a challenge in her eyes as she gestured towards the dance floor with her head. With the first dance wrapping up, we were expected to join in as best man and maid of honour, and we walked across the open space of the dance floor towards each other like two magnets being drawn together until we met in the middle.

"May I have this dance?" I asked formally, bowing to her in a way that I knew would make her laugh.

Sure enough, her beautiful blue eyes shone as she grinned. "Do you know how to dance? Maybe we should have practiced this ahead of time."

"I'm available for practice whenever you like," I teased her back, holding out my hand, and she stepped into my arms like we'd done the move a million times before.

"So, they really did it," Holly said as her hand slid over the top of my shoulder, close to my neck, sending a tingle of excitement through my body. "After being engaged to Edwin for six years, I never would have guessed that Gemma would be married to someone else a year after breaking up with him."

"Sometimes, you just know when a thing is right," I pointed out. "It's got nothing to do with time."

A hint of sadness flashed in Holly's eyes as she looked away from me. "Or sometimes, things that seem right fade over time."

That was the biggest glimpse she'd ever given me into the world inside her head, but before I could ask her to explain what she meant, she turned back to me with her smile back on, as if that little moment had never happened at all.

"I'm here for three weeks now, until New Year's." I knew that already; Gemma had mentioned it to me several times. "I know Gem's got some plans for me, but she's hardly a native New Yorker. What are the can't-miss things I need to see while I'm here?"

Taking the bait, I began to tell her about some of my favourite places, the list growing bigger as I kept thinking of more things she should see.

"I think I'm going to need you to write that all down." She laughed as I twirled her across the floor.

"I'd be happy to show you around," I offered, completely unplanned. "I've taken most of the rest of the month off. Since Cole's out of the office, there won't be any major deals going on, so my work can all wait too. I might have to stop in every now and then, but most of my time is free."

Holly looked up at me in surprise, her face tantalizingly close to mine as we moved to the music. "You don't have any plans? What about your family? Aren't you going to spend the holidays with them?"

The details of my family life were hardly the kind of light-hearted talk suitable for a wedding dance, so I kept my answer vague. "I mostly planned to relax. I've got a few days booked in to babysit Noah, but otherwise, I'm pretty flexible. If you're interested, I'm at your service."

She raised an eyebrow at me, a smile playing on her lips as her gaze dropped down my body and back up again. "Exactly what kind of services are you offering?"

I knew she meant it as a joke. Flirty and upbeat had always been our dynamic, but after everything I'd been thinking about all day and watching my best friend get his happy-ever-after, I couldn't bring myself to smile back. The implication was perfectly clear: Holly only wanted me in the way she always had, and nothing more. I hadn't really expected her position to have changed, or at least I had told myself that I hadn't expected it, but it stung anyway to hear her say it.

Luckily, the music drew to an end just then, so I gave her a quick kiss on the cheek to avoid answering. "Thanks for the dance, Holly." Without giving her a chance to reply, I turned around and headed for the outdoor terrace, needing to get some air.

After a few minutes of pushing through the crowd, I finally made it out into the night air and breathed deeply as I tried to push down the lump in my throat. Why was I so disappointed? She'd made it clear enough the year before that she only saw me as a good time. Why should I have hoped for anything else?

"Hey, are you okay?" Holly's British accent cut through my self-pity, forcing me back to the present. She stood just behind me as I turned around, a worried look on her face. "Did I say something wrong?"

"Of course not," I lied. "It was just getting a little stuffy in there."

"You're not a very good liar." She saw through me immediately, but her expression was soft and kind. "You don't have to tell me if you don't want to, but can I at least make it up to you?"

She held out her hand with a peace offering: one of the candy cane favours Gemma had ordered to complement the red and white colour scheme. They were raspberry vodka flavoured rather than peppermint and dangerously good. Gemma and I had tasted a few a couple of nights earlier and managed to get ourselves a little tipsy, though she had a better excuse than I did since she hadn't been drinking for the last year because of her pregnancy.

"Thanks." I took the candy from her and opened it while she unwrapped one of her own. Turning back to the view of the skyline, I put the end of the candy cane in my mouth and Holly did the same with hers, coming to stand beside me.

"You grew up here in Manhattan, right?" she asked as we looked out over the city lights together.

"Right," I confirmed. We had talked about that briefly the year before. "Up in Washington Heights. Born and bred."

"Have you ever wanted to live anywhere else?"

I looked over at her, trying to gauge if her question held a deeper meaning, but her eyes remained focused on the skyscrapers as she twirled the candy cane absent-mindedly in her mouth.

"I can't really imagine calling anywhere else home, at least not permanently. This city has an energy all its own. It's like it won't let you just sit back and wait for life, you need to go out and find it. I've travelled a lot through my work and I've never found anywhere like it."

I sucked a second longer on my candy cane before biting off the end of it, and Holly turned to me with a grin. "That was hardly more than a minute! I thought you'd last longer."

I had no idea what she was talking about. "Last longer at what?"

"Your candy cane," she explained, still smiling as she gestured to the piece that was left in my hand. "At school, we used to try to suck the whole candy cane without taking a bite, and it's a lot harder than you think. It's so tempting to snap it off. You need to have a lot of self-control."

"I have plenty of self-control," I teased her right back. "You just didn't tell me what we were doing. I bet I could hold out longer than you if you'd told me the game."

Something flashed in her eyes, looking almost like desire mixed with hesitation. "I'm not so sure about that, Jackson. I bet I could get you to give in first if I really tried."

She stepped closer to me and her hand brushed against the front of my pants, subtly but obviously not accidentally. Combined with what she'd said on the dance floor, her meaning couldn't be clearer: she still wanted to get into bed with me, but she had no idea how much self-control I really had.

The time had come for me to be clear about that too. I took hold of her hand and kissed the back of it before looking her straight in the eye. "Holly, nothing has changed for me. I still think you're beautiful and fun and smart and all-around amazing, and I would love to give whatever this is between us a proper shot. But I'm not going to sleep with you unless we're in some kind of committed relationship."

Her lips pursed, showing her disappointment. "I really don't understand," she said, the frustration clear in her voice as well. "You just said you find me attractive, and I've made it pretty clear that I feel the same. Why can't we just have some fun and then see where it goes?"

"Because that's not the kind of guy I am, Holly. I told you that last year."

"You did, but it still doesn't make sense to me." Her brow furrowed as she tried to understand. "You're not the guy who does a one-night stand, fine. What kind of guy are you, then, Jackson Hanmer?"

There was a challenge in the question and I took a deep breath before deciding to tell her the truth, a truth I'd hardly told anyone before.

"I'm a virgin."

Chapter Two

THE CHALLENGE

~Holly~

Beneath the New York night sky, I stared blankly at Jackson's handsome face, certain I had misheard him.

He *couldn't* be a virgin. Incredibly hot, successful, funny, charming, pretty much the perfect guy, he must have had women throwing themselves at him for years. It just didn't seem possible.

"Does that mean something different over here than it does in England?" I asked, only half-joking as I tried to wrap my head around what he'd just said.

He chuckled softly, his eyes never leaving mine. "No, I'm pretty sure it means the same thing. I've never slept with anyone, Holly."

Well, that seemed to mean my secret fantasies for that night were not going to become a reality, but I still didn't understand. "Why not?" I blurted out before I could stop myself. "Were you in prison or something? In space? On some kind of solo underwater trip for the past ten years?"

He smiled wider, looking genuinely amused, but something else lingered in his eyes too: that same vulnerability I had seen during our last conversation before he left London. The look that had haunted me ever since that day.

"It's not that I haven't had the opportunity," he said drily. "You should know that better than anyone. It's simply been my choice."

I did know that. I had offered, and I was sure dozens, or even hundreds of other women had as well. What on earth was he waiting for?

"Is it some kind of religious thing?" I asked, still completely confused and thrown off by his confession.

Again, he laughed. "No. I'm no monk, if that's what you're thinking. It's not that I set out to save myself or anything. When I was 16, I would have died if you told me I was going to be a 28-year-old virgin. That was never part of my plan."

"Then, what happened?" I prompted. "Shouldn't you have lost your virginity at your prom? I thought that's what all American teenagers did?"

I meant it as a joke, but the way Jackson's face tightened made me immediately regret my words.

"I'm sorry, I didn't mean..."

"It's fine, Holly." He gave me another smile, though this one felt a bit more forced. "I intended to, actually. I'd been seeing a girl for a few months. I got the hotel room and the limo, all the trimmings. I spent a fortune on it. And I didn't grow up like Cole, where money like that was no big deal. I saved for months to be able to afford it all."

"So, what happened?" My voice was quiet, but even so, Jackson glanced around us at the other random people out on the terrace. They were all caught up in their own conversations or looking out over the city. No one seemed to be paying us any attention.

When he felt certain we wouldn't be overheard, Jackson turned back to me. "She spent the night in Cole's room instead."

"What?!" The word came out much louder than I intended, and despite Jackson's precautions, a few people turned to look at us, but I was so outraged that I didn't care. I did, however, lower my voice before continuing. "He stole your girlfriend at your prom? And you're still friends with him? I'm going to give him a piece of my mind right now..."

I had turned halfway around before Jackson grabbed my arm, holding me in place and surprising me with his firmness. I hadn't realized he was quite that strong.

"Holly, it happened more than ten years ago," he reminded me, sounding more like his usual easygoing self with an amused tinge to his voice. "I don't think you need to yell at him about it on his wedding night."

He had a point, and I turned back sheepishly. "Alright, fine, but please tell me you tore him a new one at the time."

His gaze dropped to his hand that still rested on my arm, and he let me go while avoiding my gaze. "It wouldn't have done any good. It wasn't his fault."

Immediately, my back went up again. "How could it not be his fault? He just tripped and fell into her vagina?"

Jackson laughed, looking back up at me in amusement. "I don't think so, no, although that's an interesting image."

"So, explain it to me," I requested, crossing my arms as I waited for his reply. "How does your girlfriend end up in your best friend's bed and it's not his fault?"

Jackson sighed, rubbing a hand down his beard, which drew my attention to his strong jawline. With every gesture, he grew more attractive, and I had to force myself not to stare. "He didn't know she was my girlfriend. She went to another school and I'd never introduced them. All the girls at our school would try to make friends with me to get to Cole. Between his money and the whole bad-boy vibe he had going on, girls were all over him. They were falling at his feet. When I met this girl, I thought she was different. I didn't think she even knew Cole's name."

My stomach started to sink as I began to fill in the blanks. "But she did know?"

He nodded. "Yeah. It turned out I was just her ticket in. She ditched me as soon as we got to prom and Cole disappeared too. Later, I found out they'd hooked up along with his own date. Cole thought she was just some random girl. He never knew she came there as my date."

I blew a long breath out through my mouth. I supposed Cole really couldn't be blamed for that, though the whole situation still seemed surreal to me. "Teenaged Cole was a bit of a horndog, huh?"

Jackson laughed again, appreciating my humour as always. I never had to explain myself to him like I had to with other men I'd dated. We always seemed to be on the same wavelength.

"You do know how Cole and Gemma met, right? Some things really don't change."

I had to concede that, and as our laughter died off, I thought over what he'd just told me. As enlightening as it had been, it didn't answer my main question. "Alright, so prom sucked," I summed up bluntly. "I can see why you didn't get laid that night. But what about every night since then? You must have had other girlfriends?"

He nodded slowly, the soft light from inside the building playing across his handsome face. "Of course. But I didn't have any for a while after that, not for a few years. I went on dates but I didn't get close to anyone. That whole experience, being used by someone I thought I could trust, it made me a bit paranoid. I know that probably sounds silly."

He looked down at the end, out of embarrassment, it seemed, so I quickly reached out and took his hand. "It's not silly at all. I get it, Jackson. Honestly."

I knew all about the feeling of not having been good enough for someone and being passed over for someone else. If I could relate to any of what he'd said, that would be it.

"But eventually, you got serious with someone?" I prompted, still not sure how we got from the trauma of prom to a decade later with him still a virgin.

He nodded again. "Yes, but for one reason or another, we just never got to that point. If you don't mind, I'd rather not go through the whole litany of my failed relationships right now."

His words were accompanied by a smile, but I heard the hint of loneliness underneath, another feeling I recognized all too well.

"And eventually, it just began to feel like I'd waited so long, I wanted to make sure that when it finally happened, it turned out to be something worth waiting for. I didn't want it to be a random hookup or a woman I'd see a few times and then never see again. I wanted it to be 'the one'. Which probably sounds hopelessly lame…"

I cut him off, reaching up to run my hand along his beard the same way he'd done earlier. "I think it's sweet."

His eyes closed at my touch, making my heart contract. He really was a good guy. It seemed impossible that he hadn't found someone who recognized that yet, someone far less broken than me who could give him what he deserved.

"Look, Jackson, I'll be honest with you. I don't think I'm 'the one'. However, I also think that fixating on that might be holding you back a bit. You've built it up in your head so much, thinking that you have to find the perfect woman, that you're missing out on the other things you could be experiencing and enjoying. I'm not even sure you *can* know if someone's the one until you know that you enjoy each other in bed."

"What makes you so sure you're not the one I've been waiting for?" he asked, the sincerity in his deep blue eyes nearly taking my breath away. It could almost make me believe it might be possible.

Almost.

"Because I know myself," I answered, forcing myself to hold his gaze. For a long beat, neither of us spoke. Though we were only inches apart, I could feel the distance that existed, the gulf between what he wanted and what I could provide. It seemed too large to cross, but maybe somewhere, there might be a bridge across, at least temporarily. "I know my strengths and weaknesses, and one of my strengths is that I know my way around the bedroom. I could show you what you've been missing."

When his jaw clenched and his body shifted, I knew I'd succeeded in turning him on a little bit, just as I'd hoped. I pressed ahead while I had that advantage.

"So, I have a proposal for you. Try a few things with me. Just a few warm-up exercises, not the main event. I'm not going to force you to have sex with me if you don't want to, but I think that once you get that candy cane in your mouth, you might not be able to resist taking a bite."

I raised my eyebrows at him in challenge, teasing him as usual but also secretly praying that I hadn't pushed it too far. For some unknown reason, knowing about his inexperience made me want him more than ever. I wanted to be the one to show him how good it could be. To be entirely truthful, the thought of being the first woman to make him come had my body tingling in anticipation.

Jackson swallowed hard, thinking things over before giving me a tight smile. "Counter-proposal?"

"Sure," I readily agreed. I would entertain whatever he might have in mind if it meant I could get at least some of what I wanted.

"You let me take you out. Dates, romance, the whole nine yards. Let me woo you, Holly. And after each date, we can try something I haven't done before. However, we won't go all the way unless you agree to be my girlfriend."

As he had, I took a moment to think it over. The idea of leading him on when I knew nothing would come of it made me a little uncomfortable, but I'd been as honest as I could be about my feelings. The payoff certainly seemed worth it. "And you're that certain you can resist me?" I teased.

His eyes sparkled in reply. "I told you I've got excellent self-control. The real question is: can you resist me?"

Honestly, that *was* a good question. Looking into his handsome face, for the first time, I didn't feel entirely sure, but given the incentive he'd offered, I was still willing to try.

"Are we setting a deadline?" I asked, and Jackson grinned at my implicit acceptance.

"How about Christmas Eve? I'll plan something special. If you agree to be with me then, you can spend the night with me."

"Or you might just invite me to stay anyway," I countered, giving him a cheeky smile of my own which made him shake his head in amusement. "Alright, that sounds fine to me. I'm in."

I held out my hand to shake his but Jackson ignored it, leaning in to kiss me instead; a sweet, lingering kiss that made my heart beat faster and all the hairs on my arm stand up.

"Game on, Holly," he whispered in my ear before walking away, heading back into the reception.

Left on my own, I looked out over the skyline, at the lights twinkling almost in rhythm to the dancing of the butterflies in my stomach. No one had made my stomach flutter like that for a very long time, and I'd been determined to run far away if it ever happened again. Instead, I'd just agreed to run headfirst towards the cause of it.

What on earth had I gotten myself into?

~Jackson~

My heart beat so loudly as I walked back into the reception that it seemed entirely possible that anyone close to me would hear it even over the chatter of conversation and the melodies drifting over from the dance floor.

What had I just done? Although I was thrilled that Holly had agreed to go out with me, even if only for a specified time period, I couldn't ignore the worry inside me either. Would I really be able to say no to her? Although I was sure I couldn't even imagine everything that she had in mind, I could guess at a few things she might want to try with me, and just the thought of them had me straining dangerously against the zipper of my tuxedo pants. If we got to a point where we were naked together with her trying to seduce me, did I really have the willpower to turn her down?

Could *anyone* resist?

One thing was for certain: I needed to come up with a plan to make sure I won her over before she took me down.

And for the time being, I definitely needed to distract myself before anyone noticed the situation I was in. So, I put on my best charming smile and worked the crowd for a while, visiting with Cole's family, all of whom considered me practically one of their own, as well as many of our work colleagues.

Occasionally, my eyes scanned the room for Holly, but I never caught more than a glimpse of her blonde hair or a stray note of her laughter as she did the same as me, chatting and laughing with the gathered guests though she hardly knew anyone there before that night. No one could accuse her of being a wallflower. Finally, after at least an hour of schmoozing, I headed to the bar for a drink, but before I could place my order, Gemma suddenly appeared in front of me.

"There you are!" she exclaimed, sounding like she'd already hit the bar a few times without me. "I thought you'd run off without giving me a dance."

"Never." My brow furrowed as I took in her flushed cheeks and bright eyes. "Are you feeling okay? How many candy canes have you had?"

She giggled, letting me know I'd hit the nail on the head. Gemma wasn't usually the giggly kind. "Not enough. Come and dance with me."

She pulled me towards the dance floor before I could protest that I hadn't had a chance to get a drink yet. An upbeat song played as we joined the dancers, but the tempo quickly changed to a slower one and Gemma leaned fully against me, letting me take nearly all her weight.

"Where's your husband?" I asked her, scanning the room for Cole. Maybe he didn't realize just how much of a lightweight his new bride was these days?

She giggled at that too. "My husband," she repeated, scrunching up her nose in amusement at the sound of Cole's new title, "is probably out finding some Christmas lights."

"What?" I couldn't even be sure she knew what she was saying. Why would Cole need Christmas lights?

She pulled my head down so she could whisper in my ear. "He promised to tie me up with them later."

"Okay, Gemma, too much information," I told her, trying not to laugh. She definitely wouldn't have told me that sober. "I think we better cut you off."

She just grinned at me, completely unbothered by what she'd just revealed. "You need to find someone to tie you up too, Jackson."

"Do I?" I asked, growing more amused by the second. "Is that what I need?"

"Yes." She nodded solemnly before dissolving into giggles again. "Well, maybe not that exactly. But you need someone who will make you lose control. Someone who's going to let that inner beast out."

She clawed playfully at my chest while I shook my head at her, but her words brought thoughts of Holly rushing back to my mind, front and centre. If anyone could make me lose control, it would definitely be her.

Holly was such a mix of everything I found appealing in a woman. Quick with a laugh and a joke, she could also be fierce when she needed to be. She was a complete professional in the office but a little bit wild outside of it. I knew she could have me eating out of her hand in an instant, but something lurked in her eyes, something I caught in those rare unguarded moments, that made me want to wrap her up in my arms and take care of her.

I hadn't won her heart the previous December in London, but then, I hadn't really tried either, not like I planned to do this time around. We had hung out together but we hadn't dated. If I gave it my full effort, surely, I could sweep her off her feet.

And Gemma might be just the person who could help me with that, especially if I could get some information out of her in her current less-than-guarded state.

"I think *your* inner beast needs a nap," I teased the bride as we continued to dance, or at least sway clumsily to the music. "But can I pick your brain about something? I promised to show Holly around a bit while she's in town. What kind of things does she like to do?"

Gemma's eyes sparkled, making me immediately wary of whatever might be about to come out of her mouth. "Well, she doesn't like to be tied up, but she would probably do it to you if you asked nicely."

"I'll keep that in mind," I replied, rolling my eyes which only made her laugh more. "I'm serious though, Gemma. What does Holly like?"

"Hmmm..." Gemma hummed thoughtfully, though I had no idea if she was actually thinking about my question or if her mind was still on the Christmas lights and her plans with Cole later. "Well, she likes drinking and men. That's a good place to start."

Getting a straight answer out of her might be harder than I thought. "Where does she like to go drinking?"

"Places with drinks!" She laughed so loudly at her own attempt at a joke that a few people nearby turned to look at us. I just shrugged my shoulders at them while they smiled at the bride indulgently.

"Okay, Miss Comedian, let's try this again: imagine Holly could do anything she wanted to do tomorrow. What would she choose to do?"

Gemma did her best to concentrate, but her expression melted into confusion. "She's coming to brunch with me tomorrow."

My eyes closed in a mixture of frustration and amusement. "It doesn't have to be tomorrow. Pick any day."

Her face scrunched up further as she tried to understand my words. "No, I'm pretty sure the brunch is tomorrow."

Just as I concluded this conversation wouldn't get me anywhere, Cole arrived to retrieve his new wife.

"Come on, Gorgeous." He hooked his arm around her waist and pulled her away from me. "Let's get out of here. The fresh air will sober you up a bit."

"The fresh air will sober you up a bit," Gemma repeated in her best attempt at mimicking Cole's New York accent, and that time, I laughed out loud along with her.

"Almost nailed it," I assured her as Cole simply raised his eyes to the ceiling.

"Don't encourage her," he muttered at me.

"Or what?" I challenged. "You'll tie me up with your lights too?"

Gemma snorted and, to my shock, Cole actually blushed. It had to be a miracle. I had *never* seen Cole Stamer blush before.

"Someone has definitely had too much." He turned to Gemma with a much softer expression. "Say goodnight, Gemma."

"Goodnight, Gemma," she and I both said in unison, both of us seeing that coming a mile away, and we cracked up again.

Cole rolled his eyes once more. "You two are spending entirely too much time together."

Although he meant it as a joke and not in a negative way at all, I couldn't help feeling the sting of the words anyway. Because they were true. I had been spending far too much time with the both of them. They were married and had a baby, and it was really well past time that I focused on my own life instead.

"We'll see you tomorrow for brunch, right?" Cole asked me as they both turned away.

"Absolutely," I agreed. I'd been planning on it anyway, but with the confirmation that Holly would be there, I definitely wouldn't miss it. "Congratulations again, both of you."

Cole gave me one of his rare, genuine smiles. "Thanks, Jackson. Enjoy the rest of your night."

They walked away from me but I wasn't alone for long. I knew Holly had come up beside me before I even saw her. Something about her mere proximity made the skin on the back of my neck tingle.

"Did Cole actually just smile?" she asked, sounding so surprised that I had to laugh.

"It's unusual, but it does happen. They're heading out now, so I think we're officially off the hook for our best man and maid of honour duties. How are you doing? Are you still jet-lagged from your flight?"

As soon as I mentioned it, she stifled a yawn before slapping my arm playfully. "Thanks for reminding me. Now, I'm feeling it. I don't suppose you'll be a gentleman and help me back to my hotel?"

"Of course I will." I was ready to go too. "You're at the Plaza, right?"

I didn't really need to ask. I already knew, and she probably knew I knew, but she didn't call me out on it.

"That's right," she confirmed instead. "Can we walk from here?"

"We could. It depends how much you want to walk in those shoes, I suppose."

She groaned as she looked down at the high heels that made her legs look absolutely incredible. "Okay, they weren't bothering me either until you just mentioned them. Have you got some kind of magic power of suggestion?"

I certainly hoped so. That would make the two weeks ahead go a lot better for me.

"Let's get a cab, then," I suggested. "Come on, Holly. Time to show me where you're going to be spending the night."

~Holly~

The December air felt chilly on my stocking-covered legs as we stepped out of the heated lobby of Rockefeller Center onto the busy street outside.

"Why are there so many people?" I asked in confusion. The crowds wouldn't be out of place during rush hour in Leicester Square back home, but it must have been nearly midnight. Although I'd heard that New York was the city that didn't sleep, it still seemed a little extreme.

Jackson just laughed at the question. "Come here, I'll show you."

He took my hand and led me down the street to where the crowd swelled even more. His hand felt warm around mine, and as we walked, I caught a glimpse of our reflection in the windows of the building next to us. We looked good together, I had to admit, especially in our formal evening wear. Anyone who happened to see us together would certainly think we were a couple. On the surface, we were a great match.

Reaching the end of the huge building we had just been inside, we rounded the corner and I couldn't help gasping in surprise.

In front of us stood the biggest Christmas tree I'd ever seen, towering above a lighted skating rink where more trees and lights twinkled. People filled every foot of the plaza, holding take-away coffee cups with their mittened hands, wearing toques and scarves, and taking selfies with the tree.

It looked just like every New York Christmas film I'd ever seen.

Jackson beamed at my stunned reaction. "You couldn't come to Rockefeller Center and not see the tree. I'd offer to take you skating, but it's a little too late tonight."

His words immediately reminded me of how we had gone skating together the previous December at Somerset House in London. I could still almost feel his hands around my waist as he pushed me across the ice, racing against Gemma and Cole. That had been the closest he'd come to really touching me other than the occasional casual hug.

That would change, very soon, since he'd agreed to let me show him some things he'd never tried before. The thought of it immediately made my body heat up, the chill of the cool air forgotten as a warm, pulsing heat spread through me.

How soon were we starting our little challenge? He had told me it was 'game on' back up on the terrace and at the moment, we were heading to my hotel. Could there be a chance for something to happen that night? My thighs pressed tighter together beneath my dress to try to relieve the growing ache brought on by the mere possibility.

Even if we didn't go too far, I would take anything he wanted to give me that night. Standing there in his tux and dress coat, his warm eyes smiling back at me, he looked like something out of a film himself.

"Let's get that cab," he said, reading my mind, or maybe just the look in my eyes. At least, I thought he had, until he added, "You must be tired."

Maybe he couldn't tell what I was thinking after all.

Still holding my hand, Jackson stepped over to the curb and in no time at all had a taxi pulling over for us, a yellow one, just like on TV. I thought about mentioning that to him, but I didn't want to sound silly. He'd lived there all his life, and he travelled all over the world with his work. It would sound foolish if I let it slip how excited I was to be there or that this was my first time outside of Europe. In fact, I'd only really travelled to the continent before because of Gemma or the men I'd been dating, when they'd been the ones paying.

Although I made very decent money as the managing director and lead interior designer of Anchor Design, the business that Gemma and I ran together, I still couldn't bring myself to spend it on things like travel. I knew what it felt like to have very little, and I saved as much as I could to make sure I never had to live that way again.

To my surprise, though, Jackson was the one to bring up my home as soon as we were settled in the back seat of the taxi. "It's not quite as roomy as the London black cabs, is it?"

It wasn't, but since it meant I got to sit closer to him, I didn't really mind.

Jackson pointed out a few things to me, both of us looking out the window as the car drove the few blocks to the Plaza hotel. Gemma and Cole had offered to let me stay with them, but between the fact that they were technically honeymooning, even though they weren't going away until the New Year, and the fact that they had a 3-month-old baby, I thought it would be easier for all involved if I stayed at a hotel instead.

Cole had then insisted on getting me a suite at the Plaza since the flagship Stamer hotel was under renovation, to my own new designs, so the Plaza was where I was staying, feeling like an imposter the second I walked in the front door. But that night, as Jackson paid the taxi driver and walked into the lobby with me, his hand on the small of my back, I didn't feel like quite as much of a fraud. Once again, people looking at the two of us would have simply seen a successful, well-dressed couple. No one had any reason to think I didn't belong there.

"Would you like me to walk you to your door?" Jackson asked politely as we made our way to the lifts. "Or can you take it from here?"

Once again, my ideas of what the evening might bring appeared to be dashed. "You don't want to come in for a while?" I asked straight out.

Though he smiled at me, I could see an uncharacteristic tightness in his lips. "Not tonight. I need to take you out first, remember?"

"We were just out," I pointed out. "You showed me the tree. That doesn't count?"

Jackson laughed, the tension in his face disappearing. "No, that certainly doesn't count. Trust me, you'll know when you've been on a date with me. And besides, you should get some rest. You've got a busy day tomorrow."

"I do?" All I knew about was the wedding brunch, which would be happening right there at the Plaza.

He smiled even wider. "You do if you're still up to our challenge. I already have plans for tomorrow afternoon. Who knows, you might be in love with me by the end of the day."

I smirked back at him, trying not to show how worried his confidence made me. "And after that, you'll come upstairs with me?"

"That's the deal. I'll see you at brunch and we can figure out the rest from there."

"Sounds good." I hoped he didn't notice the way my voice wavered. "Are you going to give me any hint about what we're doing on our date? How should I dress?"

"Wear whatever you like to the brunch," he suggested. "When I see you, I can let you know if you need to dress up or down from that. Your room's just upstairs, so I don't mind waiting if you need to change."

He definitely had something specific in mind even though we had only agreed on the challenge a couple of hours earlier. How did he already have a date planned?

"Have a good night, Holly." His voice grew huskier as he leaned closer to place a kiss on my cheek. His masculine scent, spicy and warm, flooded my senses, and I closed my eyes as I inhaled more deeply. All too soon, his lips left my skin and he pulled back, a smile on his face but something more complicated in his eyes. "I'll see you tomorrow."

He stepped back but waited until I got in the lift before leaving. I gave him a little wave as I stepped inside and he nodded back in acknowledgement, the smile on his lips the last thing I saw as the lift doors closed in front of me.

The next morning came quickly since I fell asleep nearly before my head hit the pillow. I woke up early, still on London time, so I had some time to kill before brunch, and I decided to use the hotel gym, where I found several businessmen with the same idea. My entrance earned me several appreciative looks and a few friendly hellos, and I knew exactly what they were thinking: they were wondering if there was any chance of drinks and a bit of fun later. They wouldn't be interested in more, and normally that would have been fine with me, but that day I had other plans, even if I still had no idea exactly what those plans were.

For brunch, I dressed as Gemma had requested. She told me she planned to wear her most garish Christmas jumper and she wanted me to match, so I had brought along a bright red jumper with a picture of a curvaceous snowwoman on it, along with the text: 'I'm sexy and I snow it'.

After pairing the jumper with my favourite skinny jeans and boots, I spent a little more time on my hair and make-up than was strictly necessary, but when I stepped back to assess the results, I gave my reflection a satisfied nod. The goal was to have Jackson thinking about coming back to my room from the second he saw me, and looking the way I did, I seemed destined to succeed.

All I had to do was hope that whatever he planned for our date wasn't going to give him the upper hand before that could happen.

Chapter Three

FIRST DATE

My attire was a lot more casual when I stepped back into the Plaza hotel the next morning for the wedding brunch than it had been the night before. Gemma had instructed everyone to wear Christmas sweaters, or 'jumpers' as the invitation called them, so I had found one that should be Christmasy enough to appease her, in shades of blue with a bit of red and some snowflakes and reindeer in geometric patterns, but also wouldn't look entirely out of place where I planned to take Holly afterwards. Wearing the sweater along with a worn-in pair of jeans, I felt a little out of place among all the men in suits and women in their Sunday best in the Plaza lobby, but I didn't really care. As long as Holly thought I looked good, nothing else mattered.

However, as soon as I walked into the small, private dining room where we would be eating brunch, all thoughts of impressing Holly went out the window.

She was directly in front of me, bent over across the table to hand Gemma something, her perfectly-shaped ass in the air right in my line of vision, and it felt like someone punched me in the gut, knocking all the air out of me. A rush of blood ran straight to my dick as I tried hard not to imagine what she would look like in that position with nothing on at all.

Would I find out that night?

She really wasn't playing fair, and she hadn't even done it on purpose. What would it be like when she actually started trying?

As she straightened back up, I realized that she had been handing Gemma a couple of aspirin, which Gemma quickly swallowed, followed by a big gulp of water. "Are the candy canes catching up with you?" I asked with a laugh, alerting them to my presence as I tried to direct my thoughts to safer subjects.

Both women turned to look at me while Gemma winced. "Not so loud, please," she begged, placing her fingers on her temples. "It's touch and go right now as to whether I'm going to make it through this meal."

As I murmured an apology, my eyes dropped to their Christmas sweaters, both loud and bright with ridiculous puns, and I laughed again, but quieter. "Okay, next time you are shopping for those, you have to pick one up for me."

"You could wear Cole's," Gemma suggested. "I bought one for him but he won't wear it."

I rounded the table to give the bride a hug. "That does not surprise me."

"Because I have some taste," Cole's voice interrupted as he also came into the room, dressed in his usual suit and clearly having caught the last part of the conversation. "And some self-respect."

He followed up that remark by giving my sweater a rather critical look, but before I could defend myself, Holly did it for me. "Jackson makes that jumper look good, and at least he's following your wife's request."

Cole raised his eyebrows at her in amusement. "I don't think my wife has any complaints. Do you, Gorgeous?" He shot her a smirk and Gemma rolled her eyes in response, but we all noticed that she didn't disagree.

"Are we complaining about Cole? I have a whole list if we've got time." That voice belonged to Cole's sister, Isabel, also joining us as the room began to fill up.

She gave her brother a teasing grin as Gemma ran over to take Noah from her. "I missed you, beautiful boy," Gemma cooed at her son while Isabel's kids and husband came in behind her.

"Uncle Jackson!" Jennifer and Darryn ran straight to me, bypassing their actual uncle who shook his head in mock disbelief.

Hugs were eventually given all round and Holly looked a little surprised to be included. As I watched her, I realized I didn't know anything about her family. Did she have brothers and sisters, nieces and nephews of her own? We'd never talked about it, no more than we'd talked about my family. We still had a lot to discover about each other, and I couldn't wait to learn it all.

Last to arrive were Cole's parents, and once they did, we all took a seat around the large square table, talking about the wedding and Christmas plans and a bit of Stamer Hotels business, which seemed unavoidable whenever the Stamer men got together. Both Cole and his father had dedicated their lives to their business, so when they were in the same room, it seemed bound to come up. Waiters in pressed uniforms served us course after course of every brunch food imaginable, each one delicious, and mimosas flowed freely.

"This is nice," Holly whispered to me as the meal began to wind down. She and I were sitting next to each other with Gemma on my other side and Isabel's husband next to Holly. At first, I thought she meant the meal itself until she clarified a bit further. "Gem never had a family like this. I'm so happy she has one now."

Wistfulness lay beneath her words, but I couldn't tell if it was on Gemma's behalf or her own. I would have to ask her about it later when we were on our own.

As the meal drew to an end, Holly and I stood at almost the same time to say our goodbyes. "Do you two have plans?" Gemma asked curiously, looking back and forth between me and Holly.

"Yes. Like I told you last night, I'm going to show Holly a bit of the city, and I'm starting with your suggestion."

Gemma's eyes widened in surprise. "My suggestion? What did I suggest? I don't remember that conversation at all."

The laughter of everyone around us made it clear that we all knew exactly why that would be. "I thought you might not," I told her, giving her cheek a kiss. "But if Holly hates it, it's on you."

Gemma looked over at Holly with a shrug and an expression somewhere between confusion and apology, which Holly simply laughed at. "It's okay, Gem. I'm sure we'll have fun no matter what it is."

I felt just the same. As long as Holly and I were together, I was pretty sure we were going to have a good time.

Once we'd said goodbye to everyone and walked out to the hall, Holly turned to me. "Are you going to tell me what we're doing now? And what I need to wear?"

"Actually, I think you're perfect just as you are." I definitely didn't want her to change out of those jeans. "Just grab your coat and your keys and I'll take care of the rest."

Her raised eyebrows suggested she didn't quite believe me, but she didn't argue either. I waited for her by the elevators and it didn't take more than ten minutes before she reappeared, ready to head out. A line of taxis waited outside the door so we were able to jump straight in, and I gave the driver the address rather than the name of the venue, trying to keep it a surprise for as long as possible.

My precautions proved founded, since Holly seemed to be looking for clues. "Where are we going?" she asked again as the taxi pulled out onto the street. "What did Gemma suggest to you?"

The memory of my conversation with Gemma and how I'd arrived at my plan for the day made me smile. "Well, she was very helpful. I asked her what you like to do, and she told me you like drinking and men."

Holly's hand went to her mouth to hide her smile as she tried to give me a disapproving look. It didn't quite work though, not when I could still see the twinkle of amusement in her eyes. "Okay, based on that, I'm going to guess... strip club?"

She always knew how to make me laugh. There were times the previous year, when we spent hours together, that my cheeks were sore afterwards from smiling so much. "No, but if that's on your list, I can look into it for next time."

Holly pretended to look disappointed, making us both laugh again. "Okay, let me think: somewhere with drinks and lots of men... maybe a sports bar?"

"A lot closer, but not quite."

She kept guessing and I kept shooting her down, right up to the moment we pulled up outside Madison Square Garden. Holly's pretty blue eyes gazed up at the illuminated arena in surprise. "We're going in here? For a concert?"

"Not in the middle of the day. Besides, I said you were close when you guessed the sports bar."

"Oh!" At last, the pieces clicked into place in her head. "We're going to watch some a sporting event?"

"Right." Though I kept the smile on my face, I also watched her reaction closely as I helped her out of the car. I didn't know if this was up her alley or not, but I really hoped she would like it. "There's a hockey game this afternoon. It's got drinking and men, just like you wanted, and if we're lucky, we'll even see some fighting.

Holly's radiant smile warmed my whole body as she put her arm through mine before I even had a chance to offer. I loved the way her body felt next to me. "You're going to have to explain it all to me. I don't know anything about ice hockey, or any other American sports for that matter."

"Well, first, it's just hockey. You don't need to say ice hockey, everyone knows it's on ice. And second, I'm pretty sure the Canadians would be offended about you calling it an American sport."

"If there are a lot more lessons, we better get a drink first," Holly suggested with a cheeky smile.

Her happiness made me even happier, so happy that I couldn't help leaning down and placing a gentle kiss on her forehead. Being there with her at that moment felt completely right, and I really hoped she could feel it too.

~Holly~

As the Rangers scored another goal, Jackson and I jumped to our feet, cheering as we high-fived each other. We must have looked a little silly being so invested in the game, but I was having a great time. I'd never been to a hockey game before, and I found all of it utterly fascinating, although when the players first came out, I complained to Jackson that I couldn't see any of their faces.

"How am I supposed to know which ones are the hot ones? That's how I always decide which team to cheer for in football: whichever team has the fittest players."

His laugh let me know he didn't feel in any way threatened by me checking out the players. "Well, we're sitting right behind the Rangers' bench and the crowd is definitely on their side, so I would suggest you cheer for the home team."

Looking around us, I could see he had a point. Everyone wore the red and blue colours of the home team and Jackson's jumper blended in perfectly. As for me, I felt a bit out of place with my bright red, silly jumper, but it didn't seem to stop several of the men sitting around us from glancing my way. Jackson noticed it too, and before long, he stretched his arm out across the back of my seat in a simple but clearly possessive gesture.

I didn't mind. In fact, having people think I was with him felt kind of nice. For the length of the date, at least, we were together and I could deal with that. Committing to him for the afternoon seemed safe enough.

Several of the people sitting around us also overheard some of the explanations he gave me about the game, along with my British accent, so they began to offer their expertise too. Soon, we had nearly the whole section offering to teach me. Jackson found it funny and I did too. Were Americans always so friendly, or did the alcohol and the home team taking an early lead put everyone in a good mood? Either way, by the end of the game, we'd made a ton of new friends and had offers to go out for dinner and drinks with several different groups.

"Sorry, guys," Jackson announced to the crowd at large. "I've got something special planned for this beautiful lady tonight."

A chorus of 'awwwws' rang out, followed by another round of laughter, with me laughing most of all. Jackson took it stoically as several of the men patted him on the back, telling him how lucky he was. He gave me a look that made me think he felt the same.

And maybe he did. He might feel that way at that particular moment in time, but we were still at the beginning. Beginnings were never the problem for me. The part that followed was where I ran into trouble.

"Do you really have something special planned?" I asked him as we made our way back onto the busy streets. The sky had turned completely black even though it wasn't six o'clock yet. "Or were you just making an excuse to get me alone?"

My reference to being alone was calculated to remind him of the visit to my hotel room that he had promised me at the end of our date, and by the way his pupils dilated, I could tell my plan worked. He was thinking about it too. However, to my disappointment, he assured me that he hadn't been kidding. "Would I really lie to a hundred of our closest new friends? I do have something planned."

Of course he did. I shouldn't even be surprised, and by that point, I already knew better than to ask what we were doing or where we were going. I simply got in the taxi next to him while he gave the driver an address.

As he leaned back in his seat, I took his hand, my fingers entwining around his larger, rougher ones, and he looked down as if the gesture caught him off guard. A moment later, his grip tightened around me, letting me know he didn't mind it at all.

"This is technically our first date," he pointed out as the taxi drove along the perfectly straight streets of the city. "Which, in my books, means dinner."

"Do you want to know what it means in my books?" I teased, pressing myself a little closer against him. The drinks I'd had at the game were certainly doing their part to loosen any inhibitions I had, and I didn't have many inhibitions to begin with. If he let me, I'd have my hands up under that jumper of his in a second, or, even better, down his jeans.

Jackson swallowed hard, attempting to keep some control. "You can tell me later. First, we need to get to know each other a bit."

"I think we already know each other pretty well for a first date," I argued.

"In some ways, but I have a feeling I haven't really scratched the surface of you yet, Holly."

What exactly did he want to know? The thought made me a little nervous, though I tried not to let it show, brushing it off with a joke like I usually did. "You can scratch me all you like later."

His sharp exhale suggested I had succeeded in getting his train of thought to line up with mine, but before I could tease him any further, the taxi pulled over.

I glanced out the window in surprise. "We're here already? We could have walked that."

"Probably," he agreed as he tapped his bank card on the reader before opening the car door. "The women I date don't usually want to walk very far. I should have asked you instead of assuming you wanted to take the taxi."

Curiosity ran through me as I followed him into the building we'd stopped in front of. "What kind of women do you usually date?"

He raised an equally curious eyebrow at me. "Is that what you want to talk about on our first date? Am I allowed to ask you the same thing?"

Fair enough. Talking about my past relationships with Jackson didn't sound like a good idea, not when we were supposed to be having fun.

"What *do* you talk about on a first date, then?" I asked, changing the subject as smoothly as I could as we got into the lift inside the building. I still had no idea where we were going, but by that point, I'd decided to just go with it.

He began listing things, ticking each item off on his fingers as he went. "Favourite movies, favourite bands, favourite books, favourite holiday destinations, all that kind of thing. What about you?"

My answer felt incomplete by comparison. Recently, all of my first dates had been pretty much the same: I asked the man involved as much as I could about himself so I didn't have to share anything about me other than the most superficial things. By the end of it, I knew whether I planned to invite him back to my flat or not, and if I did, he never stayed for breakfast.

I hadn't been on a second date in a very long time.

Since I couldn't say *that*, I simply agreed with him. "The same. Nothing too deep."

"Oh, I didn't say it wasn't deep. You can tell a lot about a person by the things they pretend to like."

A surprised laugh bubbled out of me. He never said exactly what I thought he would. "What makes you think I would pretend?"

His grin matched my mood exactly: amused and interested. "Everyone pretends. They want to look smarter or more cultured or more interesting than they feel. Nobody ever answers those questions truthfully, but you can tell a lot by what they choose to lie about."

His theory was interesting, but flawed in one fundamental way. "I would tell you the truth, if you do the same."

"Honesty is guaranteed with me, Holly. Whatever you give me, I'll give you the same right back."

Finally, the lift door opened again, and when I turned to look at what lay beyond it, my mouth dropped open in surprise. We'd travelled up so many floors that we were on a roof terrace, and just outside the doors in front of us, a row of transparent igloos sat beneath the night sky, each containing a private dining table, lit with fairy lights and decorated with flowers.

"We're eating here?" I asked in awe, taking in the beautiful setting overlooking the city lights and the warm, welcoming ambience of the table that we were immediately led to.

"Do you like it?" The question sounded so earnest and unsure that it nearly brought tears to my eyes. Nobody had ever tried so hard to impress me before, and he really didn't need to. I was already more impressed with him than I dared admit.

"It's amazing." As I took my seat, the atmosphere between us seemed to have shifted, becoming more serious, so I tried to make a joke to lighten the mood. "You know you don't have to go to all this trouble, right? I'm already taking you upstairs tonight either way."

Something flashed in Jackson's eyes, an emotion I couldn't quite recognize. "That's got nothing to do with this. I wanted to do something special for you because you're special. That's the only reason. I don't need anything from you in return."

He sounded almost offended, and I hadn't meant to offend him. Pushing down my instinctive urge to make another joke, I leaned over and placed a gentle kiss on his cheek instead. "Thank you. I really do love it. It's beautiful."

"You're welcome." He smiled at me as I pulled back, but a tension remained in his expression that hadn't been there before.

His eyes dropped to my lips, and I couldn't even say who moved first. Somehow, in the next moment, his lips were on mine and if I hadn't already felt on top of the world just by being on the rooftop, I would have felt it then.

We had kissed before in London, walking along the Thames one night, and another night in the back of the pub I took him to, but it felt different. Those kisses had been full of lust, on my part at least, an exploration to see how far he wanted to take things... which hadn't been very far at all, it turned out.

That night on that rooftop, though, his kiss felt soft and sweet and full of promise. It seemed to be telling me that no matter what happened, we had those two weeks together, so I should enjoy it while it lasted.

Be careful with this one, my heart whispered even as my body thrilled to his touch. This one, I might not be able to survive.

~Jackson~

As Holly and I enjoyed our meal, chatting easily about anything and everything that came into our heads, I tried to keep my hopes in check.

Everything about our date had been pretty much perfect to that point. She seemed to be enjoying herself and she definitely seemed comfortable with me, just as comfortable as I felt with her. And that kiss... wow. I hadn't meant to kiss her, it hadn't been part of my plan at all, but when she leaned over to me, her face so close to mine, I couldn't help it. And for that moment, the whole world seemed to disappear. Nothing existed but her and me, in our little bubble on top of the world, two people who, despite living an ocean apart, made perfect sense together.

It might have been the most perfect kiss of my life.

Only when I pulled back from it and saw the uncertainty in her eyes did the warning start sounding in my head, telling me to pull back and not to rush things, not to push too hard if she wasn't ready yet. That was where I'd always gone wrong before; I always went all-in too quickly. Women often complained about men not wanting to commit, but in my experience, women were just as hesitant. They might say they were looking for something serious, but if you mentioned love or family or the future in the first few dates, they ran just as fast as men did.

At least, the women I dated had. Each time I started to think that maybe I'd found something, that maybe this was the connection I'd been waiting for, whenever I laid my heart on the line, they would always pull away.

"It's too soon," was a common refrain.

"We should keep our options open."

"How can you say you love me when you won't even fuck me?"

That last one had particularly stung. The woman in question and I had dated for a couple of months three years earlier, and I really thought it might be going somewhere. I told her up front that I wasn't looking to get physical right away, just like I did with Holly. Actually, she was the last woman before Holly that I told about my virginity, and she said she understood. Then, I surprised her at home one night with champagne and roses, only the surprise was on me when another man answered the door wearing only a towel. The whole scenario couldn't have been more of a cliché, but that didn't make it hurt any less.

She acted like she hadn't done anything wrong since we weren't in a physical relationship yet. When I protested that I loved her, she came back with the words that had been burned into my brain ever since.

I didn't fall in love with every woman I dated; I wasn't quite *that* desperate. However, when I felt that spark, I didn't see the point of beating around the bush, and I guess I came on too strong.

Maybe they just didn't expect it from the easygoing joker that everyone saw on the outside. They didn't know about my past or the way I had been before I learned to hide my anxieties behind my smile.

"Favourite food?" I asked Holly as we continued working our way through our list of likes and dislikes.

Her gaze dropped to my lap before she looked back up at me with a challenge in her eye. "For now, it's cheesecake, but I might change my mind later."

Her saucy wink made my heart melt and my dick harden almost simultaneously. We were definitely going to have to set some ground rules once we got back to her hotel or my virginity wouldn't last the night, never mind the two weeks.

Because the issue wasn't that I didn't want to sleep with her. Of course I did. I'd have to be crazy not to. Beautiful, sexy, and confident in her sexuality, I had no doubt a night with her would be unforgettable, but the idea that she wanted *only* that from me nearly killed me. If I gave in to her and she got back on the plane after New Year's Eve, went back to London and I never saw her again, I didn't think I could take it.

Therefore, I had to hold out for more from her, no matter how challenging that might be.

Too soon and not soon enough, our dinner ended and we headed back down to street level where I stepped out to the edge of the curb to hail a cab.

"You don't want to walk?" Holly asked, reminding me of our earlier conversation. I truly appreciated how unpretentious she was, up for anything. However, her grip on New York City geography still needed some work.

"It's a bit too far to walk this time, but I'll take you out somewhere later this week where we can go walking if you like."

A taxi pulled up before she could ask me what I had in mind and I held the door open for Holly before getting in myself and directing the driver to the Plaza.

During the ride, I kept up a steady stream of chatter, not giving Holly a chance to make any kind of move before we had a chance to talk in private. When we got out of the taxi at the Plaza, I took her hand as we walked together to the elevator, my heart pounding frantically as we got in one by ourselves.

I hadn't been in a woman's bedroom for several years and now that we were on our way there, I suddenly felt incredibly insecure. Even though Holly knew I was a virgin, would she expect me to be naturally good at certain things? I had watched enough porn and, to be honest, read enough romance novels that I understood all the basic mechanics, but I suspected there would be a significant learning curve between reading about something or watching it and doing it myself. What if I couldn't please her?

"Hey." Holly's voice sounded softer than usual as she placed a gentle hand on my cheek and turned my head towards her. "You don't have to be nervous, Jackson. We don't have to rush anything."

I mustn't have been hiding my nerves as well as I'd hoped. Though I tried to smile my usual casual smile, it felt forced. "I think maybe I'd feel better if we set some limits first."

Holly nodded. "Of course. You can decide what you're comfortable with."

As the elevator door opened, we both fell silent for the walk down the hall to Holly's suite. Her kind and understanding response alleviated my worries somewhat, but I was still having trouble hearing myself think over the thudding of my heart.

I didn't usually get so worked up, but then, I usually knew how an evening would end. That night, I had no idea, and being there with her felt... risky.

As soon as we were inside, Holly offered me a drink. "Cole's paying for everything," she explained as she pulled a bottle of wine out of the mini-fridge. "We might as well make the most of it."

That made me laugh and I accepted gratefully. With our wine glasses in hand, we sat down on the couch in the living area, close to each other but not quite touching.

Though I didn't know how to begin, Holly had no such qualms. She dove right in. "So, let's talk limits. What have you done with a woman before?"

Her curious tone sounded warm and not at all judging.

"I really haven't done much. Some heavy petting, I guess you'd call it. Under the clothes but over the underwear."

Saying it out loud made me feel ridiculous, but to my relief, Holly didn't act like she found it shameful in any way. "You've never been naked with anyone?" she clarified.

"No."

"Okay." Taking a drink of her wine, she blinked a few times, thinking it over.

"I'm sorry," I apologized, rushing to fill the silence. "This is hardly sexy, trying to decide beforehand what we're going to do."

Holly shook her head immediately. "You're wrong. Consent is always sexy, and it goes both ways. I don't want you to be uncomfortable, Jackson, and if I came on too strong earlier, I'm sorry."

The last thing I wanted was for her to feel guilty or, God forbid, to stop flirting with me. I loved her flirting and teasing and her sexy confidence. It had only been when we got back to the hotel that it all felt suddenly very real and I began to panic.

"You have nothing to apologize for. I'm flattered that you want me, Holly, and I love that you don't hide it. I want to be with you too, just... not quite yet."

"So, we're both sorry and we both say we don't need to be," she summed up with a laugh, leaning back and taking a sip from her wine glass. "In that case, let's negotiate. I'd love to see you naked, Jackson, but if that's too much tonight, just tell me so."

"Maybe not tonight," I agreed, wincing as I waited for her disappointment.

It never came, though. She accepted my choice willingly, raising her eyebrows at me instead. "Can I see you in your pants, then?"

In confusion, I glanced down at my jeans. "You mean just taking my shirt off?"

Holly laughed again, the sound of her laughter calming me even more than the wine did. "I guess that's a British term. I meant your underwear."

Okay. That wasn't too scary, not really much different from going swimming, and plenty of women had seen me do that. "And you'll take your clothes off too?" I asked, wanting to make sure I understood her plan.

"If you want me to."

God, I really did. "Okay, so should we just..." I trailed off, placing my wine glass down and grabbing the bottom of my sweater to pull it off, but Holly put out a hand to stop me, giving me a gentle smile.

"Hold on. Let's play a little game first."

Dropping my arms, I exhaled, leaning back against the couch as I tried to get myself under control. I did feel better now that we'd talked about it, but I also felt like I'd just drained all the romance from the evening. Did she even still want me after all of that? I really hoped she wasn't talking about Monopoly. "What kind of game?"

Holly leaned forward, a challenging twinkle in her eye. "A guessing game. The bra and knickers I'm wearing today have two different colours and a pattern. See if you can figure out what they are. For each guess you get wrong, you take a drink. When you guess right, I'll give you a kiss. And once you get all three, then you get to see them for yourself. What do you think?"

I thought this woman couldn't get any more damn perfect if she tried, but I knew I couldn't say that to her. Not yet. Not until I knew she felt the same.

Chapter Four

GUESSING GAME

Jackson's face lit up when I suggested the guessing game, and I breathed an internal sigh of relief. He had been growing more and more tense, his face tight and his shoulders stiff, ever since we got in the taxi. Racking my brain, I tried to figure out what had caused the shift in his mood. Had I come on too strong? Made one too many innuendos over dinner? Did he think I would argue with him when he told me he wanted to stop?

When he suggested setting some limits before we did anything, I thought that would be a great idea. That way, I would know exactly what he expected out of the evening and I wouldn't have to worry about crossing any lines he didn't want me to cross. As much as I wanted him in my bed, I wanted his trust and respect even more.

However, once we agreed to take off our clothes and get down to our underwear, I also didn't want to just strip off and stare at each other awkwardly. No matter how big a step it might be for him, it should still feel organic, like it happened naturally just as it would on any other date. With our endpoint established, getting there should be the fun part. That had been the idea behind the guessing game I suggested, and thankfully, Jackson jumped fully on board. "I think that's a great idea, Holly."

With his agreement secured, I shuffled back on the couch, keeping my eyes trained on him. "Make your first guess, then," I prompted. "I already told you my favourite colour over dinner. Do you think I'm wearing it tonight?"

The question served as a test for him as well as part of the game; I wanted to see how much attention he'd been paying to my answers over dinner. His answer had made me both groan and smile when he said his favourite colour was blonde, like my hair. He could be such a charmer.

But did he remember what I'd said?

"Black?" he guessed, raising his eyebrows hopefully.

So, he did remember, but he didn't realize that I'd been setting him up. With a wicked laugh, I shook my head. "You fell right into my trap! It's not black."

He joined in with my laughter, looking a hundred times more relaxed than he had a few minutes earlier. Following my rules, he took a swig from his wine glass before his gaze returned to me, looking me up and down as if he might be able to see through my clothes if he just stared hard enough.

"White?" he guessed next, and I shot him an incredulous look.

"Do I really look like a plain white kind of girl?"

Jackson grinned, shaking his head. "You're right, I don't know what I was thinking."

As he took another drink, his Adam's apple bobbed as he swallowed, sending a rush of anticipation through me. I couldn't wait until I could kiss his neck, running my hands through his hair or maybe over his chest, feeling his hard, firm...

"Red?"

Jackson's next guess shook me out of my daydreaming. "Nope. You're going to be too drunk to get home tonight if you don't start making some better guesses."

Gamely, he took another drink before giving me a scrutinizing look. "Alright, let me think. You looked incredible in that bridesmaid's dress yesterday, and Gemma told me you picked it out yourself. Based on that, I assume you must like pink, so I'll guess pink."

I didn't answer him with words; I simply swooped forward towards him until our lips met.

Like it had at the restaurant, the kiss started soft and sweet but quickly turned more needy. The thought of getting him out of his clothes had me worked up, and clearly, he felt it too. His lips moved firmly against mine as his hands cupped my face, warm and gentle, and the taste of the wine on his lips combined with the smell of his cologne left me feeling a little drunk.

"Okay," I managed to gasp as I pulled back, nearly breathless. "That's one. You still need to guess one more colour and the pattern."

"Right," he agreed in a tone that made it clear he'd all but forgotten about the game. His deep blue eyes looked down into mine curiously. "So, it's pink and something else."

Looking for clues, he glanced at my hair, tenderly brushing a stray strand from my face.

"How about yellow?"

Either he'd made a lucky guess or he could read my mind. Either way, I rewarded him with another kiss, even deeper than the one before. His lips parted against mine and my tongue slid between, tasting the wine stronger than ever, along with a slight mintiness that must have come from a breath mint he snuck while I wasn't watching him.

With my excitement rising, I couldn't wait any longer to touch him and my hands slid up the back of his jumper. His skin felt warm beneath my fingers and he sighed into the kiss as I ran my hands up his back, feeling the muscles tense and react to me all on their own.

It surprised me when he reached for the bottom of my jumper in return, but I pulled back, teasing him now that I knew he felt more comfortable. "Hold on. You still need to guess the pattern."

Although he groaned in frustration, his eyes sparkled, showing me he enjoyed the challenge just as much as he disliked it.

"Polka dots?" he suggested, but I shook my head.

With a sigh, he picked up his wine glass from the floor and took another drink, keeping it in his hand in case he guessed wrong again.

"Flowers?"

That was a good guess, but still wrong. "Nope, sorry."

He took another drink, a smaller one, anticipating the game might go on for a while.

"Can I have a hint?" he begged. "I don't know how much more I can take."

Did he mean the wine, or waiting to get our clothes off? I knew which one I had on my mind, so I took pity on both him and myself. "It's one of the patterns on your country's flag."

His eyes lit up once more. "Stripes?"

I couldn't hold back my laugh. "No, the other one! Come on, you had a 50/50 chance!"

Technically, he should have taken another drink, but as he put his glass down and leaned towards me, I had no plans to enforce the rules. Our lips connected once more and he wasted no time in plunging his tongue into my mouth, taking control of the kiss in a way he had never done with me before. I wouldn't give in so easily though, fighting back with my own passion and desire until he pulled away, declaring a draw.

"Can I see it now?" he asked, his voice nearly hoarse with anticipation.

"Go ahead." My arms stayed at my sides, letting him take the lead.

Tentatively, but still with determination, Jackson reached down and grabbed the bottom of my jumper. Slowly, he lifted it higher, his eyes glued to the skin being revealed, until his breath caught, his lips parted and he froze, apparently lost for words.

Seeing his struggle, I took over, taking the jumper from him and pulling it off the rest of the way so he could see the full picture of my pink bra with yellow stars and a yellow bow in the middle.

"Is it how you imagined it?" I teased, arching my back ever-so-slightly to give him the full effect.

"So much better," he breathed, his eyes finally moving up to meet mine again. The desire I saw in them nearly took my breath away. "You're stunning, Holly."

"Just wait," I promised, standing up to show him the matching set.

His eyes didn't leave my hands as I undid the button and pulled down the zip of my jeans, opening them to reveal the bikini-cut knickers with another little yellow bow on the front. When I felt sure he'd had a good glimpse, I pulled the jeans the rest of the way off, peeling them off my legs and dropping them on the floor next to me.

"Your turn," I reminded him as he continued to stare at me as if I were some kind of work of art. "Come on, Jackson. Let's see what you've got."

~Jackson~

The wine helped to lessen my nerves, but not nearly as much as kissing Holly did. I wanted to kiss her again. I *needed* to, so if I had to take my clothes off to get to that point, I would happily do so.

With her toned, tanned body and her beautiful curves, covered only by her bra and panties, pink with yellow stars, she looked like the poster on a teenage boy's wall come to life. Already, I knew I would never, ever forget what she wore the first time she got undressed for me. It had been burned into my memory for all time.

As much as I wished I could make anywhere near as much of an impression on her, my plain black boxer-briefs were nothing out of the ordinary. I doubted they would capture her imagination, but she stood there anyway, waiting to see them, so I hurried to oblige.

My shirt came off first, yanked up over my head as quickly as I could. When I stood to undo my jeans, I glanced up at Holly for just a second. Her teeth were holding onto her bottom lip, her chest rising and falling almost hypnotically as she watched my hands, waiting to see what they would reveal.

With a grunt as the zipper brushed against my hard dick, I pulled it all the way down. I'd been hard since the first time she kissed me, and watching her undress had only made it worse. She couldn't fail to notice it as I pulled my jeans over my hips and dropped them to the floor before looking back over at her.

Holly's eyes ran over my whole body, slowly and deliberately, but to my surprise, it didn't make me uncomfortable. After our earlier conversation, I already knew she would respect the boundaries we'd set, and since seeing each other in our underwear fell within them, it didn't worry me. After all, I couldn't stop looking at her either.

Still desperate to kiss her again, I reached for her, but Holly took a step back before taking my hand. "Come with me," she whispered before turning and leading me towards the bedroom.

I followed her like a lost puppy, willing to go anywhere so long as I got to be with her.

She turned to me with a soft smile as we entered the room. "We'll be more comfortable in here, if it's okay with you."

I loved that she asked me, but I couldn't even get an answer out, not when her lips were so close. Instead, I reached for her again, and that time, she came straight into my arms without hesitation. As my mouth claimed hers, her chest pressed against me and the feel of the smooth fabric and the hint of her hard nipples against my skin made my legs feel weak.

Holly's hands ran over my shoulders and around to the back of my neck, pulling me even tighter to her, while my own hands went around her waist, luxuriating in the feel of her soft, supple skin. Although our upper halves were pressed tightly together, I held my hips back, afraid of how turned on I was, afraid of her knowing it and afraid it would get worse if her body touched me there.

I lost all track of time as we kissed, our hands exploring each other, but when we finally came up for air, Holly gestured towards the bed. "Do you want to lie down?"

Again, she put the decision in my hands, letting me set the pace, and a wave of both desire and affection ran through me. "Sure," I agreed. Lying down would be good, actually, since I felt a little light-headed, partly from the wine but more from the intoxication of touching and being with her.

She climbed onto the bed first and when she reached for me, I was there right behind her. For a moment, I hesitated, wondering whether she would want me on top of her or if she would go on top, but instead, she lay on her side and pulled me down to face her.

"How is this so far?" she asked, genuine warmth and concern in her eyes. "You feeling okay?"

I answered her with total honesty. "I feel amazing, but not as good as you feel."

She grinned at me, clearly pleased with that answer. "I might have to argue with you there. Because this right here?" She ran her hands across my chest muscles, sending little shivers through me everywhere she touched. "This is incredible."

It felt so good when she touched me, I wanted to try to return the favour somehow. Hardly believing this could really be happening, I brought my hand to her face. "You want to talk about incredible?" I teased her right back as my fingers trailed down her neck, past her collarbone, down to the swell of her breasts above her bra. She inhaled sharply as I rested my hand directly over the cup of her bra and gave it a gentle squeeze. "*This* is incredible."

"You like that?" she asked breathily. "You should try the other one then."

With a laugh, I wasted no time in doing just that, running my hand across to her other breast and squeezing it the same way. Her stiff nipple strained against the fabric, pressing into the palm of my hand.

"Jackson." Her eyes were closed as she murmured my name and it sent a rush of blood to my dick stronger than anything I'd ever felt before. I thought I knew what it meant to be turned on, but she was quickly redefining the whole experience.

"Holly," I groaned in response before kissing her again, even harder than before.

Once again, time lost all meaning. I couldn't guess how long we stayed that way, kissing each other and touching each other. At one point she rolled me onto my back so she could kiss my chest. The feel of her lips against my skin, her tongue flicking lightly across my nipples, made my whole body nearly vibrate with pleasure. Energy flowed through me so strongly, I felt I could nearly levitate right off the bed.

She began to kiss lower, down to my stomach, and my dick jumped within my underwear, protesting at the restraint. *Traitor*, I reprimanded my body, trying to keep the blood in my brain instead. Just as I began to wonder how much farther she would go, her kisses began to move upwards again, ending at my mouth, where she kissed me until I flipped us both over to return the attention.

Her sweet floral scent flooded my senses as I buried my face in her neck, kissing and licking and sucking on the tender skin as she wriggled beneath me, her hands tangled in my hair. Just as she had, I moved lower, until I was confronted with the most beautiful pair of breasts I had ever seen, separated from me only by the thin fabric of her bra.

It would be easy to take it off her, or at least pull it down enough to free her of the fabric covering her, and I knew without question that she wouldn't object if I did. However, I didn't want to change the limits that I'd set. If we changed one, we'd be tempted to change more, so I kissed her over the fabric instead, finding her nipple with my teeth and giving it a gentle nibble.

"Are you sure you haven't done this before?" Holly sighed, and my heart filled with pride, so happy that I could give her even a portion of the pleasure she gave me.

When I'd kissed my way down to her stomach and back up again, following the example she had set me, I returned to her mouth and gave her one last, long kiss before rolling off her and onto my own back.

I had to stop there. If I didn't, I wasn't sure I would be able to stop at all.

For a moment, neither of us said anything. On my part, my body buzzed with exhilaration, completely satisfied and craving more all at the same time. Hopefully, she felt the same.

Eventually, Holly turned to me with a smile. "So, that just happened."

I laughed, grateful that she hadn't changed her way of speaking to me after everything we had just done. "Yeah, I think it did."

"So, did I win? Do you want to stay the night?" she challenged, and I laughed again, knowing that she didn't really mean it. She might be testing the waters, but she didn't expect anything.

"Only if you tell me you love me," I teased her right back.

Something deep and pained flashed within her eyes, the amusement completely gone. "If I was going to love anyone, Jackson, it might be you. I just don't think it's going to happen, though, and not because of anything you do or don't do, so please, don't take it personally."

Her words washed over me in an icy shock, dulling the fire she'd so recently stoked inside me, and I sat up, wanting to see her properly. She sat too, although she wouldn't meet my eye.

"What do you mean you're not going to love anyone? Why not?"

"It's a long story." Though she said that, I knew what she actually meant: she just wasn't ready to tell me yet. "And you need to get back home, right? How far away do you live?"

"My apartment's on the Upper East Side. It's not too far. You'll have to come see my place before you go."

Relieved that I had accepted her change of subject, she finally looked me in the eye again, only a hint of her previous hesitancy remaining. "Is that our next date, then?"

"I haven't decided for sure what we're doing next, but I'm afraid tomorrow, I'm unavailable. I've promised to watch Noah while Gemma and Cole take care of some paperwork, some documents they need to sign now that they're married."

"That's okay," Holly quickly assured me, but I could have sworn she looked a little disappointed.

"Of course, you're always welcome to come and babysit with me," I offered, saying the words as soon as they popped into my mind. "We could watch a movie and make out on the couch when he takes his nap."

Holly laughed, just as I hoped she would. "Like a couple of horny teenagers?"

I grinned back at her, the mood between us light and teasing once again. "Exactly. What do you say, Holly? Want to come and play house with me?"

~Holly~

As I grabbed my phone to check my schedule following Jackson's invitation, my mouth dropped open in surprise when I got a look at the time. We had been back at the hotel for nearly two hours. Honestly, I couldn't remember the last time I had spent that much time with someone simply kissing and touching them. Would it have been in school? Maybe I never had.

I also couldn't remember the last time I'd been with someone that I enjoyed touching so much. Jackson's body was amazing, far more toned than I'd been expecting from the slightly goofy persona he usually projected. He must work out, and I found myself wondering for a second if he would be interested in us working out together, until I remembered that he had the task of suggesting activities outside the bedroom, not me.

As impressive as his physique was, though, it didn't fully explain why I had enjoyed making out with him so much. More than just the way he looked, I loved the way he reacted to my touch and I loved the way he touched me too, somehow hesitant yet confident at the same time; like it terrified him a tiny bit, but he needed to do it anyway.

And the idea of touching him more, in places we hadn't explored yet, had my body humming in anticipation. I had honestly never got the hype about virgins or why men were so often obsessed with being a woman's first lover. However, as I glanced over Jackson's amazing body once more, the idea of being the first woman to get to see him and touch him was an incredible turn-on. Maybe those guys I'd always thought of as jerks were onto something after all.

Shaking my head at my train of thought, I unlocked my phone and pulled up my calendar just to double check that I hadn't forgotten anything I'd promised to do the next day, but a blank calendar page stared back at me.

"Looks like I'm free," I told Jackson, who grinned in delight. "I'm yours if you want me."

"As if you need to ask," he replied, charming as always. "I can come and pick you up here around noon if that's okay?"

"Don't you live close to Gemma and Cole? It will be completely out of your way to pick me up." I felt pretty certain that Gemma had told me that before.

"Nothing is out of my way when it involves you," he assured me.

"So smooth." As usual, I teased him to try to cover the way my stomach fluttered when he said things like that or looked at me that way, as if I were the only woman in the world.

We walked back out to the living room where we'd left our clothes and Jackson got dressed again while I grabbed a bathrobe from the bathroom. I had no plans to go anywhere else that night, so I didn't need to put my clothes back on. Although I would have loved to go further with Jackson, surprisingly, I didn't feel too unsatisfied. Just being with him had been really nice, and I knew we had more nights ahead of us. I had no doubt that eventually, I would see exactly what he had hidden beneath those sexy black pants of his.

"Have a good night, Holly." Jackson gave me a gentle kiss on the lips as he said goodbye. Though tame in comparison to the way we'd just been kissing, it somehow made me shiver anyway.

After he'd gone, I sank down onto the couch, my head spinning. That had been quite a day, starting with brunch with Gemma and Cole and his family, which had really been an eye-opener for me. Other than in films, I'd never seen a family that got along like his did, teasing each other, laughing together. Gemma's family was certainly nothing like that. I'd been her best friend for six years, since we were in uni together, and in all that time, her father had never bothered to learn my name. I'd only met her brother once.

It genuinely delighted me that she got to be part of such a loving family as part and parcel of marrying the love of her life, but it dragged up old feelings of self-pity too. Once, I'd had dreams of being accepted into a family like that, like Gemma had, but I'd learned my lesson the hard way. It would never happen, and I simply had to accept that.

I couldn't help noticing that Jackson fit right in with the Stamers too. Cole's parents clearly loved him and so did Isabel and her kids. And why wouldn't they? Who *wouldn't* love Jackson? Anyone with a heart would.

What a shame, then, that mine was too broken to work like that. No matter how enticing he made it seem, I simply couldn't take that leap. Not again.

Shaking my head at myself once more, I got up from the couch and went to bed.

The next day, I was ready to go long before Jackson arrived to pick me up and feeling even more nervous than I had the day before. Going out with him had been one thing. I'd had a great time at the hockey game and at dinner, but that had all been somewhat typical date stuff, even if Jackson managed to take it to another level. Staying in with him seemed more dangerous, since there were fewer distractions and fewer ways I could divert away from talking about myself.

Except for Noah, of course. Thank goodness for my friend's newborn. Hopefully, we would focus on him and avoid any really personal conversations.

I went down to the lobby to wait for him so that I could jump in the taxi when it arrived, and in no time at all, we were standing outside an elegant apartment building on Madison Avenue. I hadn't been to Gemma and Cole's apartment before, so I had no idea what to expect. I knew that Cole had grown up wealthy and that he had no problem spending his money when he thought something was worth it, so I expected to be impressed. I'd also seen bits of their flat in the background when Gemma and I chatted over video and she walked around the space.

Even so, my mouth dropped as the lift door opened directly into one of the most beautiful homes I'd ever seen.

"They've got the whole floor?" I asked in wonder as Jackson stepped into the living space ahead of me.

He laughed at my awestruck tone. "They do, though I'm not sure why. It's not like Cole has any other friends to come over."

I laughed at that too. As much as Jackson liked to tease Cole, he obviously cared about him a lot, making me curious about their friendship and how they had ended up so close. Maybe I could ask him about that during our afternoon together, to keep the conversation away from myself.

"We're here!" Jackson called out into the empty space, and a few moments later, Gemma came around the corner, dressed in a jade silk blouse and black trousers, her red hair up, looking effortlessly beautiful as always.

"Hi!" she greeted us, giving Jackson a quick hug before turning to me. "Sorry if he roped you into this. I know babies aren't really your thing."

Jackson gave me a curious look, but I kept my eyes on Gemma. "When it's your baby, that's a different matter. I'm sure we're going to get along great."

"Well, Noah's pretty easy to please. If you've got a bottle, you're his best friend. Come on, I'll give you a quick tour before we head out."

She pulled me away as Jackson wandered off to find Cole.

"So, what's going on with you two?" she asked as soon as we were alone, stopping to give me a quizzical look. "Are you dating? Is it something serious this time?"

She looked so excited at the prospect that I had to let her down gently before she got her hopes up too much. "We're spending some time together, but it's not going to lead to anything."

As I expected, disappointment clouded her expression. "Hols, I know you've got a hard time trusting people, but believe me, Jackson is not like most guys. He's something special and he really likes you. You should give him a chance."

To my great annoyance, tears began to gather in the corners of my eyes, but I quickly blinked them away. "I know he's special. That's why he needs someone better than me."

Her eyes narrowed into a disapproving look. "I dare you to find me anyone in the world better than you."

That made me laugh, thankfully, drying my eyes completely. "You might be just a little bit biased there, Gem. Now come on, show me this amazing home of yours!"

Obviously, she didn't appreciate me avoiding the topic, but the truth was that she didn't know all the details of my past either. She knew a bit about the men I'd dated and that it had ended badly, but she didn't know everything. I had been too embarrassed to tell even my best friend since she could never understand, not growing up the way she had.

Like it or not, though, Gemma accepted my request for a tour, leading me through room after room, each one more beautiful than the last. "Who designed it?" I couldn't help asking. As an interior decorator, I was extremely impressed.

Gemma gave the name of a designer I certainly knew by reputation. "Brenda Watts. She did a hotel for Cole in Bermuda and he liked it so much he had her do this place too."

Of course he did. What Cole wanted, he usually got.

As we continued down the hall, Gemma skipped past one door even though we'd peeked into every other one so far. "What's in here?" I asked, stopping outside the door.

Gemma avoided my gaze, a sure sign that she didn't want to answer. "Just a supply room. Can you believe Cole has someone come in to clean the apartment every single day? I don't think we make that much of a mess!"

Her obvious lie and attempt at distraction only raised my curiosity even more. "Not buying it, Gem. What's in there?"

Her cheeks turned slightly pink. "Honestly, it's nothing. Now, come see the kitchen..."

I planted my feet firmly on the floor of the hallway. "You know I'm not moving now until you show me what's inside. You might as well just get it over with."

She resisted a second longer before, with a sigh, she gave in. "Alright, fine. But don't judge me, okay?"

"When have I ever judged you?"

She grimaced. "You're right, I'm sorry, I didn't mean that. And I'm not really embarrassed about it, it's just... kind of private."

Each word made me more curious than ever as she pressed her thumb to a special control panel on the wall and the door clicked open.

Though I couldn't say for sure what I expected, it definitely wasn't what I walked into. A large bed dominated the room with various chains and loops set up around it. To one side, a wall had been covered with a variety of toys and implements, and a couple of other pieces of equipment stood dotted around the room, items that I didn't know the names for but I definitely knew what their use was.

After taking it all in for a few seconds, I turned back to her in disbelief. "You guys have your own sex dungeon?!"

"Shhh!" she shushed me, turning back to the door to make sure no one was there. "Don't call it that! It's just for fun, and Jackson doesn't know about it, so please, don't tell him. I don't think he's really into anything kinky, it might shock him."

She must not know about Jackson's virginity if she only 'thought' he didn't have a kinky side. I had no plans to tell him, but as I looked back over the room, along with my surprise, I also felt proud of Gemma. It wasn't my thing, but if it worked for her, then good for her for going and getting it.

"Do you think it's weird?" she asked hesitantly, and I quickly shut that down.

"Not at all. If the two of you like it, that's amazing. Do you get to tie him up too sometimes?"

I had a hard time picturing Cole letting anyone else take control.

"Not often, but sometimes," she admitted, and my eyebrows raised in surprise, making her laugh. "Don't look so shocked, Hols! People aren't always what they seem."

She didn't need to tell me that. I could say the same for myself, and for some reason, her comment brought my mind back to Jackson too. All things considered, how much did I really know about him? Maybe the time had come for me to dig a little deeper. Maybe he wasn't exactly what he seemed either.

Chapter Five

Two Truths and a Lie

~Jackson~

"How was your date yesterday?"

Cole's question took me by surprise as I sat down across from him, since I didn't know he even knew about my date with Holly.

I'd found him in the main living room, Noah stretched out on his lap with his little feet kicking against Cole's chest. It still felt weird to me to see Cole with a kid. He'd sworn for so long that he would never get married or fall in love again, but all of that was in the past. Gemma had completely rewritten everything he thought he knew.

"The date was really good," I answered honestly. After I got home the night before, I lay in bed replaying the whole day in my mind, everything from brunch to the time on Holly's bed. I didn't really see any way it could have gone much better, except for that thing she'd said to me right at the end of the night about how she wasn't going to love anyone. I still needed to get to the bottom of that.

"Did you spend the night with her?"

Cole had always been blunt, so that question came as less of a surprise. I'd learned how to deal with those kinds of questions from him a long time ago. "You know I never kiss and tell, Cole. Nice try."

He grunted at me before leaning down to make a funny face at his son who grinned up at him in response. "Gemma is desperate for you two to hook up, just so you know."

That didn't come as news to me. Gemma hadn't made any secret of the fact that she thought Holly and I would be good together, but I had tried to avoid putting her in the middle. Being friends with both of us, it would be hard on her if things went badly and she felt she had to take sides.

Besides, Cole had oversimplified things. "I think she wants us to get married and live next door to you, not just hook up."

Wearing his usual smirk, Cole shrugged. "Same difference."

To him, maybe. For all the time Cole and I had spent together over the years, I'd managed to keep a few secrets from him, including my virginity. More times than I could count over the past few years when he hired himself an escort for the night for some event or another we were attending, he would offer to get one for me too. Once or twice I had even been tempted, thinking maybe I had built it up in my head so much that I should just sleep with someone to get it over with and get rid of all the pressure I'd put on myself.

But each time, I would think about the future woman that I wanted to share that experience with, and I had to turn Cole down. I hadn't waited all that time for no good reason. I wanted it to be special, and it would be. I would make it so.

"How long do you think you guys will be out?" I asked, trying to change the subject.

"A few hours. We've got to go to the lawyer's, the bank and to the office for a while. Depends how many people we run into along the way."

"And you're really signing over half of everything to her?" Cole had told me he planned to make Gemma an equal partner in everything he owned, but I could still hardly believe it. After what happened with his ex-fiancée, I thought that if Cole ever did manage to find someone to marry, he would insist on a pre-nup and separate bank accounts and the whole nine yards. Instead, he trusted Gemma so completely, he planned to do the exact opposite.

"Yup," he replied matter-of-factly, his face scrunching up again as he played with Noah's belly, drawing a shrieking noise from his son. "Did you hear that? Was that a laugh?"

He looked up at me with such an earnest look on his face, so unlike his usual smirk, that I couldn't help laughing myself. "Not quite, but it won't be long until he's laughing at you, don't worry."

Cole's face instantly reverted to his more typical unimpressed expression. "Very funny. Anyway, he needs a nap in about an hour. Gemma just fed him but he'll need a bottle when he wakes up. It's in the fridge. Do you need anything else?"

I shook my head since I'd watched Noah a few times already and felt pretty confident with the basics. Eventually, they were going to hire a nanny, but Gemma wanted to take some time at home with her son first. Since she could do most of her work from her home office, it didn't interfere with her work too much, and Cole was just as involved whenever he was home. So far, he loved being a father. It hadn't quite made him a softie yet, but there were moments I could see some real tenderness peeking through, and I imagined there were a lot more of those moments in private.

"Have you gone over everything?" Gemma asked as she entered the room with Holly right behind her.

Cole stood up, his son still in his arms. "Just finished. You're all ready?"

With a nod, Gemma bent down to give Noah a kiss before taking him from his father and handing him to me. "If you need anything, just call and we'll be right home."

"We'll be fine," I assured her as Noah grabbed onto one of my fingers and pulled it into his mouth. "Don't worry."

After a few more rounds of goodbyes and reminders, they finally made it out the door and I sat down on the floor, placed Noah down on his stomach and grabbed a few toys to keep him entertained.

"You're good with him," Holly observed, still standing beside the couch where she'd been since she came into the room. "Do you have a lot of experience with kids?"

Normally, I didn't talk much about my family, but since I wanted Holly to open up to me, I'd have to be open with her too. "Yeah. My mom wasn't around very much growing up, so I helped to raise my younger brother and sister."

"How old were you?" she asked, taking a step closer. Though her eyes were on Noah, I could tell she was paying close attention to my answers.

"When I started looking after them? About eight, I guess. Layla was two and Josh was just a baby."

As I spoke, Noah tried his best to reach one of his toys I had placed just out of reach, but when he couldn't reach it, he let out a frustrated cry and Holly winced. "Is he okay?"

I put the toy a little closer so he could try again before offering Holly a smile. "I'm guessing you *don't* have much experience with kids."

She shook her head as she returned my smile. "It's that obvious, huh? But no, I don't; I'm the youngest in my family."

That might have been the most personal detail about herself she'd ever given me. Trying not to sound too invested, I asked a follow-up question. "How many other kids are there?"

"I've got three older brothers and two sisters." She took another step forward and tentatively lowered herself to the ground, still watching Noah curiously.

"Wow, that's a big family. That must be fun."

I hadn't pictured her coming from a big family, for some reason. Maybe because of how private she was?

When she winced again, I immediately regretted my assumption and tried to offer an alternative viewpoint instead. "Although sometimes, the more people there are, the more problems you have."

"Yeah, I guess." Her noncommittal reply seemed to close the window she'd briefly opened into her life as she changed the subject. "So, what are we supposed to do with him?"

My focus returned to Noah, happily gnawing on the toy he'd managed to reach, his little legs kicking away. "This is pretty much it for now, just keep him happy until he's tired. You could sing to him or read to him if you want to, but he's pretty content just as he is."

Holly flashed me a teasing smile. "You haven't heard me sing. Nobody wants that."

We moved on to talking about other things, music we liked and concerts we'd gone to as we played with Noah until he started to look sleepy.

"Do you want to help me put him down?" After getting to my feet, I reached down to lift up Noah's tiny little floppy body. Immediately, he burrowed into my chest, trying to get comfortable, and when I looked over at Holly, the almost wistful look on her face took me by surprise. As soon as she caught me looking at her, the emotion quickly disappeared.

Clearing her throat, she also got to her feet. "What does that involve?"

In Noah's nursery, I showed her how to change his diaper before putting Noah down in his crib. His eyes were already closed even before he hit the mat.

"This baby stuff isn't so hard," Holly whispered as we made our way back out to the living room.

The fact that she'd reached that conclusion after one hour made me chuckle. "Noah's pretty great, but you haven't seen him upset yet. It's not always that easy."

Taking a seat on the couch, Holly looked around. "So, you want all of this? The wife, the kids, the fancy house?"

"I don't know if the house needs to be fancy," I protested. "But yeah, I definitely want a family. Don't you?"

Immediately, her words from the night before about not loving anyone came back to me, and that same pain flashed in her eyes again.

"I have an idea," she announced, completely avoiding my question. "It'll be a while before he wakes up now, right?"

"Right," I agreed, not entirely sure where she was going with this. When I invited her to join me for the afternoon, I had suggested we could make out while Noah napped, and I hadn't been entirely joking. However, I didn't think that was what she had in mind.

She quickly confirmed that her train of thought had gone down a different path entirely. Her eyes were bright and her smile a little forced. "Why don't we play another game? You want us to get to know each other, so we might as well make it fun. Let's play Two Truths and a Lie."

Actually, that sounded pretty good to me. Any chance to learn more about her, I would be happy to take. "What does the winner get?"

Holly winked at me, her smile turning more genuine as I agreed to her suggestion. "That's for me to know, and you to find out."

~Holly~

Jackson gave me his usual sexy grin, sitting just out of arm's reach on the sofa next to me. "I guess any prize from you is worth it, so I'm in."

Unlike the guessing game the night before, the game I'd just suggested wasn't going to end with us stripping, at least not right away. I did have a definite plan in mind for what the prize would be but it would have to wait until we were completely alone. We couldn't risk Gemma and Cole walking in on us in any kind of compromising situation, not when Gemma was already sniffing around about us getting together.

Despite her hopes and Jackson's determination, that still wasn't going to happen, and the reason I suggested the game was that it would give me a chance to open up to him in a controlled way. Once he knew some of the things about my past, he would understand why I couldn't be the woman he wanted me to be. I didn't want him to be hurt when I couldn't give him what he was after, and it might hurt him less if he understood the reasons for it, which had nothing to do with him.

So, I'd made the choice to share some of it with him, but I didn't want to just blurt it out as if I were at a psychiatrist's office. If we made it into a game, it could be a good way to get some of those hard truths out there in a playful, less heavy way.

I sure hoped so, anyway.

"Who's going first?" Jackson's eyes glimmered with excitement at the prospect of learning some of my secrets. He truly had no idea.

"Since I suggested it, I'll go first. You know the rules?"

"I think so. You tell me three things about yourself. Two are true and one's a lie, and I have to guess which is the lie."

He had it exactly right. "You've got it, so let's start with a fairly easy one. First, I used to have a tongue piercing. Second, I'm descended from royalty. And third, I can bench press 35 kilograms at the gym."

Jackson's face scrunched up in confusion at the last one. "How much is 35 kilograms?"

A dramatic, disappointed sigh left my lips. "You know the metric system is better, right? Americans."

As usual, he laughed at my joke. "I have no firm opinion on that, but what's the conversion? How many pounds is 35 kilograms?"

"It's about 80 pounds."

The way his eyebrows raised suggested he found that impressive. After taking a second to think over everything I'd just said, he made his guess. "Well, I believe that you work out, and I also wouldn't be terribly surprised if you had a piercing. So, I'm going to guess that the lie is that you're descended from royalty?"

Feeling smug, I gave him a cheeky grin. "Wrong! I can actually bench 110 pounds, not just 80."

"That's just sneaky," he protested with a laugh. "I didn't realize we were being that specific with the details!"

"You should have asked." With a wink, I pulled out my phone to make a note.

Jackson tried to peer at my screen over the top of the phone. "What are you doing?"

"Keeping score. That's a point to me. I don't want you to accuse me of cheating when I win."

He laughed again as he leaned back. "So, you really did have a tongue piercing?"

My smile turned sheepish. "I got it when I was fifteen, in my rebellious phase, but I got rid of it when I went to university."

Jackson's eyes shone in anticipation. "I would love to see a photo of rebellious teenaged Holly. Please?"

"Not today." Even if I wanted to show him, I couldn't. "Those only exist on my laptop at home and they haven't seen the light of day in a long time."

His pout was really kind of adorable, but he only wore it for a few seconds before moving on. "And you really are descended from royalty?"

"Very loosely. I can trace my family tree back to Edward III, but so can about a quarter of all British people. I'm not going to get called up to take the throne anytime soon."

"Fair enough, but be warned: now that I know we're playing dirty, I'll adjust accordingly."

"Bring it," I challenged, making him laugh again.

"Alright." He rubbed his palms together as if preparing for a fight. "My turn, then. For my first three things, I'll tell you that I was in the army but only for a month, my first kiss was with Cole's sister, and I studied ballet for three years."

I leaned back in my seat, exhaling deeply. That wouldn't be easy to decipher, but I did my best to think things through logically. "Well, I would say that Cole would have kicked your ass for kissing his sister, but I've met Isabel too and I think she can stand up for herself. She's also beautiful, so I can understand why you'd want to kiss her. Therefore, I'm going to say that one's true."

He inclined his head, which I took as a concession that I had it right. That just left the other two to decide between.

"I know you've got a great body and I can definitely picture you in tights, so I'll say the ballet lessons are true too. And since I don't really think of you as a quitter, I'm going to guess the army thing is the lie. How did I do?"

"You really want to see me in tights?" Even though he was teasing, I couldn't help dropping my gaze to his muscular legs and remembering how they'd looked last night when he took his jeans off.

"Definitely."

Our eyes met for a second, a moment of heat passing between us before he shrugged. "Sorry, but you're wrong. I never did ballet. I wanted to, but we couldn't afford it."

That surprised me. I thought he grew up wealthy like Cole. Well, maybe not quite like Cole, since there weren't many people in the world who were wealthy like Cole, but I had just kind of assumed that he came from money too, from that same world.

"You quit the army?" I asked, equally as surprised about that as I was about him saying he couldn't afford dance lessons.

A brief look of regret flashed across his face. "I joined up when I turned 18, but then my mom disappeared again and I needed to go home and look after my brother and sister. So, I ended up going to college instead so I could live at home and take care of them."

That opened up a whole raft of additional questions. "What do you mean your mum disappeared 'again'?"

I remembered that he said before that he had to look after his younger brother and sister because his mum wasn't around a lot, but I thought he meant she'd been at work or something like that.

Looking uncharacteristically vulnerable, Jackson looked down, avoiding my gaze for a moment before he took a breath and raised his eyes again. "That's something I'd like to tell you about, but maybe after the game. We can keep a list of things to come back to."

He pointed to the phone that I still held in my hands, and I obligingly started a new note of things to discuss later. First entry: Jackson's mum.

When I looked back up, his smile had returned. "And that's a point to me too, don't forget."

With a laugh, I entered a tick against his name.

"Your turn," he invited.

Just as he had, I took a deep breath. He had just shared quite a lot with me and it only seemed fair that I do the same. I'd proposed the game for that reason in the first place, so I could let him in a bit, and if I didn't have to talk about the specifics until later, that made it a bit less scary to share it in the first place.

Screwing up my courage, I blurted out my three facts: "I was the first person in my family to go to university. Since we're talking about first kisses, my first kiss was with the lead singer of a British punk band. And I was proposed to and dumped on the same day."

My heart beat fast as those words came out of my mouth, and Jackson's eyes widened in surprise. "Who proposed to you?"

I forced myself to smile. "Remember, that might not be true. That one could be the lie. You have to guess first, so which one do you think is false?"

He didn't return my smile that time. The concern and sympathy in his eyes were so strong that it nearly brought tears to my eyes.

It felt like he could see right through me.

"Holly. What happened?"

Chapter Six

OPENING UP

~Jackson~

I didn't know which of the other two things Holly told me was the lie, but at that moment, I didn't really care. I had absolutely no doubt that what she said about someone proposing to her and breaking up with her on the same day had been the truth. Her voice wobbled, just a little, in vivid contrast to her usual confident delivery, and she pressed her hand firmly against her leg as if to stop it from trembling.

Those were little tells that I might not have picked up in anyone else, but from Holly, they practically screamed out at me, telling me that the words out of her mouth were very private and important to her.

Knowing that, I couldn't care less about the game. I just wanted her to talk to me.

However, when I asked her to tell me what happened, Holly bit her lip, looking away from me. "I thought we were going to go into more detail about things later."

Damn it. I didn't want to push her too hard, not when she had just shared something so personal and so obviously painful, but it killed me not to know what had hurt her so badly. It had to be related to what she had said to me the night before. She had the same haunted look in her eyes as when she told me she wouldn't ever love anyone.

We seemed to be getting to the heart of the matter, right there and then, and as much as I didn't want to upset her, I couldn't just let it go either. "I said that we could go into more detail when the game is over, and I'm conceding the game to you right now. You win, Holly."

"Are you sure?" Although she tried best to stay composed and tease me as always, I could still hear an undercurrent of worry in her tone. "You don't even know what the prize is."

"You can have any prize you want." After the previous night, I felt confident she wouldn't ask more of me than I was willing to give. "Just tell me what happened. Please."

I tried to keep my voice as soothing and undemanding as I could, to let her know that whatever she had to say would be safe to share with me, and I forced my body to relax even though every nerve felt on edge.

Holly swallowed, still looking into the distance a moment longer before finally turning back to me. "Alright, but this is just between us, okay? Gemma doesn't know about it."

She hadn't even told Gemma? Why not? Why wouldn't she have gone to her best friend for support after something like that? I had so many questions, but I pressed my lips together to keep from asking them and simply nodded instead. I needed to let her take the lead.

Taking a deep breath, she brought her legs up so that she sat cross-legged on the sofa, facing me. I couldn't do the same since my legs were too long, but I turned towards her as fully as I could, matching her position as closely as possible.

"So, I need to back up a little bit to give you the full story."

My eager nod couldn't have been more sincere. I wanted to hear all of it, as much as she was willing to share with me. "Please. I've got nowhere else to be."

She smiled, knowing we were both stuck there until Gemma and Cole returned, but her smile faded as she began to talk.

"I grew up poor," she started bluntly. "Only five miles away from the house where Gemma lived, but I didn't know her then and it might as well have been on a different planet. We lived in a council flat and my parents were on benefits. I don't know the equivalent of that here in America, but we were poor, that's the point."

I understood that far better than she probably realized, but I didn't want to interrupt and make it about me. We were focused on her story; I could share my own with her later.

"My older brothers got in trouble with the police, all kinds of anti-social behaviour. My sisters were pregnant before they left school, and nobody expected any different from me. That rebellious phase I told you about? Mostly, that was just me trying to be who everyone expected me to be. My teachers considered me a lost cause. I could have done well in school, but I didn't really try. I was going nowhere."

"So, what changed?" I couldn't help asking, though I had told myself not to interrupt.

Something in her memory made her smile, almost wistfully. "We took a school trip to the Design Museum to do a workshop. I almost didn't go when some of my friends decided to wag off and I nearly went with them, but at the last minute, I changed my mind and went along anyway. That visit absolutely changed my life. A designer by the name of Norman Honeywell led the workshop. He's a big deal, but I'd never heard of him at the time. He gave us an assignment to start the day off and see how creative we could be. We were asked to design a bedroom for ourselves with a bunch of recyclable material that had been donated. I'd never tried to do anything like that before, but as soon as I started, something just clicked in my head. I could see the completed image before I even started and I completely lost myself in it. I didn't even realize until I finished that he'd been standing over my shoulder, watching me."

"That's amazing." I meant it sincerely. That kind of natural talent had always eluded me, and I'd always admired people who possessed it.

The praise almost made her blush, but she pushed on as if I hadn't said anything. "Well, Mr Honeywell seemed to like it. He was so impressed that he got in touch with my school and offered me an internship to come and work in his workshop. That led to some evening classes, and eventually, I got a scholarship to go and study at Cambridge. That's where I met Gemma, on one of my first days there."

I knew that Gemma and Holly had gone to university together, but my knowledge didn't extend much further than that. Everything else Holly just told me, I'd never heard before.

"She came from a different world than me, like I said. Her family was extremely well off and upper class. She already knew so many people there, people she'd gone to boarding school with, and her boyfriend at the time, Edwin. Since I didn't know anyone, I fell in with her group, and for a while, I thought I fit in with them."

Once again, I could relate, but I stayed silent, waiting for her to continue.

"One of Edwin's friends asked me out shortly after we met. His name was Harry, and I'd never gone out with anyone like him before. The guys I dated back in London were from families like mine. They didn't have any money, so our dates were usually just hanging out at the chippy or going to their flats. For fun, they played football and drank beer and watched telly. But Harry was completely different. He played polo and drank wine and went to the theatre. He was studying law and planning to be a politician, things that no one I grew up with would ever dream of."

She could have almost been narrating parts of my own life. The parallels were uncanny.

"When he asked me out, I couldn't really believe it. I couldn't believe he would be interested in someone like me. He took me out to dinner and even though the restaurant wasn't even all that fancy, no one had ever taken me anywhere like that before, somewhere where the waiter actually came to your table. That sounds so stupid."

She cringed with embarrassment as she said the last sentence, and I quickly jumped in. "Not at all. I get it, Holly, honestly."

She didn't look like she believed me, but she kept going with her story anyway. "After dinner, we went back to his room and we slept together. It was my first time but I didn't tell him that. He didn't act like having sex on the first date was a big deal, so I didn't want to make a big deal out of it either. I never slept with any of the boys I dated before because I didn't want to end up like my sisters, and I knew those boys didn't love me anyway. They would only be doing it because they were bored and wanted something to do. But Harry was so different in every other way, I thought he would be different in that too. I thought it really meant something to him. That *I* meant something."

The last sentence came out in the quiet, vulnerable tone I'd so rarely heard from her, and my heart ached for her and for that rather naïve girl she had been.

The story also confused me, though. I thought I had a pretty good idea where it was going, and it didn't involve a proposal.

Holly quickly confirmed that. "The next day, I had planned to meet up with Gem and the whole group to go to some event. I got there a bit early and Gemma hadn't arrived yet, but Edwin and a few of his friends were there, including Harry. They didn't see me walking over so I caught the end of their conversation."

She took a deep breath and I tried to brace myself for what I suspected was coming.

"Edwin told Harry that Gemma had asked if Harry planned to see me again. Harry laughed and said that he'd seen all there was to see, then he asked the whole group if they could imagine him taking someone like me home to meet his parents. They all laughed like they'd never heard anything more ridiculous."

"Fuck." I didn't often swear, but the situation called for it. What a fucking bastard. "What did you do?"

"I ran away. I'd never been so embarrassed, not only by what he'd said but that I ever thought he would actually be interested in me in the first place."

"He asked you out and slept with you," I pointed out. "That usually means someone's interested. It's not an unreasonable assumption."

The smile she gave me had no humour in it. "In any case, I suppose I should have learned my lesson then, but I didn't, and the next time was even worse."

~Holly~

I could hardly believe the words that were coming out of my mouth. The things I told Jackson, I'd never told anyone. I hadn't intended to tell him so much, but once I started, I couldn't seem to stop. Maybe it had to do with the way he listened to me so attentively, or maybe it came down to the caring look on his face, concerned but not pitying.

I didn't know for sure what made me start, but since we'd already got to that point, I figured I might as well keep going. Once he knew it all, he would understand why we couldn't be together. Hopefully, it wouldn't affect the time we'd planned together before Christmas, because I still wanted to go out with him for those two weeks, and I definitely still wanted to stay in with him at night too.

Would he even still want to after I told him my pathetic story? I didn't know, and yet for some reason, I kept talking anyway.

"So, that was Harry. After that, I didn't date anyone else from Edwin's group of friends. I might not have been the brightest girl at Cambridge, but I knew a dead end when I saw one. My next sort-of serious relationship involved a guy named Nigel."

Jackson wrinkled his nose at the name, making me laugh. He could always make me laugh, no matter what we were talking about.

"I know: not a great name. He came from a less upper-class background than Harry, but still way above me."

Jackson's mouth opened as if he wanted to say something to that, but he quickly closed it again, shaking his head. "Sorry. Keep going."

"We dated for a few months and it seemed to be going well. He told me he loved me, the first guy to ever say that to me. I thought maybe I loved him too. We had a good time together, anyway, and when the holidays came, he took me home to meet his parents."

A slight shift in Jackson's posture told me that he anticipated where this might be going, but again, he didn't interrupt. He waited patiently for me to tell it.

"Apparently, they decided within the first minute of meeting me that I wouldn't be a suitable partner for their son, though they didn't say so to my face. Once again, I only found out by accident. They had a guest suite out in the garden where they put me up for the night, so I said goodnight and went out there, only to realize I had left my phone in the house. I went back to get it, and when I walked by an open window, I heard my name. Nigel and his parents were inside talking, and I got to hear how anyone who met me would know in two seconds that I was basically trash. Not the words they used, but that was the gist of it. They said that if my accent didn't give me away, my lack of social graces would, and he would be embarrassed to have someone like me at parties when he became an important businessman and all the other men had 'proper' wives."

"What the hell is wrong with these people?" The words burst out of Jackson like an eruption, like he'd been trying to hold them in and couldn't do it any longer. "There is nothing wrong with your accent or your social skills, Holly. That's bullshit."

"Well, to be fair, I've done a lot of work since then," I admitted. "After Nigel broke up with me, once his parents made it clear that it came down to me or his monthly allowance, I went and got myself some lessons. It took me months to save up for them. I found myself a dialect coach who made me sound more like Gemma, and I took etiquette classes. And before you ask: yes, those are really a thing."

Although he humoured me with a smile, I could see the anger still lurking in his eyes, and I hadn't even got to the kicker yet.

"Finally, in my last year of university, I met Paul. He came from an upper-class background too, but not Edwin's circle. Gemma knew him and his family from social occasions, but they didn't know each other well. And that time, I fell hard."

Paul's face flashed in front of me, his easygoing, carefree smile similar to Jackson's in so many ways. He was the only other guy I had ever told about Harry and Nigel. He promised me he was nothing like that. He swore he'd stick with me through thick and thin, that we were made to be together.

Those kinds of promises were overwhelming for someone like me, and I wanted so desperately for them to be true.

"I met Paul's family pretty early on, and that time, it went well. I sounded right and I did all the right things, and they accepted me with no problem. Whenever they'd ask about my own family, I'd only say that they were working class from London, and they would all praise me for how hard I had worked to better myself. I didn't realize at the time how patronizing that was, I just took it as a genuine compliment."

Jackson's jaw clenched as he leaned forward. He seemed to sense, rightly, that we were getting to the end of the story.

"We dated for just over a year, but we spent all our time in Cambridge or with his family or on holiday. We never went to see my family. The day we moved into our new flat in London, after graduation when Gemma and I were just about to open up Anchor Design, Paul proposed. He got down on one knee amongst all the moving boxes and asked me to marry him, and it was the happiest moment of my life."

I could still see that moment so clearly in my mind and almost feel it in my bones. The smell of fresh paint on the walls of the flat, the sound of traffic outside the window, and the heavy pounding of my heart as I realized Paul held a ring box in his hands.

"He told me he'd arranged a party for that evening where we could announce it to our families and celebrate. Through my excitement, I realized he'd said families, plural, and when I asked him to clarify, he said that he'd contacted my family and invited them too."

"And he'd never even met them before?" Jackson asked, before his eyes widened. "Sorry, I didn't mean to interrupt."

"It's okay," I assured him. He must have had a lot of questions, and I was doing my best to answer them all before he had to ask. "No, he'd never met them. He had gone into my contacts to get my mum's number, and he had arranged for cars to go and pick them up and bring them to the venue."

My eyes closed in shame as the scene played across my memory.

"The party had already started when we got there. Paul hadn't told anyone about the proposal, he'd said the party was to celebrate our new flat and the start of our new lives in London. My family hadn't arrived yet, and I began to hope that maybe they wouldn't come. That hope didn't last long. They turned up, and I'll never forget the look in Paul's eyes when he saw them. My dad in his mismatched suit, my brothers with their tattoos, and my sisters, both pregnant, with an army of little ones in tow. He probably didn't realize that people like them existed in real life."

Both my pain and my anger came back in equal parts as I recalled the last part of the story.

"After talking to my parents for no more than five minutes, Paul asked to speak to me. I'd never seen him so rattled before. He had always been the joker, never taking anything too seriously, but when we were alone, he turned to me and said he finally understood why I was ashamed of my family."

"Fucker," Jackson muttered under his breath, making me smile. I'd hardly heard him swear at all before and it sounded strange coming out of his sweet mouth.

"The problem was: he was right. I *had* been ashamed of them, but in that moment, I finally realized how wrong that was. I had nothing to be ashamed of and neither did they. They might not be middle class, but they're decent people doing the best they can with the lives they have, and I had spent the last four years trying to pretend they didn't exist and that I sprang fully-formed from somewhere that didn't include them. And for what? So I could marry someone who thought I should be ashamed?"

"You stood up to him?" Jackson guessed, and I nodded.

"Anger got the better of me and I was harsh, probably harsher than he deserved, honestly. After all, I hadn't given him any reason to think I was anything other than embarrassed about my past. I had tried so hard to be the girl he wanted me to be that I had ignored all the other parts of me. And when I told him that there was more to me than he realized and I didn't want to hide it anymore, he withdrew his proposal."

Even though Jackson knew where the story would end, he still stared at me in disbelief. "He just took it back?"

"He said we were lucky we hadn't told anyone about the engagement yet so there wouldn't have to be a big scene. He said he'd find his own place and move out of our new flat as soon as possible. And just like that, our relationship was over."

"Wow." Jackson leaned back, running his hand through his hair as he processed all of that. For a moment, neither of us said anything. He seemed to be waiting to see if I would add anything else, but when I didn't, he spoke again. "Thank you for telling me, Holly. Really. It means a lot to me that you would share this with me, but I have to ask: why haven't you told Gemma?"

For the first time since I'd started speaking, tears came to my eyes. "How could she understand? She has no idea what it's like to feel judged based on your class. She is the one person I have met who honestly never did that, and she had her own problems with Edwin at the time, so I didn't want to burden her. Besides, I didn't need her to explain it to me. Obviously, I'm not the marrying kind, at least not for the kind of man I'm attracted to. I'm a girl who's fun to have around for a while, and I've found plenty of men to do just that with. That's all I look for now, and it's all I need. Can you understand that?"

At last, we'd come to the crux of the matter. I needed him to see why a relationship between us would never work, and to understand it had nothing to do with him as a person.

Jackson's reply sounded tentative and cautious. "I understand that you've had some terribly bad luck, but it doesn't mean it would happen again."

"The first time might have been bad luck. The second, I chalked up to experience. But by the third time, I have to accept there's a pattern. It went really well until it didn't. They all thought I was great until they didn't. Each time I let myself believe it would be different, but it wasn't, and I can't do it again, Jackson. I don't want to live through the moment when you realize I'm not the woman you thought you wanted."

His expression grew more unhappy by the second, and he opened his mouth to respond, but before he could say anything, we heard the gentle ding of the lift followed by Gemma's voice. "We're home!"

~Jackson~

After everything Holly just told me, I wanted her to know she was even more the woman I wanted than she had been before, but I hadn't managed to get the words out before Gemma called out from the hall, letting us know that she and Cole were back.

I glanced down at my watch in surprise. They hadn't even been gone for two hours and Noah hadn't woken up yet. Their timing could hardly be worse. At least Holly had finished her story, but we still had a lot more to talk about.

She had no idea how much I could relate to so much of what she'd said. Not to having an engagement taken back, I hadn't gone through anything like that, but so much of the rest of it: the feelings of inadequacy around people of a different social class, the need to hide things about her past that would make people uncomfortable, feeling like she didn't quite fit in anywhere she went. All of that was very familiar to me.

"We're coming in, so it's your last chance to make sure all your clothes are on..."

Gemma's voice got closer and closer until she appeared in the doorway, peering in eagerly as if she really expected to find us naked. When she saw us sitting on the couch, not even touching and fully clothed, her face fell in disappointment.

Cole hadn't been kidding about how much she wanted Holly and me to get together.

"Why are you back so soon?" As soon as the words were out of my mouth, I winced at how they sounded. Obviously, they could return to their apartment whenever they wanted; I just wished it hadn't been right when we were making such good progress. Sure enough, Holly stood up to give Gemma her full attention, our conversation clearly at an end.

"Someone forgot her passport," Cole teased his wife, giving her a kiss on the temple. "We had to cut the day short."

"I blame the baby brain," Gemma protested before giving Holly and I an apologetic shrug. "It's a real thing."

"How long do you get to use that excuse for?" Holly asked, making Cole's lips twitch in amusement as she took his side.

"As long as she wants to." I jumped in on Gemma's behalf so she wasn't completely outnumbered. "She grew a human being. That deserves some credit."

"Thank you, Jackson." Gemma gave me a grateful smile before looking between me and Holly. "What were you two up to? Noah's still asleep?"

"He is, and we were just talking." Though I tried to catch Holly's eye, she refused to look in my direction. Did she regret opening up to me as she just had? I really hoped not, and I would have to show her she had no reason to.

If Gemma noticed any tension between us, she didn't show it. "Well, if you don't have anywhere else to be, why don't you stay for the afternoon and have dinner with us? It would be so nice to hang out, all four of us."

Her plan to maneuver more time for Holly and I to be together couldn't be less subtle, and normally, I'd be grateful for it. However, at that particular moment, I really wanted to get Holly alone somewhere to continue our conversation.

Before I could answer though, Holly jumped in. "That sounds great. I don't have any plans until later."

With those words, she gave me a wink, which both pleased and confused me. Did we have plans later? I hadn't made any plans, but perhaps she meant her prize from the game that I'd conceded. I didn't know whether to worry about that or look forward to it.

The rest of the afternoon went surprisingly quickly. As Gemma suggested, hanging out as two couples rather than just the three of us made a nice change. Often, I ended up feeling like the third wheel to Gemma and Cole, but with Holly there, things balanced out. Holly was charming and funny and just as appealing as always, all traces of the hurt and scarred woman she'd shown me earlier completely wiped away. If what she'd told me wasn't so firmly imprinted on my mind, I would have begun to wonder if I had imagined the whole thing.

We played with Noah a bit more and Holly even held him for a while as Gemma and I made supper and Cole made a few phone calls. She might say she was no good with kids, but I saw the soft smile she gave Noah when she thought no one could see. On his part, he found her blonde hair fascinating, reaching out to grab it whenever he got a chance.

Gemma sent Holly and Cole off together to pick out a wine for dinner from their specially designed wine closet before turning to me eagerly. "So?"

She only said the one word, but I knew what she was asking. "We had a good talk." Of course I couldn't tell her anything Holly had told me in confidence, but maybe I could find out a bit about what Gemma knew about it. "What did you think of her boyfriend, Paul?"

Gemma's eyes went wide. "She told you about Paul? Wow." The last word was almost whispered under her breath, but I heard it anyway. "I honestly don't know what happened there. One day, they were moving in together and the next, they were broken up. She just said they decided it wouldn't work. She swore he didn't cheat or anything like that."

No, he hadn't done that, at least, but I didn't know how much consolation that was.

"But if you're asking if they were good together? Yes and no. She seemed happy, but always a little bit on edge too, almost like she was waiting for something bad to happen. She was never really relaxed with him like she is with you."

Really? Gemma thought Holly seemed relaxed with me? Before I could ask her to explain, Holly and Cole returned with the wine and the conversation quickly moved on to other things.

When dinner ended, Holly and I made our excuses and headed out together. Gemma gave Holly a hug as they said goodbye and whispered something in her ear before they both glanced over at me and smiled at each other.

Well, that didn't give me any reason to feel self-conscious or anything.

We didn't say much in the elevator, but when we got out onto the street, Holly turned to me with a bright smile that I had started to recognize as a sign that she didn't want to talk about anything too deep. "You live near here, right? Are you ready to show me your place?"

"Is that your prize?" I asked curiously, still not having a clue what she had in mind for the evening.

Holly tossed me a teasing wink in reply. "Part of it. I'll tell you the rest of what I won when we get there."

It seemed pretty obvious she didn't want to have further serious conversation, so what exactly did she have in mind? A few of the same nerves I'd had the night before fluttered up again, but I also remembered how supportive and patient she had been with me, and I pushed my worry back down. She already knew my limits, so she shouldn't be disappointed, and maybe if I could prove to her that I wanted her just the same way after everything she'd told me, it would help her to understand that my feelings for her weren't going to change. She seemed convinced that they would eventually, but that simply wasn't the case.

With all that in mind, I held out my hand to her. She hesitated only a few seconds before gently placing hers in it, and we walked together hand-in-hand for the few blocks to my own apartment, keeping the conversation light and fairly impersonal as we went.

My building and my apartment were far less grand than Cole's, just a two-bedroom apartment with a small balcony. Cole paid me very well in my position as acquisitions director for Stamer Hotels, but I didn't feel the need to spend it on anything flashy just for me. I had saved a good amount to be ready to buy a house when I found the woman I wanted to settle down with. I even had a townhouse picked out not too far away, my dream house for when I found my dream woman.

What would Holly think of that house? I'd like to find out, but not that evening. For that night, I took her inside and gave her a quick tour of my apartment before we settled in my living room with a glass of wine each, much like we had in her hotel room the night before.

"What do you want for your prize?" I asked her straight out once we were comfortable, unable to take the suspense any longer.

A beguiling mix of confidence and vulnerability played across her face. "Well, earlier I shared quite a lot about myself with you, and it's left me feeling a bit exposed."

"You never have to feel that way with me," I tried to tell her. "I'll never..."

"Jackson, hush." She cut me off by pressing her finger against my lips, a smile playing at the corners of her mouth. "Let me finish. Earlier, I exposed myself to you emotionally. I think that's fair to say?"

I nodded in agreement, her finger still preventing me from speaking.

"As my prize for winning the game, I want you to return the favour. I want you to expose yourself too, but it's not the emotional side of you I'm interested in."

My heart beat faster as I finally put together what she was saying.

"What do you think, Jackson?" she asked, raising her eyebrows at me in that very sexy, challenging way of hers. "Are you ready to show me everything?"

Chapter Seven

A Wrong Step

~Holly~

Despite the smile on my face, my heart continued to race just as it had for the last few hours. I couldn't remember the last time I felt so sick with nerves. Ever since Gemma and Cole returned to their flat, I had felt off-balance and disoriented.

Why on earth had I told Jackson all of that about myself? What could I have been thinking? When it was just him and me talking, he'd made it seem comfortable and almost safe but as soon as the rest of the world intruded, I began to realize just how much I had revealed and I wished I could take it all back. Of course, by then, it was too late.

All I could do was what I always did when I felt insecure: deflect the attention away from anything personal and focus on the one side of myself that men had never failed to find attractive. Maybe no one wanted to marry me, but no one had ever turned down a night in my bed either.

Not until Jackson, at least.

If I could turn the heat up between us, maybe it would help to get back to a place where I felt comfortable and in control. Maybe that would get rid of the twisting feeling in my stomach that had been making me feel ill ever since our talk.

However, when I suggested to Jackson that I wanted to see him naked, he leaned back from me, his brow furrowing into a look of uncertainty.

"I'd be happy to show you the real me." He spoke softly, as if he didn't want to upset me. "But maybe I could do that in the same way you did? I could start by telling you about my mom if you want. You said earlier that you wanted to know more about her."

I had said that. I still had the note saved on my phone and I did want to know about his mum, I really did, but not at that exact moment. Talking wouldn't help to ease the dread I felt.

"You conceded the game to me," I reminded him, trying to keep the panic out of my voice. "You said I could have any prize I wanted, and this is what I want, Jackson."

As he looked away from me, his internal conflict clear from the look on his face, my stomach sank even further.

He was taking it back.

Although logically, I knew the two situations weren't comparable, all I could see in that moment was Paul asking for his ring back, telling me that he had changed his mind.

Jackson must have changed his mind too, the attraction he'd previously felt for me evaporating once he knew how I'd never managed to hold a man's interest in the long term. One after another, they all realized that I was defective in some way, and now, he thought so too

Why hadn't I just kept my mouth shut?

I couldn't take back what I'd said, but I didn't have to sit there and wait to be rejected again either, so I grabbed onto the one bit of control I still had left.

"You know what? Never mind." My hand shook as I placed my wine glass on the end table, getting to my feet. "I'm tired. I'm going to head back to the hotel."

The hotel had a bar where I could get something stronger to drink and even find some male company if I wanted to. Somebody out there would be happy to help distract me and tune out the thoughts of self-recrimination echoing around my head.

"Holly, wait," Jackson pleaded as he also stood up. "We don't have to talk if you don't want to. We could just hang out and watch a movie, or we could go out somewhere..."

By the time he got that far, I'd already made it to the door, shoving my feet back into my boots. "No, thanks. I need some time by myself."

Though his lips tightened, he didn't try to stop me. "Okay, if that's what you want. Let me call you a taxi."

"I can walk." A little more forcefully than necessary, I grabbed my bag and pulled the door open.

"It's thirty blocks and it's cold out," Jackson protested as I stepped into the hall. "Do you even know where you're going?"

"I'm pretty sure I can figure it out," I snapped at him. His concern felt patronizing for a grown woman who lived in a major city. I had my phone and I could read a map. I didn't need him looking after me.

Again, he didn't argue, though he didn't stop talking either. "Can I call you later? I had some ideas about what we could do tomorrow..."

If he finished that sentence, I didn't hear it. I'd already closed the door behind me.

Although the cold air nipped at my skin when I stepped out the front door of Jackson's building, I hardly noticed. My cheeks were flushed hot with embarrassment. I had *never* been so completely shot down like that, at least not when it came to sex. Seduction had always been my safe place, the one situation when I never had to worry about whether I would be good enough.

But apparently, for Jackson, I wasn't.

Bitter tears stung my eyes as I started walking, not entirely sure which direction I should go. When I got to the next intersection and realized the numbered streets were going higher when I needed to go lower, I spun around with a frustrated groan and walked back in the opposite direction instead.

That was fun while it lasted, I thought angrily as I wiped my face dry before the tears could freeze on my skin. I couldn't even manage two full days of playing at being in a relationship with Jackson before it went wrong. And why was I even so upset? The only reason it made sense would be if I had actually believed there might be something real between us. Even though I had told myself it couldn't happen, some part of me must have hoped for it anyway, and with his rejection, that hope had just been crushed.

My phone buzzed with a text, the device vibrating against my hand that I'd shoved in my pocket for warmth, and though I wanted to ignore it, curiosity got the better of me. I thought it would be from Jackson, but it came from Gemma instead.

Everything okay? Jackson just asked me to make sure you got back to the hotel alright. Do you need to talk? Gem

Why was everyone so obsessed with talking? I sent her back a two-word response – *I'm fine* – before shoving the phone back in my pocket.

Eventually, my breathing evened out, and as I continued walking, I began to cool down, both in body and mind. Without the blood rushing through my ears, my head became clearer, and I began to get embarrassed for a whole new reason.

What had I just done?

Talking with Jackson about my past had not only dredged up those old feelings of inadequacy, but apparently, it made me behave like a child as well, throwing a tantrum instead of just telling him how I felt as an adult would do.

If he hadn't been turned off by me before, he certainly must be after that.

By the time I made it back to the hotel, cold and tired, I was no longer angry, only a little sad instead. Bypassing the bar, I headed straight to my room where I pulled out my phone and sent Gemma a better reply, apologizing for my earlier curtness. She quickly texted back and assured me she'd taken no offense, and repeated her offer to talk.

I did need to talk, but not to her. I had to apologize to Jackson instead.

That much, I knew, but what to say would be tricker. Should I try to be funny? Sincere? What would he appreciate? My first message failed on all levels, so I deleted it and started over again. Halfway through my second attempt, a message came in from the very man I was thinking of.

With some trepidation, I opened it, only to be greeted with a picture of his naked shoulder.

I stared at it for a moment in confusion before another one popped up, that one of his chest, quickly followed by one of his abs.

He looked incredibly sexy, but the photos bewildered me. What did they mean? What was he doing?

The next text just had a message with no photo. *Should I keep going? How much do you want to see?*

Immediately, guilt rushed through me. Of course I wanted to see him, but not that way. Not because he felt he had to appease me after my appalling behaviour.

I quickly deleted the text I had been typing and wrote a new one instead. *I want to see it all, but in person, when you're ready. I'm sorry for tonight. I was out of line. It's cliché, but honestly, it was much more about me than you.*

Almost immediately, my phone rang and Jackson's voice came through the line.

He didn't even bother with 'hello'. "I'm sorry too, Holly. I didn't mean to push you. I really appreciate that you shared so much with me, and I did promise you a prize if you answered my question. It wasn't fair of me to change the rules afterwards."

With a sigh, I leaned back, resting my head against the sofa as I covered my eyes with my free hand. "We keep apologizing to each other. That's got to be a bad sign."

He disagreed. "Actually, I think it's a good sign. It means we can see each other's point of view and admit when we're wrong. Nobody's ever going to be perfect all the time and it's not realistic to expect that, but if we can talk it out afterwards, that's what matters."

How could it even be possible that he wasn't angry with me for how I behaved?

"And I know it's not exactly what you had in mind, but I *am* naked right now, talking to you. That's something I've never done with a woman before."

He was actually fully naked? The images he had just sent me took on a whole new meaning and I couldn't help asking: "Were you really going to send me a dick pic?"

His warm laughter began to ease the nervous ache in my stomach. "Maybe? I'm not sure. I might have chickened out, but I was thinking about it at least."

"Well, now I'm definitely thinking about it too."

He laughed again, making my heart even lighter. "Are you going to give me something to think about, Holly?"

Could he really mean what it sounded like? "Jackson Hanmer, are you suggesting we get dirty over the phone?"

"I'm game if you are," he offered, and finally, my queasiness vanished entirely, my body starting to respond to his tone and the idea that he didn't want to give up on our challenge even after our disagreement.

"In that case, tell me what you want me to do."

~Jackson~

After Holly ran out of my apartment, I texted Gemma to ask her to make sure Holly got back okay before I sat back down on the couch to try to figure out exactly how things had gone so wrong so quickly.

Her request had taken me by surprise. I didn't see the correlation between the game we played and me getting naked for her. It seemed completely random, and despite her best efforts to convince me otherwise, I didn't think it was even what she really wanted. When we had been in her hotel room the night before and we had taken our clothes off, she had been encouraging and patient with me, and there had been real desire and maybe even affection in her eyes. That night, though, I could only see fear and that lingering hurt from when she told me about her past.

So, I offered to tell her about something painful for me instead, thinking that made more sense and might help her to feel closer to me, the same way learning about her past had made me feel more connected to her. Instead, she completely shut down and shut me out.

It didn't make sense to me in the moment, but as I thought back over what she'd said, I started to get an idea of where I had gone wrong.

She told me that talking about her past relationships had left her feeling exposed, so she wanted me to expose myself too. By offering to talk to her, I'd been trying to do that, but maybe opening up about my mom didn't feel like exposing myself in the same way she had done. Talking to Holly about anything, even my mom, still lay pretty firmly in my comfort zone, whereas she had gone way outside of hers when she told me about her past rejections.

Perhaps, her suggestion that I get naked wasn't as random as I had originally thought. She knew it would be a stretch for me, and she asked me to take a risk, just as she had done in opening up to me.

And what did I do? I refused.

Damn it.

I still had my doubts about whether stripping for her was the best thing for either of us at the moment, but maybe we could have found a compromise that would have still satisfied her. Instead, I took it upon myself to offer to do something that, from her point of view, didn't begin to compare, and *that* was why she got upset.

By opening up to me that afternoon, she had proven her willingness to give me an honest chance and share things with me that she didn't share with anyone else, and the time had come for me to do the same.

So, when Gemma texted me back to say that Holly had made it back to her hotel, I made up my mind. I would do something I'd never done before and push myself out of my comfort zone, and hope that it would show her that I was just as willing as she was to be vulnerable.

Taking my phone into my bedroom, I quickly removed all my clothes, doing it fast so I couldn't second-guess myself. In the stark, unforgiving light, I started taking photos and sending them to her. My shoulder first, because I thought it might make her laugh. My chest would give her a clearer indication of what I intended.

When I asked if she wanted to see more, I found myself holding my breath as I waited for a response. Was she still angry with me? Would she accept my peace offering?

When her apologetic reply came in, I hit the call button right away, needing to hear her tone and for her to hear the sincerity in mine. I felt rather silly admitting to her that I was fully naked, but when I heard the desire and the humour in her reply, sounding so much more like her usual self, I knew immediately that it had been the right call. We had both done something new for us, which put us back on a more even footing, just as I'd hoped.

And for some reason, I didn't even feel that strange about being naked and having her know about it. When she suggested that we go a little further, my body responded instantly, my dick jumping in anticipation as the blood flow increased with the mere thought that she might be thinking about it.

"I've never done this before," I told her, though she had probably already guessed that. "But I'll give it a try."

Her voice through the receiver felt warm and soothing and seductive all at the same time, wrapping me up in its heat. "That's all I can ask. Since you're already naked, what do you want me to take off?"

It didn't take much effort to picture her in her hotel room, waiting for my instructions and willing to obey them, and the thought sent another wave of longing through me.

"Take off your shirt first." My voice sounded a little more throaty than usual as I imagined her doing just that.

She had been wearing a buttoned blouse that day, so it took her a moment to undo the buttons, but she counted them off for me as she opened them. In my mind, she wore the same bra as the day before, the memory of which still burned bright in my mind, but I quickly realized I didn't have to assume. I could ask her to describe her lingerie to me.

"What are you wearing underneath?"

Holly's voice also sounded a little lower than usual as she replied. "It's a red bra with a black lace overlay and lace trim. I'm running my fingers along the edge of it now."

Oh, God. I could see it so clearly in my mind, the fabric covering the swell of her breasts perfectly, and my dick throbbed again, growing harder by the second.

"Is it a matching set again?" My words sounded breathless, even to me.

"Let's see," she teased me, as if she didn't already know. The sound of the zipper on her jeans came through the phone and I exhaled loudly as the blood rushed through my now fully erect dick.

A moment's pause followed, building the anticipation even higher before she spoke again. "Yup, the knickers are a match, except they're a little wetter than the bra is."

I stifled a moan and she chuckled, her voice warm and sweet as honey. There was something about her using the word 'knickers' that struck me as insanely sexy. It wouldn't sound like that in an American accent, I was certain.

"Take them off." The words surprised me as they came out of my mouth. I probably wouldn't have been so bold in person, but somehow, the distance made it feel a bit less intimidating.

It must have taken her by surprise too because another brief pause followed, only for a moment. "Yes, sir," she teased, but I could hear the slightly breathy quality to her voice that told me she was turned on too. A moment later, she confirmed it. "They're off, but now I'm even more wet than before."

Taking a deep breath, I decided to step even further out of my comfort zone, just like she'd asked me to. "I'd like to know what that feels like."

With her answering groan, a surge of pride ran through me. I was actually doing okay at this, but just when I thought I had things under control, Holly firmly took the reins. "Are you hard now, Jackson?"

Did she really have to ask? "I don't know if I've ever been so hard," I told her honestly.

"Are you touching yourself?" Her voice sounded hot and breathy, and I made a strange hissing noise I could hardly believe came out of me.

"Do you want me to?"

"So badly," she sighed, making me groan in response. *Damn, I had no idea this could be so hot.* "Will you do what I tell you?"

"Of course," I agreed readily. At that point, I would have done anything she said.

"I'm going to touch myself now." Her words made my dick twitch again. Somehow, it kept getting harder. "I want to come when you do. Is that okay?"

I nodded before remembering that she couldn't see me, so I forced out a reply, my voice so tight that it barely sounded like me. "That sounds good."

"Put the phone on speaker and put it down so you can make yourself comfortable," she instructed. "I'll do the same."

Quickly, I turned on my speaker as she said, grabbed some lube from my bedside table and lay down on my bed, closing my eyes so I could better picture Holly the way she had looked the night before, laying on her bed in her bra and panties.

"Take your cock in your hand." Holly's voice sounded like something out of a dream as I lay there with my eyes closed, grasping my painfully hard dick just as she said. "Give it a squeeze. Pretend it's my hand."

I inhaled sharply as the jolt of pleasure ran through me. "What are you doing?" I managed to ask, wanting to make sure she was enjoying herself too.

"I'm starting slow on my clit, but I'm going to put one finger inside while you start stroking yourself. Are you ready?"

"Yes." Even getting the one word out felt like a struggle, I found it so hard to breathe.

As my hand moved up and down my dick, slowly but firmly, Holly sighed into the phone. "I'm so wet for you, Jackson. I'm imagining it's your fingers right now, deep inside me."

Holy hell, this wouldn't take long at all. I hoped she didn't expect me to be able to wait.

Maybe I could say something too. Would it help her along to know how much she affected me? Summoning all my courage, I tried to put it into words. "I'm rock hard for you, Holly. I've never wanted anyone so bad."

Her soft sound of pleasure filled the air as my hand started to move faster. I really couldn't take much more and her next words only made it more difficult. "My nipples are so hard. I loved you biting on them last night. I'm imagining it right now."

"Fuck, Holly." The curse was out of my mouth before I realized I'd even thought it, and she exhaled again with a gentle laugh.

"That's definitely what we're working towards." She inhaled again, her breathing as clear as if she were right there in the room with me. "I'm so close, Jackson."

"Thank God," I muttered, and we both laughed, only for a second before the sound turned to moaning once more. "I don't think I can wait. I'm going to come now, fuck."

My whole body tightened as I edged nearer to my release, and when Holly cried out my name, I had to let it go. The whole world faded as my pleasure washed over me, leaving me aware of nothing but the bliss of the orgasm and the sound of Holly's laboured breathing on the other end of the phone.

How could it be possible to feel so connected to someone who wasn't even in the same room?

For a moment, neither of us spoke, but soon, her voice filled the air again, gently teasing as always. "So, that's phone sex. What do you think?"

I laughed, since she meant it as a joke, but I didn't speak the words that were in my head. I felt closer to her than ever and I wanted her even more than I had before. If I let her know just how badly I wanted to do that in person, I didn't know if I could find the will to stop it from happening, and she still hadn't given me any sign of being closer to falling in love with me than she had been when we started.

I was in so much trouble.

~Holly~

The morning looked bright and sunny as I pulled back the curtains in my hotel bedroom. Jackson and I had talked for a while the night before after our mutual climax and I felt a lot better about everything. Not *only* because of the orgasm, although that had certainly helped, but even more so because we talked through how our argument made us feel and why we both reacted the way we did.

I'd never really had a talk like that with a man before, analyzing my emotions and their origins. Being so open with someone felt strange to me, but actually kind of nice too.

For that day, I had plans to see Gemma again at her apartment. Cole would be at work, and Gemma and I needed to review some things for our business. Most of the time, we could do our work virtually, but since we'd known that I would be coming for a visit, we'd been saving a few designs to go over in person. Stamer Hotels were expanding in Europe over the coming year and Anchor Design had six different hotel projects on the go for them, two refurbishments of existing buildings and four completely new designs. The contract we had signed with them had certainly elevated our business to a whole new level, not to mention what it had done for Gemma's personal life.

However, Jackson had told me that he'd like to take me out once Gemma and I were finished, so at five o'clock on the dot, he knocked on Gemma's home office door. He seemed to be able to let himself in and out of their flat at will.

"What amazing things did you ladies design today?" he asked cheerily as he walked in, giving Gemma a kiss on the cheek before doing the same for me.

Seeing each other for the first time since our steamy phone call the night before, he blushed as our eyes met, and an unfamiliar affection swelled within my chest. He really could be adorable.

Gemma showed him a few of the blueprints that we'd been working on before turning to us both with a smile. "You're both technically on holiday right now, so that's probably enough work talk. What do you have planned for this evening?"

That was a good question. Once again, I had no idea what Jackson had up his sleeve. He seemed to enjoy keeping me in the dark, which was fine with me as long as I got to have him in the dark a little later

"It's a typical New York night out," was all he would say as we walked back to the lift and he helped me into my coat. "Are we still on for Friday, Gemma?"

"Friday?" I repeated curiously. "What's happening Friday?"

Gemma rolled her eyes. "Cole wants to take Noah to see Father Christmas at Macy's, but he doesn't want to wait in the queue like everyone else so he's booked out the whole place for twenty minutes, no matter how much I try to tell him that Noah does not care and will either sleep or cry through the whole thing. It seems a waste to me, but Jackson's excited about it at least."

"I can't believe you're *not* excited about it!" he laughed. "You're the most Christmas-mad person I know. You just don't know how great it's going to be because you've never been. Holly, you'll have to come too."

His contagious enthusiasm made me smile, and I had no other plans anyway. "Of course, I'd love to go."

"That's settled, then. Have a good evening." Gemma gave me a wink that I assumed was meant to be subtle, but Jackson must have seen it too. "I'll talk to you later, Hols."

As we rode the lift down and stepped out onto the street together, Jackson and I made easy small talk about the day. Since it was December, the sky had turned dark already, the air chilly but not too cold. Jackson offered me his arm like an old-fashioned gentleman, and though I rolled my eyes at him, I took it anyway. I liked the feel of his warm body next to me, and being so close to him, I couldn't help thinking about the phone call from the night before. Now that we'd opened that door, would he be willing to go farther that night? I couldn't wait to find out.

"Are you going to give me any hint where we're going?"

He gave a partial answer. "Well, we're making a few stops, but first up is the park."

"The park?" He said that like I should know what park he was talking about.

He grinned at my confusion. "You haven't been to Central Park yet, I take it?"

Oh, *that* park. "No, not yet."

"Well, we'll change that right now."

The entrance to the park sat only a block from Gemma and Cole's apartment, and as we stepped through the gates onto one of the paths, the city quickly disappeared behind us. If it weren't for the sound of the traffic, it would have been easy to forget we were in a huge city at all.

"Did you play here a lot growing up?" I asked as we passed a small playground tucked in behind some trees. "It must be an amazing city to be a kid in."

The part of London I had grown up in didn't have any green spaces like this. The city centre had the royal parks, but my friends and I never strayed too far outside our own postcode.

His smile felt a little wistful. "I didn't have a lot of time for playing, but I tried to bring my brother and sister here about once a month when I was a teenager. We went out on the lake in a boat once. I lied about my age since we were supposed to have an adult with us, but luckily, the girl working there was about my age too and she didn't care enough to challenge me on it."

"You mean you flirted with her until you got your way," I teased him, and he gave me a wider, cheekier grin in return.

"Maybe a little."

I could imagine. He was such a charmer, I could guess he'd talked himself into and out of a lot of things in his life.

"Where do your brother and sister live now?" He'd mentioned them a few times but I didn't know anything about them.

"Hold that thought."

For a moment, I didn't understand why he was putting me off, until we rounded a corner and saw the horse-drawn carriage waiting there. It looked like something from a fairy tale: a white horse in front of a white carriage, the driver wearing a top hat.

"Are we going for a ride?" I asked in surprise as Jackson steered us in that direction.

"Would you like to?" His eyes were filled with such hope that even if I hadn't wanted to, I wouldn't have been able to say no. However, I actually did want to. I'd never done anything like it.

"I suppose a carriage is okay. No champagne and roses though?" I teased, and Jackson's face immediately fell. With an internal groan, I rushed to reassure him. "I'm just kidding, Jackson. I don't need all that, this is perfect."

As we walked up to the carriage, the driver tipped his hat to us in greeting. "Good evening, folks. Lovely evening, isn't it? There are some blankets back there to keep you warm. Anything else you need, just let me know."

Jackson helped me up into the carriage, still playing the gentleman, and I settled down on the seat as he pulled himself up and grabbed a few of the fake fur blankets to drape across ourselves. When we were cozy, he reached over in front of me and pulled a piece of fabric off a little platform to reveal...

"Champagne and roses, as requested."

He looked so pleased with himself as my mouth fell open in surprise that I couldn't help laughing.

"Wait a minute! If you had this planned, why did you look so sad when I just mentioned it?"

"Because you spoiled my surprise. Shall we?"

With a practiced hand, he grabbed the bottle of champagne from the bucket of ice and popped the cork as the carriage began moving through the park. Once we both had our glasses filled, we leaned back beneath the blanket, his thigh pressed right up against mine. Old-fashioned street lamps cast a twilight over the whole scene as we travelled through the park. Only a touch of snow would have made it better, but I wasn't about to complain.

"This is amazing," I told him sincerely. "I've never seen anything so romantic. You're not playing fair, Jackson Hanmer."

"I'm just trying to make us even," he whispered in my ear, his breath hot in the winter air. "I haven't been able to stop thinking about last night."

A shiver went through me that I knew had nothing to do with the cold. "I haven't either," I admitted. The phone sex with him had been better than actual sex I'd had with several other men.

When he leaned back, I immediately missed his warmth. "So, I needed to give us something else to think about. What do you think? Will this do the trick?"

With the arm furthest from me, he gestured to the whole scene: the magical park, the carriage, the champagne and roses. It couldn't have been more perfect, but as soon as that thought crossed my mind, I remembered other moments I thought were perfect too. My problem wasn't finding the perfect moments, it was that it could all be pulled out from under me at any time with no warning at all.

"Hey." Jackson's voice was soft and filled with concern as I glanced back over at him. "Where'd you go there?"

"Still thinking about last night," I lied, not wanting to bring down the mood with more talk of my past. "This is amazing, Jackson, but if you think it's going to make me less determined to get you naked instead of more, you're seriously confused."

He laughed as he took my hand in his. "Well then, let's talk about something extremely unsexy. Let me tell you about my mom."

Chapter Eight

A Perfect Son

~Jackson~

The sudden distance in Holly's eyes confused me. One minute, she looked happy and maybe even a little bit charmed by the experience I'd put together for us, and the next, her eyes had taken on that slightly haunted quality that made me want to take her in my arms and kiss all the fear away.

Her explanation about what she'd been thinking about didn't feel entirely truthful, but it gave me an opening to move on to what I wanted to talk about anyway. The day before, she asked me about my mom, and just before we got in the carriage, she asked about my brother and sister. After she'd been so open with me about all the things from her past, I didn't want to keep anything from her. So, taking a sip from my champagne glass to steel my nerves, I dove in.

"My mom was really young when she had me: sixteen years old and not ready to be a mother. My grandparents took care of me a lot as a baby and toddler. The first real memory I have of my mom is her coming home after a long period away and me thinking that she was a babysitter."

Holly switched her champagne glass to her other hand and reached out to me under the blanket, placing her hand on my knee to show me she was listening. "Where was your dad?"

"I've never met him. He wasn't involved at all, but when I was about five, my mom met a new guy and decided to settle down. They got a little apartment up in Washington Heights and they took me to live with them. His name was Brian and he worked in construction. He was a really good guy. He loved her and he treated me well even though I wasn't his. My mom got pregnant pretty quickly and my sister, Layla, was born, followed by Josh about a year and half later. For a little while, things were pretty good. We didn't have much, but we were happy."

Holly gave me a curious look when I said we didn't have much, but I didn't want to make that the focus of my story. First, I had to get through the stuff about my mom, and I could tell her more about the rest of it later.

"After Josh was born, things changed. I suspect now that my mom must have gone through some kind of postpartum depression, but at the time, I had no idea. She started going out more and more, not wanting to be at home, and finally, one day she just didn't come home at all."

Holly's hand squeezed my knee and I put my own hand on top of it, letting her know without words that I recognized her concern as I pressed ahead.

"Brian was at a bit of a loss. He did the best he could, but he worked long hours and he had to work to support us all, so a lot of responsibility around the house fell to me even though I was only eight years old. He got one of the neighbours to watch Layla and Josh while I went to school, but I had to get them up and ready in the morning, make them breakfast and make supper when I got home. It didn't leave a lot of time for just being a kid."

"How long did that go on for?" Holly's voice was quiet beside me, as if she hadn't wanted to interrupt but couldn't help it.

"The first time? Just a few months before my mom came back. But even when she was back, she wasn't fully there, not like she had been before. It always felt like she was just waiting for something better to come along, and after about a year, she left again."

"That must have been so hard." The words were plain and sympathetic, and I pressed down on her hand gently to let her know I appreciated them.

"It wasn't easy," I agreed. "I didn't understand why we weren't good enough that she'd want to stay with us. I thought I must be doing something wrong."

Holly inhaled, her breath a bit shaky, but I tried to move on before she could say anything. I really wasn't looking for pity, I just wanted her to understand where I was coming from.

"Of course, I realize now it had nothing to do with me, or Layla or Josh, or even Brian. It was about her and her own mental health, but when you're a kid, you can't help but take it personally. The more often she left, the more I tried to be the perfect son, so that when she came back, she would want to stay. I worked really hard in school to get the best marks. I found that I could make people laugh and I liked doing it, so I became something of a joker too. I never let people know that anything was bothering me, because I figured that nobody liked to be around someone sulky and sad all the time."

"But she still left again?" Holly guessed and I nodded.

"Every time. It got to be that she'd only be home for a few months and then she'd be gone for a year or more. I have no idea where she went or what she did; she never talked about it and Brian never asked. When she came home, he'd act like nothing had changed, like she'd only been gone for the day instead of a year. I think he was afraid of driving her away again if he ever tried to ask her about it."

Maybe I had learned some of my coping behaviour from him. I'd never really considered that before.

"One good thing came out of me trying to be so perfect, anyway: my teachers put me forward for a scholarship to go to a really prestigious private school in Midtown, and I was accepted. I went from being in a run-down, overpopulated school full of kids like me to taking the bus every day to this completely different world, full of kids like Cole."

"That's where you met Cole?" Holly asked, and I nodded again.

"He was a total ass then. I mean, not that much has changed in that regard."

She smiled, knowing I didn't really mean it.

"He was the first person who wasn't really charmed by me, or at least not fooled by the carefully crafted face I'd made for myself. We got in a fight not long after I started at the school. I made a joke about something he'd said and he called me out for it, saying I was deflecting my own insecurities onto him. Which was completely fair, since I probably was. But I didn't back down, I just pointed out how he used his 'I don't care about anything' persona to do exactly the same thing, and we ended up in a fistfight. Once the bleeding stopped, from that day on, we were best friends."

"Men," Holly exclaimed in disbelief, shaking her head with a little smile. I smiled back at her, glad to see something other than pity on her face.

"I loved the school and I worked hard there, but at times, it felt like living a double life. During the day, I'd hang out with these kids who had drivers and housekeepers and spent all their free time doing whatever extracurriculars would get them into the best Ivy League school. When school was over, I had to go home and look after the apartment and cook for Layla and Josh and make sure they were taken care of."

A cool blast of wind hit us as the carriage came around a corner, and Holly pulled the blankets tighter around herself. "Did Cole know about your mom?"

"I told him the basics. He knew she wasn't around much and he knew how we lived. He came to our apartment a few times. He kept telling me his dad would give me a job if I wanted it, but I couldn't work on top of school and caregiving; I just didn't have time. He tried once to just give me some money for something I needed, but I shot him down so hard that he never tried again."

In hindsight, I felt a bit guilty about that. Cole had only been trying to help, but he couldn't know how unwelcome his pity was, being someone who'd never been pitied a day in his life at that point.

We were nearing the end of the story, so I tried to keep it moving along as the carriage continued to meander through the pathways of Central Park.

"I'd planned to go to college when I was done with high school. I'd earned a few scholarships, and I planned to work to make up the rest of the money I needed. Naturally, I'd still live at home to make sure Layla and Josh were okay. I had the whole thing worked out, but a few months before graduation, Brian had an accident at work. Someone left some electrical wiring exposed and he stepped onto a live wire. His heart stopped immediately."

"Oh, Jackson." Holly leaned into me, her arm around my waist, and for a moment, we simply sat there, letting the words sink in.

"My mom came back from wherever she'd been. She promised me she'd stay that time so that I could go ahead with my plans, but I had to reevaluate everything. Spending four years in college didn't seem so smart when we needed money right away to keep the apartment and everything else. So, I decided to join the army instead so I could support my brother and sister and hopefully still end up with a decent career in the end. Cole didn't like it, but he accepted it was what I wanted to do. I joined and started my basic training, but not even a month in, I got a call from Layla telling me that our mom had disappeared again."

That was the first time I remembered being angry with her. Every other time she'd left, I blamed myself, but that time, I blamed her.

"So, as I already told you, I dropped out and went home. I'd just started looking for other jobs when Cole called and told me he'd found this scholarship that I'd be eligible for that would cover all my expenses and pay me a small allowance too, enough to cover our rent, so I could stay at home and go to college and support everyone too. It seemed like a miracle, just what I needed."

Holly caught on immediately. "Cole was the scholarship, wasn't he?"

"Yeah." I gave her a sheepish smile. "I didn't figure that out until a lot later. I guess I wanted it to be true so badly, grasping at straws, that I didn't dig too deep. He knew I wouldn't accept it if he just offered me the money, so he created a whole foundation and had it all go through there. It looked pretty legit."

In Holly's eyes, I could see her respect for Cole increasing, but her expression turned cooler when she asked about the other key player in the story. "And your mom?"

I shrugged. "Not much has changed. I see her from time to time. She appears, stays a few days, and disappears again. Josh is in the army now, following my not-so-illustrious footsteps in that regard, and Layla's married. She and her husband live in Chicago, so most of the time, it's just me."

I finished my summary with a smile, trying to pretend I was okay with all of it, but I knew she wouldn't be fooled, not any more than I had been at the end of her story the day before.

With that, she knew where my broken edges were, just as I'd learned about hers. In my eyes, it seemed like if we lined my shards up with her own shattered pieces, they'd fit together to form something good. The question was: could she see the picture of our future the same way I did?

~Holly~

As Jackson finished his story, he turned to me with a smile that I recognized completely. It mirrored the one I gave him the day before, a smile that said: 'I'm not quite as put together as you thought, but please, don't pity me.'

I had no intention of pitying him, but I admired him more than ever. The story he told me would have been a lot for anyone to go through, and especially someone as tuned into other people's moods as Jackson had shown himself to be, always so aware of and responsive to how I felt. I had no trouble imagining how he would have taken it upon himself to try to make sure everyone else was happy and that everyone else's needs were met, long before he worried about himself.

His brother and sister were very lucky to have him, and I hoped they realized that.

And though I wouldn't have blamed him at all for being bitter or angry towards his mother, I didn't pick up any of that from his words. When he spoke of her, I could hear some sadness, but it felt like sadness for all of them equally, the whole family, including her.

Hearing just how much he had been through, I knew more than ever that he deserved someone who could give themselves to him fully, someone just as amazing as he was. As much as part of me wished I could be that woman, I still didn't see how it would work.

At some point, something would go wrong, and whereas before, I had been worried about how I would cope when that happened, after what he'd just told me, I knew that I couldn't do that to him either. He didn't deserve to be let down again. It would be far safer for both of us to keep our relationship clearly casual so that no one got hurt.

So, as much as I wanted to continue spending time with him on my trip, both on the amazing dates he kept putting together and back at my hotel, if he would be hurt when it ended, maybe it was better that we didn't go any further. I had to give him an exit clause, and if he decided to take it and stop our challenge, I would accept that, no matter how much it disappointed me.

I tried to ease into that discussion by giving him a warm smile. "Thank you for telling me all of that. If I didn't already think you were amazing before, I would now. You're a really good man, Jackson.

He immediately blanched at my choice of words. "That's got to be one of the least interesting things you can say about a person. I'd rather you tell me I'm fascinating or unpredictable or even, I don't know, challenging. Anything but 'good'."

I wrinkled my nose back at him. "I don't mean it as a bad thing. You *are* fascinating and unpredictable and challenging, but more than all of that, you're good."

Jackson's eyes were fixed on me, trying to read between the lines. "But?"

"I never said there was a 'but'," I protested, but I couldn't fool him.

"You were going to, though." In his soft words, I could hear his disappointment, and I felt terrible that I'd already let him down.

"But..." I continued reluctantly, "it means that you deserve someone just as good in return. I'm not like you, Jackson. I'm a mess. I put myself first, over and over again. You gave up everything for your family, and I pretended mine didn't even exist."

"It's not a competition, Holly." He sounded frustrated as he turned to look out over the park, his jaw clenching. "I'm not looking for someone exactly like me. Do you want to be with someone exactly like you?"

I shuddered at the thought, which made him laugh, and instantly, the tension that had started to build between us dissipated. He had a real knack for doing that, keeping things light when they could so easily get bogged down.

"Why don't you tell me what's really bothering you?" he requested, turning back to me as he took another sip of his champagne. "It can't just be that I'm 'good'."

I took a deep breath as I tried to figure out how to explain myself to him. "I don't want to hurt you..."

"So don't." Cutting off what I'd been about to say, his words made it sound far easier than I knew it to be, and my lips pursed at his oversimplification.

"I wouldn't do it on purpose, but I'm worried that you're going to get your hopes up for something between us that doesn't work out. Sometimes, things just fall apart, even things that you think are going really well."

"Trust me, Holly, I know that."

Again, he spoke simply and directly, and I couldn't help grimacing. Of course he knew that. He just told me how things had fallen apart for him, over and over again.

"But that's not when you walk away," he continued, his blue eyes searching mine hopefully, and almost desperately. "That's when you dig deeper to make it work."

I knew he had a point, but on the other hand, if he knew so much about how to make a relationship work, why wasn't he already in one? "What about all the other women you've dated? There must have been a lot. Why didn't you dig deeper with them?"

His eyes closed as he sighed, and I thought for a second that I had pushed him too far. However, when he opened them again, I could only see resignation in them, not anger.

"You're right. I could have tried harder to make it work, but there has to be something there in the first place that's worth fighting for. With the other women I've dated - and there haven't been all that many, I'll have you know - by the time we got to the hard stuff, it never felt worth the effort. But this here, between us? This is something I haven't felt before. Even when you're arguing with me and putting your walls up, I feel it. I guess what you really need to decide right now is whether you feel it too. Is there something worth fighting for here, Holly? Or do you want to call it quits right now?"

The question took me completely off guard. I had been trying to offer *him* the out, to get him to make the decision, and instead, he put the ball firmly back in my court. If I meant it when I said I didn't want to hurt him, I should walk away, and he'd just given me the opportunity to do so.

But looking into those sweet eyes of his as they caught the light from the street lamps, no sound around us but the clopping of the horse's hooves, and feeling the chill in the air in strong contrast to the heat of his body, I couldn't deny it.

I felt something too.

Though I couldn't define it, it felt different from what I had felt for Harry, Nigel, or even Paul. Something about it spoke to me on a fundamental level, like something deep inside me was drawn to something inside of him.

Jackson had already seen sides of me those other men never had. He knew about my family, knew about my rejections, had already been on the receiving end of my short temper, and still, he sat beside me, not scared off at all.

Maybe it was selfish of me since I still didn't see a long-term future for us, but at that moment, the last thing I wanted to do was walk away.

"I don't want to call it quits."

Jackson let out a long breath, his lips curling into a relieved smile. "Good, because I really don't want to either. I appreciate that you're worried about hurting me, Holly, I really do, but we can't go through life expecting that we'll never be hurt. We have to take a chance on the things that are worth taking the risk for."

He looked so convinced that I was one of those things, and for the first time in a very long time, something stirred inside me that felt a lot like hope.

I didn't know for sure if he was right, but for the first time, I hoped that he was.

~Jackson~

Well, that hadn't been quite the romantic carriage ride that I planned. As the driver exited the park in front of the Plaza, I realized Holly and I had been so busy talking, we hardly looked at the park at all. Still, I didn't regret it too much, not when I had finally got Holly to admit that she had feelings for me.

Okay, she might not have said it in those exact words, but her meaning had been clear to me. She didn't want to end our challenge yet, which could only mean that she felt *something*, and that she saw at least a possibility of it ending well. That was the first step.

Next, I just needed to convince her that our feelings weren't going anywhere, and neither was I.

At the Plaza, I climbed down from the carriage first and told Holly to hand me the open bottle of champagne along with the roses before I helped her down.

"Are we done for the night?" As she looked over at the hotel entrance, I could hear the hint of longing in her voice, letting me know that she hoped we were heading up to her room, and it sent a shiver of anticipation down my spine.

However, that wasn't my plan, at least not yet. "We haven't eaten," I reminded her. "The night is still young, but I thought I'd run the champagne and roses up to your room while we're here and then we can head out again. No point in letting them go to waste."

Holly agreed, handing me the key to her suite as she took a seat in the lobby, and a few minutes later, I returned. Offering her my hand, we headed back out into the city.

The rest of the evening was, as I had promised her, a typical New York evening. After walking down through Times Square, we had a cozy dinner on 44th Street before walking across the street to the Schubert Theater to catch a play.

Holly raised her eyebrows as I pulled the tickets out of my pocket. "You realize we have theatres in London too, right?" she teased me. "Some might even say they're better."

"I know you do, but how often do you go?"

The purse of her lips answered my question.

"That's what I thought. Come on."

I'd chosen a comedy starring a couple of big-name Hollywood actors, and we both really enjoyed it. Holly laughed at nearly all the same things I did, our hands intertwined as we shared an armrest between the narrow seats. Afterwards, we walked all the way back to her hotel, talking about the show and laughing again at some of the funniest parts we remembered.

We were having such a good time that I forgot to be nervous about being back in her room until we were actually there.

"Should we drink more of this champagne?" Holly asked, moving over to the fridge where I had put the bottle earlier. I had placed the roses in a container I'd found in the kitchen, and I noticed that she gave them a sniff as she walked by.

"Champagne sounds good." Since she had everything under control, I took a seat on the sofa, trying to look completely at ease. It didn't take too much effort, actually. "Why don't you go to the theatre in London? You obviously enjoyed it."

Holly shrugged as she poured out the champagne into two glasses. "No one to go with, I guess. Gemma and I used to go to the odd thing with clients, but it's not the kind of thing I've ever thought about doing on my own."

"What about dates?" I knew she hadn't been serious with anyone since her hours-long engagement, but she must have dated other people.

She gave me a wry smile as she came over and handed me my glass of champagne, sitting down next to me. "The dates I go on aren't usually so romantic."

Although she brushed it off as a joke, it made my heart hurt to hear that. She deserved romance. "What kind of dates do you go on?"

I hadn't even realized I meant to ask the question until it came out of my mouth, but thankfully, Holly didn't seem to be offended by it. Instead, she took a drink from her champagne and smiled at me again.

"Well, as Gemma so eloquently put it the other day, I like drinking and men, so most of my dates involve going for drinks with men. Kind of like how this one is shaping up."

She winked and raised her glass to me in a silent 'cheers' before taking another swig.

"And they can't take you to the theatre first?" I pressed. I hated the idea of her thinking that a few drinks were all her time was worth.

She shrugged again. "I guess they don't think it's very sexy. Doesn't necessarily set the mood."

I raised my eyebrows at her. "So, you're not feeling even a little sexy right now?"

She raised her eyebrows right back at me, almost as surprised by my boldness as I was. "I didn't say that. Just how sexy are you feeling?"

Though my nerves were right there, I swallowed them down. I told her in the carriage that I wanted to fight for what was between us, and I needed to prove that to her. "Why don't you feel for yourself?"

Instantly, the air seemed to thicken around us as Holly's eyes moved from my face, down my body, to my lap. She bit her lip for a moment before taking one last drink of her champagne and putting the glass down on the table behind her. My heart beat faster as she moved closer to me, shuffling across the sofa until we were nearly touching.

Almost tentatively, her hand reached out to rest on my thigh.

Even that small contact made me exhale, the touch of her hand so close to where I wanted it, close enough to nearly overwhelm me.

"You're sure?" she asked, her eyes raising to meet mine, her hand still on my thigh.

Unsure whether I still had the power to speak, I simply nodded, and as her hand slid across my thigh, blood rushed to my dick, anticipating the trajectory of her movement.

When she finally reached her goal, her hand pressing against the growing bulge in my pants, I couldn't help groaning softly in satisfaction. Even through the layers of clothing, her touch felt amazing.

"I'm impressed," she teased as her fingers trailed gently up and down the whole of my confined length.

Despite her teasing tone, I could hear the desire in her voice too. It sounded so strong that when she withdrew her hand, it left me feeling completely confused. I thought she wanted to touch me, and I wanted it too; not to go all the way yet, but to take the next step.

Holly, however, had other ideas. "Yesterday, I tried to push you into getting naked for me before you were ready," she reminded me. I opened my mouth to protest that we were past that, but she held up a hand to stop me. "And when we were on the phone later, I told you how wet I was for you, and you said you'd like to know how that felt."

My mouth went completely dry as I started to understand what she had in mind.

"I've already felt how turned on you are, so why don't you feel just how much I want you too?"

~Holly~

A thrill of excitement ran through me as Jackson invited me to touch him. He couldn't be making it any clearer that he had completely forgiven me for the night before and that he intended to keep up his end of the bargain, to continue to try things with me that he'd never done before.

I desperately wanted to touch him properly too. Even feeling him through his trousers, feeling just how hard he was and hearing the insanely sexy sounds he made as I pressed my hand against him was enough to start my whole body pulsing with desire. I would have loved to slip my hand beneath his trousers and touch him like no woman ever had before.

However, something made me pause. If I wanted to approach his sexual education strategically, it seemed like a bigger step for me to touch him than for him to touch me. It would be something new either way, and I could still hear his sexy voice through the phone as I told him I was touching myself and he said he'd like to know what it felt like.

All things considered, that seemed to be the better option for that night. He could keep his clothes on if he wanted to and I would give him an introduction to the female anatomy. Hopefully, that would let him still feel in control as he tried something new.

When I suggested it to him, his eyes darkened and his lips parted, a heavy breath escaping through them. "I would love to touch you, Holly."

A grin spread across my face, satisfaction and anticipation running through me in equal measure. "Good. Why don't you start by undressing me, then?"

As Jackson leaned towards me, I thought he would do exactly that, but instead, he took my face in his hands. "Why don't I start with this?"

Leaning forward the rest of the way, he kissed me gently. The taste of champagne lingered on his lips and the scent of his cologne flooded my senses as my whole body reacted to the soft press of his mouth on mine. I was already wet for him just from getting the chance to touch him, but the tenderness that he kissed me with made me truly melt.

Just as I got used to his sweet kiss, he leaned forward again, pushing me down onto my back, his mouth never leaving mine. When I nipped at his bottom lip, he gave a little huff of amusement before deepening the kiss, his tongue meeting mine as I eagerly welcomed him in.

Even then, he didn't seem to be in any hurry. His body settled over mine as I stretched out on the sofa and he rested his weight on me just enough; not enough to make it hard to breathe, but firmly enough that I couldn't go anywhere, and firmly enough that I could feel his hardness pressing down on me, showing me just how much he was enjoying himself.

When we kissed in my room the other night, he didn't let me feel it that way. In fact, he'd gone out of his way to make sure I didn't, so it felt like we were making progress, and very hot progress too. Knowing how turned on he was made me want him even more.

As we kissed, our bodies began to move against each other, just the slightest friction but more than enough to amplify the throbbing between my legs, the need for him that grew stronger by the second.

When he made no move to start undressing me, I decided to take the reins and pulled the back of his shirt up, lifting it over his head and tossing it away onto the floor. He looked down at me with an expression half-teasing and half-smoldering. "I thought you were the one getting undressed."

"When you get around to it," I confirmed, giving him a wink. "But that doesn't mean I can't enjoy this first."

My hands ran across his bare chest to accompany my words, and I loved the way his muscles twitched beneath my touch. He let out a soft moan, his eyes closing for just a second before he looked back at me with a new fire in his eyes.

When he kissed me again, his hands got to work too, unbuttoning my shirt as my hands continued to explore the broad expanse of his chest, his arms, and his back. Finally, the buttons were all undone and he slid his hand across my bare stomach, sending a jolt of heat and longing through me.

"Let me see you," he whispered against my lips before lifting himself off of me just enough that he could see the bra I wore for him that day. Blue and green stripes covered me, with a little bell hanging from the bottom between my breasts. Flicking his finger across the bell, Jackson looked up at me in amusement. "What's the point of this?"

I gave him my best cheeky smile. "So you can hear me coming, of course."

With a groan, his mouth found mine again while I lifted my body up so I could pull my shirt the rest of the way off. When I'd discarded it, Jackson broke away from me once more, looking down at my bra, deep in thought, as if an internal debate raged in his head.

"Do you want it off?" I would be more than willing to take the bra off, but I didn't want to push him.

He took a deep breath before looking up at me and nodding. "Let me try."

My heart melted again as I realized what he meant: he'd never removed a woman's bra before. It struck me as impossibly sweet and ridiculously sexy all at the same time.

I lifted my back off the couch again to give him access, and his arms wrapped around me as his hands fiddled with the clasp. It took him a couple of tries, but eventually, I felt it release, and my nipples hardened even more at the mere thought of him looking at me or touching me. I honestly couldn't wait to see what he had in mind.

Slowly, he slid the straps over my shoulders and down my arms. Only when my arms were free did he pull the bra away fully. His mouth hung open as he looked down at my breasts, staring at them like some kind of treasure before he looked back up at me, wordlessly asking for permission to do more than look.

"They're all yours," I told him and I didn't miss his grin of anticipation as he dropped his head to my chest.

A soft sigh echoed in my throat as his lips made contact with my skin, kissing me just below my collarbone first before moving slowly lower. The anticipation was equal parts exquisite and agonizing until he finally reached the stiff peak of my nipple and ran his tongue across it.

"Yes," I moaned, surprised by just how strongly my body reacted to him. I had never been someone who could orgasm from nipple play alone, but that night, I felt surprisingly close.

Jackson seemed to appreciate my reaction as he took the nipple into his mouth, rolling his tongue around it while his fingers gently squeezed the other nipple between them.

As my pleasure built more strongly, I took a shaky breath. "I think you better move on. Don't forget the goal."

He looked up at me, my nipple still between his teeth, and the sight of it nearly sent me over the edge right then and there. "I thought the goal was to make you feel good," he teased as he released me.

"That's a given, but you also wanted to touch me, right?"

He swallowed, his jaw tightening as he nodded. "I really do."

"Then go ahead." My hips raised off the couch in invitation, and even that small movement and the friction of my trousers against my aching core gave me a twinge of pleasure. Fuck, this really wouldn't take long at all.

At least he didn't make me wait any longer, his hands moving down to unbutton my trousers and pull the zip down. I expected him to pull my trousers down too, but he didn't. Instead, he slipped his hand into the opening, running it across my mound, over my knickers, before sliding his fingers down further between my legs, pressing the fabric up against my entrance as I moaned again in both pleasure and frustration.

"You really are wet," he said with wonder, and I couldn't help laughing.

"Did you think I was lying?"

He looked back up at me with that charming grin of his. "Of course not. I know when you're lying to me, Holly."

"Do you?" I wanted to challenge that assertion, but the last word died off as he pressed his fingers against me harder, pressing my damp knickers more firmly between my folds. "Please, Jackson. Don't tease me."

He smiled again, though it looked a bit shakier that time, letting me know how much the experience affected him too. "I thought that was our whole thing."

I opened my mouth to reply, but when his fingers hooked around the side of my knickers, pressing directly against my skin and brushing over my clit, the words died on my lips.

"God, Holly," he muttered, exhaling loudly. "You feel amazing."

"You're doing great," I managed to gasp.

His eyes stayed on my face as his fingers began to explore more, rubbing over my swollen clit and gently prodding at my entrance but not going any further. It felt like he wanted to memorize my reactions, to learn exactly what I liked. Finally, just when I thought I couldn't stand it for a moment longer, he began to press a finger inside, very slowly.

"Yes," I moaned, trying to encourage him. "Deeper, Jackson. As far as you can go."

Breathing in, he did as I requested, pushing in harder and deeper until I could feel the rest of his hand against me. Rather than withdrawing it again, he began to move it around, swirling his finger gently inside me, pushing against my inner walls and brushing against my most sensitive spot.

I'd never felt anything quite like it, and I almost had to remind myself which of us was the virgin.

He pulled back, pulling his finger out, and my hips tilted towards him of their own accord, immediately beckoning him back. He seemed to get the unspoken message as he quickly thrust his finger back into me, his thumb brushing against my clit. That might have been on purpose or it might not have been, but at that point, I really didn't care.

"That's... perfect..." I gasped, the pressure inside me building stronger as he kept stroking me.

"*You're* perfect," he whispered back, and I opened my eyes to find him looking right at me with such awe that it pushed me right over the edge. My orgasm washed over me like a tidal wave, my body contracting around his finger still deep inside me, my legs trembling beneath him.

"Fuck, Jackson," I moaned as the power of speech slowly returned to me. "I think you might be some kind of prodigy. Are you really sure you haven't done that before?"

He laughed, sounding almost as short of breath as I was. "I'm pretty sure."

He gently pulled his finger out of me and out of my knickers before raising his hand in front of him, staring at the wetness covering his finger like it held some kind of magical secret.

With a satisfied smile, he looked back down at me, sexy and enticing as sin. "But I'm also pretty damn sure that I'm going to do it again."

Chapter Nine

DREAM HOUSE

~Jackson~

Looking down at Holly's beautiful face, her cheeks still flushed red from her orgasm, I couldn't quite believe that was all because of me.

At first, when she offered her encouragement, I thought she might just be humouring me. I knew that women could fake their reaction, and Holly knew I was a bit nervous, so maybe she over-exaggerated to make me feel better. It wouldn't have shocked me, but when I saw her taut nipples, and especially when I felt just how wet she was, it seemed pretty clear: she wasn't faking it. The idea of being with me, and the *reality* of being with me, turned her on. As I watched her come, the most incredible feeling of satisfaction and pride flowed through me, almost as good as if I had orgasmed myself.

Nothing I'd ever known compared to touching her. I couldn't have described it if I tried, but being inside her, even with just my finger, had been by far the most intimate thing I'd ever done with anyone. Warm and wet and smooth inside, her body contracted around my finger when she came, and the thought of what that might feel like around my dick instead nearly made me come right there and then too.

So, although I told her that I would want to do it again, I didn't mean right that second. I needed to cool off a little bit or I wouldn't want to stop. My self-control had already been sorely tested.

Luckily, Holly didn't seem to want to take things any further that night anyway.

"You can do that any time you want to," she assured me with a warm, teasing smile, shuffling back on the sofa so she could sit up. "But that's probably enough for tonight, if that's okay with you."

The time had already passed midnight and I knew she had plans for the next day. "What time is your spa appointment with Gemma?"

Cole had taken the day off to stay home with Noah so that Gemma and Holly could have some time together.

"Ten. I think we're booked in for about six hours. We're having the works done; I'll be a new woman by the time you see me again."

I couldn't help looking down at her breasts, still bare and beautiful. "God, I hope not."

Holly laughed before leaning forward to kiss me softly. "Thank you for today, Jackson: the carriage ride, the play, all of it. It was lovely."

It really had been. I couldn't remember a date I'd enjoyed quite so much, even without that amazing finale.

"Will you be up to an evening out after your day of relaxation tomorrow?" The thought of going a whole day without seeing her didn't appeal to me at all.

"I think I'm invited for dinner with Gemma and Cole, but after that, I'm free. Are you going to tell me what you have in mind?"

I shook my head with a smile. "Haven't you learned yet that I like to surprise you?"

Her gaze dropped to my hand and the finger that had just been inside her. "You do surprise me, Jackson. Constantly."

Desire sparked in me again at her tone, but I forced myself to lean back. "How about I come pick you up at the Stamer residence around eight?"

She agreed as she stood up, fetching my shirt for me to put it back on. When I was dressed again, I went over to the kitchen to wash my hands, but even then, Holly made no move to cover herself, still standing there with her pants open and wearing nothing on top. I loved that she felt so comfortable with me. What would it be like to see her naked and beautiful like that every day? Would she walk around the house naked if we lived together?

I had to close my eyes against the images that started multiplying in my mind, picturing our whole future together. We weren't there yet, I reminded myself firmly, but after that date, I couldn't help feeling like we had taken a tiny step closer to it.

The next day, I went for a run in the park to start my day and spent the rest of it making sure all my Christmas presents were sorted out, ready for the following week. I had gifts for my brother and sister, for my colleagues at work, and for Gemma and Cole. For Noah, I had a small mountain of gifts even though the kid would never want for anything. I just couldn't help myself when I saw something I thought he might like.

I couldn't wait until I could shop for my own child and shower him or her with all the little things I never had growing up. Although I wondered if Holly felt the same way, I forced myself to stop thinking about it. She was already skittish about commitment, and if I started talking about babies with her, I'd definitely send her running.

Finally, evening drew in and I headed over to Gemma and Cole's to pick Holly up. As usual, I let myself in, and found the three of them in the living room with Cole holding Noah on his lap.

"Jackson!" Gemma saw me first and waved me over to join them. "We were just talking about you."

"All good things, I hope?" My eyes moved naturally to Holly as I stepped further into the room. She looked stunning, as always, dressed in another Christmas sweater, though far more understated than the one she wore to the wedding brunch. Gemma also had a Christmas sweater on, making me guess it must have been her idea. Holly's sweater hugged her toned body perfectly and I couldn't help picturing what lay underneath, now that I knew exactly what it looked like.

Holly winked at me, teasing me as usual as she got to her feet. "You'll never know, will you? Are you ready to go?"

"Why does it feel like you're rushing me out of here? Was whatever you were talking about really that bad?"

"Of course not," Gemma assured me. "But we'll have time to catch up on Friday. We don't want to take time away from your date now."

Excitement glimmered in her eyes as she mentioned it, and Holly and I wished them both a good night before we headed downstairs to where a taxi was waiting for us.

"How was your day?" I asked as we settled in the back.

"Really good. It was so nice to have the whole day with Gemma, just like old times."

I didn't miss the hint of wistfulness in her voice. "You must really miss her."

I knew how much I appreciated having Gemma as a friend over the previous year, but I hadn't ever really stopped to think about how hard it must have been for Holly not to get to spend as much time with her anymore, given how close they were.

"I do miss her. More than I thought I would, to be honest. We still talk all the time but it's not the same as just being together, you know? Don't get me wrong, though; I'm thrilled for her that she's so happy here and I wouldn't want to change that for a second."

"Have you ever thought about following in her footsteps?" I couldn't help asking. "You'd make a great New Yorker."

Holly laughed, her eyes sparkling as she gave me a calculating look. "Very smooth. Don't think I don't know what you're up to."

I held up my hands in surrender. "It was just a thought."

"Uh huh." She didn't believe me for a second. "So, are you going to tell me yet where we're going tonight?"

"What do you think?" I asked, grinning as she gave me a dirty look.

Soon, we were on the Manhattan Bridge heading across the water and Holly peered out the window curiously. "We're leaving the city?"

"Just Manhattan. We're going to Brooklyn, which is still part of New York. Have you ever been there?"

Holly shook her head. "Pretty much all I've seen of New York is what you've shown me so far and the inside of the spa today."

"Well, then, we definitely need to explore a bit more."

I had the taxi drop us off a couple of blocks away so as not to spoil the surprise, and taking Holly's hand, we walked up to Dyker Heights Boulevard. When the first house finally came into view, Holly came to an abrupt stop, her mouth falling open.

"Oh my God."

Each year, the houses in Dyker Heights did their best to outdo each other with over-the-top Christmas lights and decoration displays. The whole street was illuminated, some houses with music and some with animated figures. It was complete sensory overload and I loved it. I went every year, but usually on my own. I had thought about bringing Gemma that year but I didn't want to take her away from her family, and I was so pleased I had the chance to share it with Holly instead.

"What do you think?"

She shook her head, a wide smile on her face. "Honestly, Jackson, I never know what to expect with you. This is brilliant!"

"Well, don't just stand there," I encouraged her. "Come on, Holly. Let's dive in."

~Holly~

Jackson's enthusiasm proved infectious as he led me down the brightly lit road, stopping to look at each richly-decorated house. All around us, other couples and families were doing the same thing, taking videos and pictures with their phones, pointing out different things to each other. Everyone was in a great mood and there I was, grinning right along with them, as if I did sweet and wholesome things like this regularly.

"Why do you think those Three Wise Men are riding unicycles?" Jackson pondered, pointing out a particularly avant-garde nativity scene.

"Because they had to keep their hands free to carry their gifts?"

He nodded sagely, trying not to smile. "That makes sense, but you'd think the tires would get stuck in the sand."

"Unless they're *flying* unicycles," I pointed out. "Maybe there's an engine we can't see beneath their robes."

"That seems unlikely. What would they do if they broke down? Where are you going to find a good mechanic in Bethlehem in 33 BC?"

I had to laugh at that, and an older lady standing just in front of us turned around with a grin on her face too. "Hang on to this one," she said to me, giving me a knowing nudge. "Trust me, that sense of humour goes a long way."

Jackson turned to her with mock offense. "Why are we brushing over my classic good looks? I thought they were my best asset."

The woman laughed again, reaching up to pinch his cheek. "For now, dear. Those'll fade though." She turned back to me with a warm smile. "You've got a good one there."

"I do," I agreed, not bothering to burst her bubble by telling her we weren't really together. Besides, I did have him for that night, at least. Still, her words brought the conversation I'd had earlier with Gemma and Cole rushing back to me.

After we finished supper, we went into the living room with Noah. I sat there quietly marvelling at how gentle and loving Cole was with him when Gemma brought up Jackson, and Cole suddenly looked over at me with that intense stare of his.

"Do you remember the conversation we had last year in London, Holly? When you threatened to haunt my nightmares if I hurt Gemma?"

I certainly did remember, but from the look on Gemma's face, she hadn't heard about it before. "What? When did that happen?"

Cole didn't answer her, keeping his eyes fixed on me. "Well, it's my turn now. Jackson was really disappointed last year when nothing happened between you two, and I know he'd be willing to give you his all. If this isn't serious for you, you should make that clear and put a stop to it. I don't want to see him hurt again."

"Cole!" Gemma sounded scandalized. "You can't just accuse her of using him. You don't know anything about it."

"It's okay, Gem," I assured her, holding Cole's gaze. "I said worse to him last year, trust me."

Cole smirked in acknowledgement.

"Jackson and I have an understanding," I told him honestly. "I can't guarantee he won't get hurt or that I won't either, but he told me it's worth the risk."

Gemma squealed in delight. "That's so sweet, Hols."

"It is." My expression softened as I remembered him saying it and the carriage ride we'd been on at the time. "He's not exactly what I thought he was."

She cocked her head at me curiously. "What do you mean?"

I shrugged, not really sure how to explain it to her. "I guess I thought he was like the guys we knew at university, the people like Edwin and Paul who grew up with money and power."

"Does that make someone a bad person?" Cole asked sarcastically. "I'd hate to think what that says about me."

My eyes dropped to the floor as I bit my tongue, trying not to point out that was exactly why I didn't want to talk to them about this. How could they understand why it mattered to me that we had our backgrounds in common?

Gemma didn't seem offended, though. "Jackson's not like Paul, you know. In more ways than that."

That might be true, but I didn't know what she meant by it. "Why do you say that?"

Her tentative smile made it clear she didn't want to push me too hard, but she explained herself anyway. "You're different with him. You're way more relaxed and happy. Maybe you can't see it, but from the outside, it's hard to miss."

Then the elevator dinged and Jackson walked in, and our conversation came to an abrupt end.

An hour later, there we were, looking to all the rest of the world like just another couple in love as Jackson held my hand or put his arm around me when we stopped to look at another house. A booth halfway along the street sold doughnuts and hot chocolate for charity, and Jackson bought some for both of us.

"It's not quite the same as the mulled wine we had at Hyde Park," he reminded me. "But hopefully, it'll do the trick."

How did he remember that? Paul had often forgotten things we'd done together, things that mattered to me, and the mulled wine had only been a minor detail on an outing that didn't even count as a date for me and Jackson, yet he seemed to remember it all.

When we got to the end of the street, a queue of enterprising taxi drivers sat there, ready to take people back home, so we hopped in the first one and Jackson turned to me with his eager, sweet smile. "Do you mind if I take you one more place?"

"Go ahead." He kept coming up with such unique things for us to do, I couldn't wait to see what else he might have planned.

The taxi took us back into Manhattan and to a quiet residential street that didn't feel all that far from Gemma and Cole's apartment. I peered out the window, trying to see why he'd brought us there, but all I could see was a quiet row of elegant townhouses.

Jackson paid the driver and opened the door for me, and once we were out on the sidewalk, he turned to me with an almost nervous smile. "This is something I've never shown anyone before, but I thought you might be interested."

He certainly had me curious, especially since I still couldn't see anything out of the ordinary in our surroundings. "Of course I'm interested. What is it?"

He raised his arm to gesture to the house we stood directly in front of. "It's this. This house."

Turning towards it, I took a closer look at the building in front of me. Other than looking almost abandoned, there wasn't much to distinguish it from all the other houses on the street. Finally, I had to turn back to Jackson. "What am I supposed to be looking for?"

His smile turned a bit sheepish. "I know it's not much right now, but eventually, I'd like to buy it and live here. When I have a family, I mean. And I'd decorate it each Christmas just like the houses in Dyker Heights and drive all the neighbours crazy."

The idea made me laugh. Looking around at all the other well-kept houses on the street with their elegant wreaths and no lights at all, I felt pretty sure no one would appreciate it. Turning back to the house again, I examined it even more closely, trying to guess why he'd chosen this house out of all the houses in New York City. "It doesn't look like anyone's lived here for a long time."

"They haven't. Not for about twenty years."

"How do you know that?" Obviously, there must be more to this than he was telling me.

"I came here for piano lessons," he explained, looking at the house as if he could see something completely different than I did. "An elderly woman that Brian knew somehow lived here, and she offered to give me lessons for free. We didn't have a piano but I came here twice a week to practice and have lessons."

"I didn't know you could play the piano." He really was full of surprises.

He smiled again, but it looked a little sadder that time. "I can't. It only lasted a few months until my mom left for the first time, and after that, I had no time for anything like that. When she came back, Brian tried to call the woman to see if I could start again, but she'd passed away. No one has lived here in the house since."

I repeated my earlier question: "How do you know that?"

With a chuckle, he explained himself further. "It's not creepy, I promise. I haven't been coming to check on the house all that time, but for me, as a little kid coming from our tiny apartment in Washington Heights, this place seemed like a palace. So, when I got my first well-paying job, I came by just to see if it looked as good in reality as I remembered it, and I could tell no one had lived here for a while. I did some digging and found out it belongs to the woman's son who lives overseas. I got in touch with him and he said he's got plans to do it up, renovate it, but he's just never gotten around to it. I told him I'd be interested in knowing when it goes on the market and he promised to let me know. We've been in touch ever since. I don't think he's ever going to do anything with it and I think I could convince him to sell it to me now."

I could almost picture him as the awestruck 8-year-old, climbing the stairs to the front door, clutching his music books beneath his arm, as if he were entering an entirely different world. The look in his eyes that evening wasn't that far off. "So, why haven't you convinced him yet?"

Jackson turned those dream-filled eyes on me. "It's not just up to me. After all, it wouldn't just be my house, and I don't want to make such a big decision without the woman I'm going to share it with."

~Jackson~

I could almost see the warning lights flashing in Holly's head as I told her I was waiting to buy the house with the woman I would share it with. I knew it would be a risk to put that out there for her, but I didn't want to hide it either. I wanted her to know that I would never be the kind of guy who would offer her something and then take it back. What I offered was as solid and real as the bricks and mortar in front of us.

To her credit, she didn't panic, at least not externally. Her gaze returned to the house, avoiding me, and she remained silent for a long moment. When she finally looked back at me, a rather forced smile graced her face. "Well, I'm sure that woman will be very grateful that you took her feelings into consideration."

Obviously, I would have preferred a different reaction, but it also could have been worse. Although she pretended she didn't know I meant her, at least she didn't run away like she had the other night or change the subject or employ any of her other defense tactics that I'd come to know. For the time being, I would leave it at that, having planted the idea in her head.

"My apartment's only a few blocks from here," I told her, not sure how oriented she was. "We can go back there if you like, or I can take you back to your hotel."

She gave that a moment's consideration too. "If your place is closer, let's go there."

When I held out my hand to her and she slipped hers into it, I noticed it tremble. "Are you cold?"

She had dressed warmly, but the air had a definite chill that evening. I'd even heard on the news that it might snow the next day. That would be nice, just before Christmas.

"If I say yes, what will you do?" she teased me, relaxing as we began to walk away from the house and settled into our usual banter. "Are you going to offer me your coat?"

"I don't think that would be very effective since it would leave me cold. Maybe we'd just have to cuddle up together."

Holly raised an eyebrow at me suggestively. "That does sound like a better idea. Maybe we can practice when we get to your flat."

I definitely had ideas about what I wanted to do when we got back to my apartment. I'd spent half the day thinking about it, but I had a request to make of her first and I couldn't predict what her response might be.

Once we were inside, I offered Holly a drink. "I can make some tea if you want. It'll warm you up and I know how obsessed you Brits are with your tea."

She wrinkled her nose at me in disapproval. "Obsessed is a strong word. We just appreciate a good cuppa, and yes, I'd love some. Do you have something without caffeine?"

She followed me into the kitchen where I opened a cupboard and pulled out six different boxes of tea. "Will one of these work?"

Holly surveyed the boxes in amusement. "And you think I'm the one who's obsessed? Why do you have so many different kinds?"

As I debated whether or not to tell her that I'd bought them all for her, she beat me to the punch as she opened one box and then another.

"These are all brand new!" she exclaimed. "Jackson, did you get these just for me?"

"I'm going to plead the fifth on that," I demurred, and Holly's brow wrinkled in confusion.

"What does that mean?"

"The fifth amendment?" I expanded, but she continued to look at me blankly. "I guess that's an American thing. It means refusing to answer something that could incriminate you."

"I'm going to have to remember that. It could come in handy." She gave me a wink that instantly had me growing harder, especially when I remembered what I wanted to suggest to her for that night.

She chose a decaf tea and I decided to try it too. We sat at the island in my kitchen as we drank our tea, talking casually about different drinks and about my apartment, keeping the conversation light and not too personal. When our mugs were empty, Holly looked over at me with an inviting smile.

"So, did you really invite me over here just for a cup of tea?"

Definitely not, but I needed to lay out my request first.

"I did actually have something I wanted to try tonight," I admitted, and her eyes sparkled with curiosity. "But if we do, I'd like you to spend the night here with me. Sleeping in my bed, I mean."

I had a couple of reasons for asking. First, it would help her to feel closer to me. If she spent the night with me and woke up beside me, maybe she could start to see how good it would be to do that all the time. The other reason was a bit more selfish. If we did what I planned to suggest, I didn't want her to leave right away afterwards, like it hadn't been a big deal. I wanted to know that it meant something to her too.

Holly took a moment to think that over, as she had so many times that evening already, but I didn't mind. I'd rather that she gave it some thought instead of going with her first impulse, since I knew that initial impulse would be to run.

"I don't have anything to sleep in," she pointed out. "Or clothes for tomorrow. Everything's at the hotel."

"I can give you something to sleep in." The idea of her wearing my clothes sent a shiver of pleasure through me. "And I'll take you back to the hotel in the morning so you can get ready there."

"Toothbrush?" she challenged. Amusement flickered in her eyes and I knew she already knew the answer even before I said it.

"I already got you one."

The smile moved from her eyes to her lips. "You drive a hard bargain, Jackson, but very well. I accept. Now, tell me..." She moved closer, sliding off the stool to come and stand directly in front of me. "What are we doing tonight?"

Chapter Ten

Another New Experience

~Jackson~

I had never had to say anything like this to anyone before, but I took a deep breath and steadied my nerves as best I could. "I thought we could switch roles from last night. I'll get naked for you, if you want me to, and you can..."

I hesitated, trying to find the least crude words, but I needn't have worried; Holly helpfully filled them in. "Give you a happy ending?"

The smile on her face assured me she had no objections to the idea. "More or less," I agreed, shifting on my stool as my dick, already twitching with anticipation, got even harder. "Does that sound okay?"

She placed a gentle hand on my cheek as she leaned towards me. "It sounds perfect."

Her lips landed on mine, soft and reassuring. In that sweet kiss, I could feel her affection for me. Maybe we couldn't call it love, not yet, but she did care for me and she wanted me to enjoy myself, that came across loud and clear. I had no doubt that she would make it good.

After kissing just long enough that I began to relax, she leaned back. "Where do you want to go?"

I supposed the kitchen wasn't really an ideal spot, so I got to my feet and took her hand, leading her to my bedroom. I hadn't had a woman in my room since I moved in two years earlier, other than my sister when she came to visit, but she didn't count, for obvious reasons. The other night, I'd shown the room to Holly from the door, but that night, she followed me inside and we sat down on the edge of the bed, still holding each other's hand.

"Do you want me to get naked too?" Her question made it clear she would do whatever made me more comfortable.

I had actually thought about it earlier, when I decided what I would ask her for that evening, so I didn't need to think about it again. "That might be a little too much. You're perfect as you are."

Though I didn't say exactly what it would be too much of, I figured she could probably guess. Too much distraction. Too much temptation. At least if she kept her clothes on, we couldn't get too carried away.

Another soft kiss followed, but with the location having shifted to my bedroom, things quickly grew more heated. Holly tasted of tea and vanilla, and I couldn't get enough. From the hunger in her kiss and the way her tongue tangled with mine, she clearly wanted more too. Her hands slid up beneath my shirt, the touch of her fingers on my skin leaving trails of goosebumps in their wake. Soon, my shirt had come off again and Holly's hands roamed my chest and stomach, tracing the lines of my muscles.

"Okay, I have to ask." With a laugh, she broke our kiss to look down at my body. "Exactly how often do you work out?"

I appreciated the compliment, since she obviously meant it as one. "Just about every day. It's the one good thing that came out of my brief time in the military: I've got excellent discipline."

"Mmmm..." she hummed, her fingers still caressing my abs. "Definitely a good thing."

A second later, our mouths were back together and her kiss distracted me so much that I almost forgot where we were heading. It all came rushing back, though, as her hands slid lower, brushing gently over the front of my pants which were already uncomfortably tight even before she touched me.

"Why don't you stand up?" Holly whispered the words against my lips, her hand still resting lightly over my groin.

The moment of truth had arrived, it seemed. Swallowing down my nerves, I got to my feet while Holly stayed seated. Her hands swept across my stomach once more before moving to the zipper of my jeans, and my breath caught in my throat as she undid the button and pulled the zipper down. My dick appreciated the extra space that gave me, and even more so as she slid my jeans down, her hands gliding over my ass as she pulled my pants down to my knees. As she stroked me again, through only my underwear that time, my dick twitched happily. It almost felt like it had a life of its own, eager to make her acquaintance after all this time.

"Is this still okay?" Holly looked up at me, giving me one last chance to back out.

At that moment, I probably wouldn't have denied her much of anything, so I simply nodded and, with a smile both warm and filled with anticipation, she reached for the waistband of my boxer-briefs. Gently, she pulled it down, over the tip of my stiff dick, exposing me to her at last.

The relief I felt at being released from my confinement mingled with apprehension as Holly's eyes travelled over me. I'd been in enough locker rooms to know that my size was pretty average, not the biggest I'd seen but not the smallest either. Obviously, no woman had ever seen me before. Although we'd never talked about exact numbers, Holly must have a few men in her memory that she could compare me to, and my heart raced as I awaited her verdict.

At last, she looked up at me again, her eyes filled with both desire and that gently teasing affection that I loved so much. "Well, damn, Jackson."

Those three words were all she said, but they were perfect. If she'd started going on about it being the biggest or best she'd ever seen, I might have thought she was overselling it. That simple acknowledgement, on the other hand, was exactly what I needed.

Almost tentatively, she reached out and wrapped her hand around my base, and as she made contact, my knees nearly gave way. "Fuck," I muttered, trying to keep my balance.

She grinned back up at me again. "Do you need to lie down?"

I would have done anything she told me to, but since she gave me the option, I decided to stay standing. Again, it seemed like there would be a little less temptation that way. "No, I'm good."

Accepting that response, her gaze returned to my erection and, almost painfully slowly, her hand began to move up the length of my shaft, all the way to my head before returning just as slowly, giving it a gentle squeeze as she got back to the base. Simultaneously, her other hand reached up between my legs, trailing lightly up my inner thighs until it cupped my balls and she gently squeezed those too.

Inhaling sharply, I fought to keep my eyes open. The sensation of her hands on me was so intense that I almost couldn't take it, but I desperately wanted to watch her too. The image of her beautiful face concentrating on me added a whole other layer to what I was feeling.

After stroking me slowly a few more times, taking her time as she let me get used to the sensation, Holly began to move a little faster. Instinctively, I widened my stance and her other hand moved up further, pressing firmly against that perfect spot just behind my balls, sending a fresh wave of pleasure through me that made the blood rush to my dick yet again. I didn't know how I could possibly get any harder, but my body seemed determined to try.

Just as the friction started to get a little rough, Holly let go and spit into her hand, coating my dick with her own natural lubricant, and when she was satisfied, she began to pump me in earnest. Each stroke felt better than the last, building and building until I knew there was no return.

"Holly, that's it, I can't..."

I tried to warn her, but it came too late. My orgasm hit me like a steam train and stars appeared before my closed eyelids as I released with all the pent-up frustration of years of self-denial. For a moment, it almost felt like I left my body, but as her hand continued to stroke me gently, she drew me back down to earth, her touch setting off additional little aftershocks to follow the main event.

When I finally opened my eyes again, a little afraid of what I'd see, I quickly realized I didn't have to worry. Obviously, she'd anticipated my ejaculation, and I had actually come into her other hand though I hadn't even noticed it at the time. The white, creamy liquid roped across her delicate hand struck me as insanely sexy.

Just when I thought nothing could top what just happened, Holly looked up at me with a satisfied smile, her eyes fixed on me as she ran her tongue across the palm of her hand, licking up everything I had just given her, and my dick twitched to life again as if it hadn't just been completely emptied.

"Delicious," she assured me in her husky British accent, before standing up and giving me a kiss on the cheek. "That was perfect, Jackson. I'm going to go wash up. Why don't you get ready for bed?"

She walked into my ensuite bathroom, looking for all the world like she'd done it a million times, and I couldn't help wishing she would do it a million more.

Among other things, obviously.

When she'd closed the door behind her, I looked down at myself, at my softening dick and my jeans and underwear still down around my knees, and I shook my head in disbelief, hardly able to believe we had actually just done that. No matter how many times I'd imagined it, in so many ways over so many years, it had never been that good.

Since she'd told me to get ready for bed, I did, discarding the rest of my clothes, grabbing a pair of cotton pants from my dresser to sleep in, and pulling out a soft t-shirt for Holly. She opened the bathroom door quickly when I knocked on it, and I held the shirt out to her. "Is this okay for you?"

She gave me another quick peck on the lips as she took it from me. "Perfect. I'll be right there."

I had a second bathroom down the hall, so I went there to get ready for bed myself, and by the time I got back, Holly had returned to the bedroom, wearing only my t-shirt. The sight made me start to harden all over again.

However, I had more self-control than that. A limit had been set for the night and we'd reached it, so all that remained was to go to sleep. "Do you have a side preference?" I asked, gesturing to the bed.

She shook her head. "Your bed, you pick."

Since she didn't care, I got in my usual side and she crawled in the other. I settled down onto my back, not entirely sure what she would want to do or be comfortable with, but to my delight, Holly immediately cuddled into me.

"Did you enjoy that, Jackson?" she asked, sounding uncharacteristically hesitant, and I suddenly realized that I hadn't said anything to her yet about how she'd made me feel. I'd been so focused on processing everything, I'd forgotten to tell her just how good it was.

Putting a finger under her chin, I tilted her head up so her eyes met mine. "Holly, that was amazing. Better than I could have ever imagined. I'm sorry I didn't say so, I was just... overwhelmed."

As she smiled, I could see the relief in her eyes. "Good. I guess we should get some sleep then."

In agreement, I hit the light switch and we lay there silently, both of us lost in our own thoughts until sleep finally came. I wanted to know what she was thinking, but I was afraid to ask, and even more afraid to tell her my own thoughts.

Like the one about how I never, ever wanted this to end.

~Holly~

In the morning, I woke up before Jackson. Although the winter sun hadn't risen yet, enough light came in from the street lights outside that I could see him pretty clearly, his handsome face turned towards me on his pillow and his lips parted ever-so-slightly. He hadn't put a shirt on the night before so his chest was still bare, his muscles clearly defined even in sleep.

It had been a long time since I'd spent the whole night with a man. In the past few years, whenever I had sex with someone, I'd go to their place so that I could leave afterwards and not have to worry about kicking them out of my flat or any awkward scenes in the morning. If they asked for my number, I came up with an excuse not to give it to them.

I left before they had a chance to leave me. My heart might be cold and a little lonely, but at least it couldn't be broken again.

That had been my failsafe method for years, but when Jackson asked me to stay over, I hadn't had to try too hard to convince myself it would be okay. We were only pretending, playing at being in a relationship to see what it would be like, me from the emotional side and him from the physical. What could it hurt to indulge him on this one thing?

Besides, the more time we spent together, the greater the likelihood that something would go wrong and he would realize this wasn't what he wanted after all. Though the thought of it made my heart ache, I almost wished it would happen sooner rather than later, before my feelings for him got any stronger than they already were.

When we stood outside that house the night before and he told me he didn't want to buy it without consulting the woman he'd share it with, I knew what he was getting at. He wanted to know what I thought of it. He was implying that I might be that woman, and when I looked back at the house, I could almost picture it: he and I sitting in the living room with the big window onto the street, maybe even with him holding a baby on his lap, just like Cole had earlier that night.

For a second, it almost seemed possible.

But how could Jackson be so sure about us after spending such a small amount of time with me? Really, in the grand scheme of things, we didn't know each other all that well. Yes, we got along well, and yes, there was an electric attraction between us. And yes, I had told him things about myself that most people didn't know, but there were still so many things *he* didn't know, things he might not trip over for years. Which of them would be the thing that made him want to back out? I didn't know, but there had to be one. There always was.

So, I pretended I didn't know what he meant, even though the brief flash of disappointment in his eyes nearly broke me. When I went to take his hand afterwards, I found myself trembling from even that small glimpse of happiness I had allowed myself to picture. Luckily, Jackson mistook my reaction for being cold and didn't question me about it.

Back at his apartment, he finally let me see him in all his naked, aroused glory, and it just might have been the sexiest damn thing I'd ever seen. Knowing that I was the first, and so far only, woman to get to see it turned me on even more. My body was absolutely aching for him, but I forced myself to focus only on him, just like he had done for me the night before, and not to go further than he expected me to. Being eye level with that enticing cock, I'd been so tempted to take him in my mouth, but I didn't think he expected it, and to be honest, I didn't mind having something to still look forward to. We might be working our way up slowly to full intimacy, but the anticipation was actually kind of sexy.

Seeing him come was way more satisfying than it had ever been for me before.

When he didn't say anything afterwards as I went to clean up and get ready for bed, I started to get worried. Did he feel awkward or regret what we did? Even after we got in bed, he didn't say anything, so finally, I couldn't take it any longer and I had to ask.

Thankfully, he explained he had just been too overwhelmed to comment, and with the sincerity in his sweet blue eyes, I instantly felt lighter. He wasn't getting rid of me just yet.

So, when I woke up still in his arms and wearing his t-shirt, just for a moment, I let myself appreciate how wonderful it felt. Wouldn't it be amazing if it was actually real?

No sooner had the thought crossed my mind than my phone buzzed from the side of the room where I had left it the night before, on top of my folded clothes, and Jackson began to stir. His arms tightened around me momentarily, pulling me even closer to him, and I could feel his cock beginning to harden. He must have felt it too because he immediately moved his hips away from me.

"Good morning," he murmured, his eyes opening just a crack to get a look at me. "Have you been awake for long?"

I shook my head, whispering my reply back. "Not at all, just a couple of minutes. I'm sorry if my phone woke you."

He shrugged sleepily. "It's alright. Do you need to check it?"

Actually, I couldn't guess who would be contacting me. All my work emails were being diverted, so the only messages I'd been receiving lately were from Jackson and Gemma. Unless someone from home needed to reach me? Maybe I should check to be sure.

"I'll take a quick peek." I tried to move away but his arms still held me tight.

"Not without a kiss first."

"Are you sure?" I teased. "You're not worried about morning breath?"

"Worth it," he assured me, leaning down to press his lips softly against mine.

Somehow, the most innocent kiss from him felt better than a full-on tongue-devouring kiss from most of the men I'd been with before.

My phone buzzed again, interrupting the moment. "Okay, I really better take a look."

He let me go that time and I stood up, shivering at the loss of the heat both from the duvet and from Jackson's body. Of course, he noticed my reaction. "Is it cold? I can turn the heat up."

"No, I think it's..." I trailed off as I got a look out the window, my phone temporarily forgotten. "Oh! It snowed."

"It did?" Jackson's eyes lit up like a little kid as he jumped out of bed and came to stand beside me.

A light dusting of snow sat on the street outside, some resting on the windowsills of the building across the road and on top of the cars.

Jackson sighed in disappointment. "Oh, that won't last too long. I was hoping for more."

His mood swings made me laugh. I loved how he never hid how he felt. "This is about what snow usually looks like in London, and we hardly ever get any before Christmas."

Leaving him at the window, I grabbed my phone and found that the texts were from Gemma. Quickly, I tapped on the first one.

Hey, hope you had a great time last night! If you don't want to ruin your day, don't read the Telegraph today, ok? I'll catch up with you later.

A second text followed, the one that had just made my phone buzz again, which said:

Cole says I shouldn't have said anything because now you'll be sure to read it. Please, don't prove him right!

It sounded like they must be together in bed, chatting with each other just as Jackson and I were. The comparison made me smile.

"What's up?" Jackson asked. I hadn't realized he'd turned to look at me, but when I looked up my phone, I could see his quizzical expression. Not having any reason to hide them, I showed him both texts and he laughed at the second one in particular. "That sounds about right. Are you going to read it or not?"

I had to admit to being curious about what Gemma thought would ruin my day. "I think the suspense will kill me if I don't. If she hadn't said anything, I probably wouldn't have even looked today."

Normally, I skimmed all the major papers as part of my job to look for news about new design projects, but being on holiday, I hadn't been doing it. Gemma must not have realized that.

"Let's look together, then," Jackson suggested, and we sat back down together on the edge of the bed as I pulled up the Telegraph app on my phone. A couple of minutes of scrolling later, I still hadn't seen anything that particularly interested me.

"I really would have had to dig to even find whatever it is," I told Jackson with a laugh as he patiently looked over my shoulder. "I can't stop now though. I need to know."

It took another minute or so before I saw the headline in the society pages, and I knew immediately it must be what Gemma had been referring to.

Christmas proposal: Lady Olivia Trowbridge and The Hon Paul Sydenham to be wed

My stomach sank as I tapped into the article. Olivia Trowbridge was one of Gemma's old boarding school acquaintances. I'd met her once or twice through Gemma. And Paul was... well, Paul. My Paul. The one who had proposed to me too, though certainly not in public.

The article explained how he popped the question in front of a crowd at the Trowbridge's annual Christmas party and gave details of their wedding plans. He must have been pretty certain there were no embarrassing relatives to come out of the woodwork of her life to propose so openly. It would be a lot harder for him to take that one back.

"Is that it?" Jackson asked, looking between me and the phone curiously. "This is what she thought would upset you?"

I nodded, trying to swallow down the lump in my throat. I hadn't even seen Paul for three years, and I certainly had no illusions about us ever being together again. It shouldn't have anything to do with me, and yet, I couldn't help feeling passed over all over again.

"That's my ex-fiancé," I managed to explain, pointing to the photo of the happy couple.

"Oh." A world of understanding infused that single word as Jackson took the phone from me and read the article. As soon as he'd finished, he switched the phone off and got to his feet, pulling me up with me. "Well, we've got no more time to waste. We've got a busy day ahead of us."

"We do?" That was the first I'd heard about it.

He nodded firmly. "Yup. You're in the greatest city in the world with an eager tour guide and the whole day ahead of us. No past, no future, just today. Let's go make some memories."

Chapter Eleven

A Perfect Day

~Jackson~

As Holly went into the bathroom to put her clothes back on and brush her teeth, I tried not to panic. I had just promised her a spectacular day out and I had absolutely nothing planned. There were some things I had been looking at and places I had been thinking about taking her, but nothing was booked.

I couldn't help myself. When I saw that haunted look in her eyes as she read the article about her ex-fiancé's new fiancée, I knew she needed a distraction. If we could go out and have a fun day together, by the time she remembered to think about Paul again, it would hurt a little less.

Through years of experience, I'd honed my skill at distracting myself from emotional pain, and I would work that magic on Holly that day, no matter what it took.

As quickly as possible, I threw some clothes on and called for a taxi to take us to the Plaza. Holly still needed to go get changed into fresh clothes and it would give me a chance to make some plans. She invited me up to her room to wait when we got there but I told her to go ahead and I'd wait in the lobby. As soon as the elevator door closed behind her, I hurried over to the concierge desk and got to work. By the time

Holly got back down, freshly showered and made up, looking absolutely stunning as always, everything was under control.

"I'm going to be the envy of every man we see today," I told her, kissing her on the cheek when she found me in the lobby. "You're breathtaking."

"And you are as smooth as ever," she replied, shaking her head at me. "How many times have you used that line?"

Was that really what she thought? "I've never said anything to you that wasn't true, Holly. It can't be a line if it's true."

Though she gave me a smile, I could still see that hint of sadness lurking in her eyes, so I took her arm and led her out the door.

"First up is brunch. I would have cooked something for you at my apartment, but the place I'm taking you is way better than anything I could make."

With her agreement, we walked a few blocks over to another hotel, one with a rooftop bar with stunning views over the city. I'd had to use the Stamer name to get us a table on such short notice, but it was worth it to see the look on Holly's face as we were shown in.

At the trendy table, she looked over the brunch menu curiously. "Is this a typical day for you? Eating out in a place like this?"

I wasn't sure exactly what she meant, but I tried to answer as honestly as I could. "Well, with my job, I spend a lot of time in hotels. I'm always looking for hotels that fit the Stamer brand that we might be able to buy, and I first visited this place on a scouting trip. Unfortunately for us, the owner decided not to sell. Even so, I loved the Eggs Benedict so much, I keep coming back."

My explanation made her smile. "I guess I don't actually know that much about what you do, other than that you work with Cole. What does your work involve?"

It warmed my heart that she wanted to hear about it, even if I felt pretty sure she only asked to keep her mind off other things. After we ordered our food, I told her about my job, how I came to work at Stamer Hotels, and exactly why I had been with Cole the previous year when we went to London.

"Even though my main role is acquisitions, Cole likes to ask for my opinion on design plans. He grew up with so much luxury, he's almost immune to it, so he likes me to look things over and make sure they're in line with what other people would find appealing. Since he's started working with you and Gemma though, he doesn't need to ask me anymore. He trusts you both entirely."

"It's kind of crazy, isn't it?" She took a sip of her mimosa as she looked out over the city spread out below us. "Gemma and Cole met so randomly, and now here they are, married, with a baby."

Was she actually thinking about them, or about her former boyfriend's new fiancée, or about her own never-meant-to-be marriage? Any of those things might be considered 'random', so I decided to bring the conversation back to us.

"It was definitely a lucky night for them both, and for me too, because if they hadn't met, I might have never met you."

She tried to smile, but at the same time, tears came to her eyes. "Fuck," she swore, picking up her napkin to dab at her eyes. "Sorry, Jackson. I'm not a crier, I don't know what's wrong with me."

Obviously, despite my best efforts, the article from the morning was still at the top of her mind.

"Nothing's wrong with you," I assured her. "Sometimes, things from our past sneak up on us when we're not expecting them and bring old feelings back with them."

"I don't even care," she said, waving her hand like she could push all the emotion away. "I really don't. He could marry twenty women if he wanted to. It's got nothing to do with me."

"Holly." I said her name softly and as supportively as I could. "Of course it's got something to do with you. Even if you don't feel anything for him now, you did at one point. You even thought you were going to marry him, at least for a little while. You've got every right to be a bit emotional."

She grimaced, clearly not satisfied with that response, so I changed tactics.

"If it makes you feel better, we can trash talk his fiancée a little bit: I mean, Trowbridge? What kind of name is that?"

Holly did laugh, at least. "It's actually a very well-respected name. Her father's an earl, the same as Gemma's. She's the kind of woman Paul always should have been with."

"So, why do you think he was with you instead?"

I didn't mean anything negative by the question, and I felt pretty sure she knew that. I was, however, honestly interested in her answer. What did she see as her good qualities?

She shrugged. "Well, you've said yourself, I'm attractive enough."

My eyebrows shot up. "That's not exactly what I said. You're gorgeous, and that's a reason anyone would want to date you, but why do you think Paul asked you to marry him?"

Her brow furrowed, and I got the feeling she'd never really thought about it before, at least not exactly in those terms.

"I guess he liked that I was ambitious," she mused, her eyes darting back and forth as she searched her memory. "He was interested in the business that Gemma and I were going to start, and I could always make him laugh. We usually had a good time together."

Those all sounded like good reasons to me. "What else?"

She shrugged again, looking a bit embarrassed as I refused to let it go. "I'm not really sure. I guess you'd have to ask him."

"I could, or I could show you this."

Reaching into my pocket, I pulled out the piece of paper I'd been carrying around for the last few days, trying to decide when it would be a good time to show it to her. It seemed like we'd reached the right moment, or at least, I really hoped so. My hand shook just a little as I slid the paper across the table to her.

Holly waited until I pulled my hand back before she picked it up, unfolding it curiously. The edges were a bit yellowed with age, but the handwritten list on it could still be read clearly.

"Sense of humour," she read out loud, glancing up at me before looking down at the paper again. "Creative and works hard. Adventurous;

likes to try new things. Passionate. Loyal; stands up for herself and her friends. Makes me feel special to be with her."

Reaching the end, she looked back up at me, her eyes searching for an explanation.

"What is this?"

"It sounds a lot like a description of you, doesn't it?"

Her cheeks coloured as she glanced back down. "But what is it?" she pressed, turning the paper over as if there might be another clue. "You obviously didn't write this recently."

"I didn't. I wrote it the night of my prom, when I went home in the limo by myself after my date ditched me for Cole."

Immediately, her eyes softened, no doubt picturing my sad and rejected teenaged self. "What does it mean?"

"I realized that night that the girl I'd been dating wasn't who I thought she was," I reminded her. "So, I wrote down the qualities that were most important to me in a woman. I promised myself that night that I was going to find the woman who checked every one of those boxes and I wouldn't settle for anything less."

Her eyes dropped to the paper again, rereading each of the lines. She couldn't argue with a single one; they all described her to the letter.

"And now, she's sitting in front of me, and all I can think is: thank God Paul was enough of an idiot to let you go."

~Holly~

For the second time in five minutes, my eyes filled with tears, but that time, they weren't necessarily sad. Jackson had just said the sweetest damned thing anyone had ever said to me, so sweet I didn't even really know how to process it.

"How can you be so perfect? Is there some kind of class that teaches you what to say?" I tried to make a joke and lighten the mood like I usually did, but he didn't laugh. He just kept looking at me with that same soft, tender expression until two teardrops slipped down my cheeks. I didn't even bother to try to stop them, though I couldn't remember the last time I cried in front of anyone. Probably not since that night with Paul, the one we were talking about, the night he retracted his proposal.

Jackson watched the tears go, his gaze following them down before he looked back up to look me straight in the eyes. "I'm not perfect, Holly, and I know you're not either, so you don't need to worry that I'm going to change my mind about you when I figure that out. I don't want somebody 'perfect'. I just want you."

Each word out of his mouth contrasted so strongly with the things that Paul had said to me that night, it almost felt like Jackson must have been there, that he somehow knew exactly what had been said and was saying the opposite to me on purpose.

Could he really be for real? Was it even possible?

"I know you're not ready to feel the same way about me yet," he continued, his blue eyes watching my reaction carefully. "And that's okay. I don't want you to feel rushed or pushed in any way, but I also want you to know exactly how I feel so there's no confusion and no wondering. I want to be with you, Holly; not just for these two weeks, but for as long as you're willing to give me, and I won't disappear or take that back, not ever."

He gave me a few seconds to reply, but honestly, I had no idea what to say. Still smarting from Paul's new engagement, I certainly hadn't expected Jackson to promise me forever, and I felt torn between two extremes and completely off balance.

When I didn't speak, the serious look on his face faded into his more typical, easy smile. "I meant what I said earlier too, about today: no past and no future. Let's do our best not to think about what's-his-name again and I won't talk about my dream woman either."

Gently, he took his list from my hands, folded it up and placed it back in his pocket.

"For today, we're just Holly and Jackson, two people who are kind of crazy about each other and going to have a wonderful day together. How does that sound?"

It sounded like some breathing room and time to think, and I appreciated it. "Perfect," I told him, finally finding my voice again. "What's our plan for today, then?"

His smile brightened even more at my acceptance of his offer. "Well, now that we're fed, we can go burn off some calories. We'll walk down Fifth Avenue and look at all the store windows decorated for Christmas. What do you think?"

He looked so boyish with his enthusiastic grin that I couldn't help but smile back. "You really want to take me shopping, Jackson? We might be there all day and we won't have time for anything else."

His laugh made the whole room feel brighter. "*Window* shopping. No going in. Unless you really want to."

I had to smile at the addition of the last condition, knowing he wouldn't deny me something I truly wanted. I never for a moment thought he would.

Together, we headed back out into the city. The air was still cold but, as Jackson had predicted, the snow that had fallen overnight had already melted. We held hands as we wandered down the street, stopping at all the elaborately decorated shop windows. I had seen Christmas window displays in London but the ones he showed me were on a completely different level, and as a designer, they fascinated me.

We stopped at Sak's, Tiffany's, Bergdorf Goodman and Lord & Taylor as well as many other smaller shops along the way. New ideas and colour schemes kept popping into my head, ways that I could incorporate some of the ideas into my own work and I took multiple photos from all different angles. Jackson asked for my opinion eagerly and listened attentively to everything I pointed out that caught my eye.

We must have spent a couple of hours out there, and I had completely lost track of time when Jackson looked at his own watch. "Shoot. We're going to be late, we have to go!"

"Late for what?" I asked as we hurried down the street, even though by that point, I really didn't expect him to tell me. He didn't, but I got my answer soon enough as we rounded a corner and saw the marquee of Radio City Music Hall.

Pulling out his phone, Jackson presented our electronic tickets to the usher outside who told us to head straight in. We were already in our seats with the lights dimming before I got a chance to ask exactly what we were going to see.

Jackson just grinned at me as the curtain opened to reveal the chorus line of the Rockettes dance troupe. "Take a look."

I'd seen them on TV before, but I never even thought about going to see them in person. For the next hour and a half, we lost ourselves in the annual Christmas show.

"That's some impressive flexibility," I said with no small amount of envy when the final kickline had ended and the lights came back up. "They're all so beautiful."

"They've got nothing on you," Jackson replied, and I rolled my eyes at the exaggeration, making him laugh. "Are you hungry yet?"

"Maybe for a snack." We were well into the afternoon already so we probably should eat something, but the big brunch we'd eaten earlier was still fuelling me.

Heading back onto the street, Jackson grabbed some hot dogs from a corner vendor, promising me it was an essential New York experience, and when we'd finished stuffing our faces with them, he hailed a taxi. That time, I didn't even bother to ask where we were going since I already knew he wouldn't tell me, and I knew it would be good anyway.

The ride took quite a while before we pulled up outside a large park with a stunning glasshouse in the distance. We had gone over another small bridge, shorter than the one to Brooklyn the night before, and I was completely lost. "Is this Central Park again?"

Jackson laughed as we got out of the car. "No, there are other parks in the city too. We're in the Bronx now. This is the New York Botanical Garden."

I never knew New York had a botanical garden, but I was eager to see why he'd chosen to bring me there, and it didn't take me long to figure it out once we got inside.

Aside from the stunning collection of plants and flowers that I expected to find, miniature trains ran around the whole space, travelling through a collection of tiny New York landmarks. As we got even closer, I could see that they were constructed not from any typical kind of building materials, but from all natural materials to match the garden theme. There were bridges made of tree bark, buildings built of cinnamon sticks and even a miniature Statue of Liberty.

"I haven't seen the real one yet!" I realized as I pointed out the tiny green lady to Jackson.

He pressed his palm to his forehead. "How did I forget that? We'll find the time, don't worry. For now, we can admire this one instead."

The whole scene was magical, lit up with fairy lights as the tiny trains went round. We took our time exploring it all, making up backstories for all the little people scattered around the scene, and once we'd had our fill, we went outside and walked through the park for a while as the sun began to set.

Only when Jackson asked me gently how I was feeling did I realize I'd forgotten to think about Paul for the last several hours. That morning felt like a lifetime ago.

"I'm feeling wonderful," I told him honestly. "This has been a perfect day. Thank you, Jackson."

His answering smile was so full of joy that it nearly brought tears to my eyes again. Honestly, what was wrong with me? When did I get so sappy?

Jackson held my hand again as we headed back to the park entrance to find a taxi. "There's just one more place I want to take you today, and then maybe we could have a quiet night in."

That definitely appealed to me. After what we'd done together the night before, I was very interested to see what he thought the next step might be on our sexual journey.

The taxi ride felt a lot shorter that time and soon, we were driving along rather run-down streets with low-rise apartment buildings. It didn't look anything like the other parts of New York that he'd shown me so far.

The taxi dropped us off directly in front of one building, and Jackson turned to look at it just as he had in front of his dream house the night before. "This is where I grew up."

With new eyes, I took in the building and the whole street around us. It really didn't seem all that different to the part of London where I grew up. I'd never taken Paul to my childhood home and I couldn't imagine what he would have thought if I did, but standing on that street and looking up at the faded apartment building where that brave little boy he'd told me about had grown up, I knew that Jackson wouldn't make any judgements.

He would understand.

Maybe he really wouldn't be scared off by anything.

Maybe everything he'd told me was real.

Maybe that time, there might be a happy ending after all.

As soon as I let myself believe it, *really* believe it, the most incredible feeling settled over me: like happiness and relaxation and excitement and anticipation all at once. My whole body felt electrified.

Almost of its own accord, my hand reached up and touched his face, turning it away from the apartment building and towards me. The action seemed to surprise him, but he looked down at me with that same expression of admiration and hopefulness that he always showed me, and I finally let myself imagine what it would like to have him looking at me like that for the rest of our lives.

If I didn't kiss him right that second, I might just burst.

I got up on my toes as he leaned towards me and our lips were only centimetres apart when the door to the building in front of us opened.

"Jackson?"

His eyes widened at the sound of the voice and he turned to the door, his mouth dropping open in surprise.

"Mom?"

~Jackson~

My mother was pretty much the last person I expected to see at that moment. Her appearance in my life always came as a surprise, without any warning, but I had never just run into her before. I always assumed that wherever she went when she disappeared must be far away from New York.

She looked just as confused about running into me as I felt. "Were you coming to see me?"

My eyes passed over her, taking in the changes since I'd seen her last. It had been nearly two years that time, and I tried to imagine what she looked like to Holly, seeing her for the first time. She was only in her mid-40s since she'd been so young when she gave birth to me, but she looked older than her age. Deep lines framed her mouth and formed craters beneath her eyes. I put money in an account for her every month but I didn't know what she did with it. Her clothes always looked worn out, like the winter coat she wore that day.

A second later, my brain processed what she had just said: she asked if I had come there to see her. Why would I go to see her there?

"Do you live here?" I asked, caught between surprise and disbelief at the thought.

She nodded. "I always liked this building and the neighbours, so I moved back in."

Still feeling off-balance, I blinked a few times, trying to make sense of that. What did she mean she always liked the building? She had done her best to stay away from it, and us, as much as she could. And how long had she been living there? Why didn't she let me know she was in the city?

She answered the last question, at least, though her reasoning sounded weak. "I was going to call you, but it's been busy getting settled. I thought maybe we could spend Christmas together."

I honestly couldn't remember the last time I had seen her at Christmas. Each word out of her mouth left me feeling more disoriented.

"And who's this lovely young woman?" my mom asked, clearly trying to change the subject as she turned her rather hesitant smile on Holly.

My mom's sudden appearance had thrown me off so much, I'd forgotten I hadn't introduced them yet. Trying my best to smile for Holly's sake, I quickly remedied that.

"This is Holly Chapman. Holly, my mother, Darla Hanmer."

"It's nice to meet you, Mrs Hanmer." Holly's words were polite, but my mom's eyebrows raised at the sound of her accent.

"Not from around here, are you? How long have you lived in New York?"

"Oh, I don't live here. I'm just visiting."

"Hmmm." The sound wasn't really an approving one as my mom's eyes flitted over to me curiously. I could tell she had something to say but didn't necessarily want to say it in front of Holly. "Well, I don't want to interrupt your date. I've actually got one of my own I need to get to."

She gestured behind me and I turned to find a man standing not far away, his hands in his pockets. I waited for my mom to introduce me as I'd just introduced her to Holly, but she didn't, simply stepping around me instead to get to the man.

"I'll call you later, Jackson. It's good to see you."

"Good to see you too," I mumbled, still feeling completely off-kilter, as I often did after any time with my mother.

She greeted the other man with a kiss and they walked away down the street together as I watched them go. She never looked back.

"I'm guessing you didn't know she lives here?" Holly's slightly sarcastic question pulled my attention back to her.

Shaking my head, I let out a small huff of disbelief. "I had no idea."

The look she'd been giving me earlier had disappeared entirely, unfortunately, replaced by one of concern. Just before my mom appeared, I saw something in Holly's eyes that had got my heart racing, a hint of genuine happiness, a promise of something, just before she almost kissed me. It felt like it meant something, but after my mom's interruption, the moment seemed to be lost.

"How long has it been since you've seen her?" There was no pity in Holly's voice. If anything, she sounded a bit angry.

I kept my answer vague. "Quite a while, but hey, we said no past today, right? That includes me as well as you, even if mine did literally turn up in front of us."

Thankfully, that brought a smile to her face.

"Let's go back to your hotel," I suggested. "We can get some room service on Cole, a little food and some wine, maybe get a little drunk too. What do you think?"

Her smile grew wider. "I think you read my mind."

As we waited for a taxi to arrive, I showed Holly a few things around the street, like the bodega at the corner where the owner used to let Layla and Josh take things they wanted on the understanding that I'd come in and pay for it later. From there, we could also see the corner of the school I'd attended until I got the scholarship for the private school instead.

Once the taxi picked us up, we rode back to the Plaza in companionable silence most of the way and Holly linked her fingers with mine in what felt like a gesture of support. I could tell she had questions about my mom, just as my mom had apparently wanted to say something to me about Holly, but as I'd already told her, I didn't really want to talk about my past that day and I appreciated that she gave me that space.

It always took me a little while to process the feelings that seeing my mom stirred up in me, and I didn't have the mental energy to do it right then, not when I'd rather be focusing on Holly instead.

Back in Holly's room, we had fun choosing the most ridiculously expensive things off the menu, things we would never order for ourselves, knowing that Cole probably wouldn't even glance at the total bill when it came in.

"Do you ever feel jealous of the life he's had?" Holly asked once we'd finished eating and were settled back with a glass of very expensive wine each. "I know he's your friend and you care for him, but does it ever strike you as unfair that some people have it so easy?"

I gave her question some serious thought before answering her. "I've never been jealous of his money, but when we were younger, I did envy him his family and how close they are. When his fiancée left him, I didn't envy him at all. He really went through hell with that. More recently, I do have to admit I've been jealous of him and Gemma a few times, at just how perfect they are together and how happy they make each other."

Holly nodded thoughtfully. "I know what you mean. Gem hasn't had the easiest life with her own family. She even told me once that she wished she was free of the restrictions of expectations, like I am, but she's had advantages too, and now she's got her own little family. I guess everyone's life has its own pros and cons."

"Definitely," I agreed, seeing my opportunity to bring the conversation back to us. "And one of my pros is being here right now with you."

I expected her to laugh that off as she usually did or accuse me of using a line on her, but instead, she just smiled at me with a rather affectionate look. "I'd count that as a pro for me too."

An unexpected level of emotion echoed in her voice, and I couldn't help it: I leaned over and kissed her, finishing what we had almost started on the sidewalk outside my old building earlier. There was a need and a vulnerability in her answering kiss that I hadn't encountered there before, and it filled my heart with hope.

As Holly pulled back, her hand gently stroking the line of my beard, she gave me a suggestive smile. "I have an idea. Since we're already taking advantage of Cole's generosity, one of the best things about this room is the absolutely massive bathroom. How'd you like to come and get steamy with me?"

Chapter Twelve

STEAMY

~Holly~

The idea of having a shower with Jackson came to me on the taxi ride back to the hotel. We'd been naked in front of each other but not at the same time, yet it felt like suggesting anything where we both got naked in bed might be a step too far for him.

However, I also suspected if I asked him straight out to have sex with me that night, he might actually agree. It felt possible. If I really wanted to, I might be able to win our challenge there and then.

But for some reason, I didn't want that. After all the time we'd spent together over the last week, and especially after that moment earlier where I finally realized he might be serious about wanting to stick around, winning didn't matter to me so much anymore, especially if I had to push him to get there.

Most of all, I just wanted to keep playing the game.

Jackson exhaled as I made the suggestion, his eyes full of desire. "That sounds amazing, Holly."

Delighted with his agreement, I grinned back at him. "Come with me, then."

Leaving our wine half-drunk, we made our way into the bathroom together, and as soon as we were through the door, Jackson's arms circled my waist, pulling me back against him, my back to his chest. His lips went to my neck and my whole body tingled in response, humming with need and anticipation. I could feel his own need in the hard press of his cock against my ass and I couldn't help smiling, remembering how only a few days earlier, he tried to hide his arousal from me.

No one was hiding anymore.

We shed our clothes one piece at a time, taking time between each one to kiss and touch each other. His hands felt warm against my skin, his lips hot, and his tongue electrifying. As it dipped into the spot above my collarbone, one hand on my breast and the other gripping my lower back, the thought crossed my mind that I could do this happily for a very long time, just kissing and touching him without being worried about getting to the usual finish line. Even going halfway with him was better than going all the way with anyone else.

Finally, all our clothes were gone and I stepped into the large shower, turning on the overhead rainfall shower head. Warm water cascaded down, running in rivulets over my body and heating my skin from the outside, but when Jackson joined me, his cock fully erect, it set off a whole other kind of heat from within.

"Can I wash you?" His hands ran over my slick body, leaving a trail of goosebumps in their wake.

"I'd love that," I told him honestly. I couldn't remember the last time I'd actually showered with a man that way. On the one-night stands that had been typical for me over the previous few years, sensuality took a back seat to more urgent needs.

In fact, I supposed the last time must have been with Paul, and as he crossed my mind, I waited for the usual sting of rejection that always accompanied my memories of him. It never came, though. All my emotions were already tied up in Jackson that night, leaving no room for anyone else.

Grabbing the bottle of body wash, Jackson squirted some into his hands and rubbed them together a moment to warm them up. As his hands went to my shoulders, pressing down with the perfect amount of pressure, a moan of pure pleasure left my lips. I couldn't remember anything ever feeling quite that good.

Not an inch of my body was left untouched. His soapy hands massaged and rubbed every part of me, interspersed with kisses in between as drops of water ran down our faces. More than once, he teased me, running his hands between my legs but without the pressure I so desperately wanted. Just when he had me ready to beg, he slipped his fingers between my folds and brushed my clit, almost making my knees buckle in both relief and pleasure. I clung onto his wet, sturdy arms for support as he began to circle my clit with his thumb, his fingers playing against my entrance but not actually going in.

"Jackson," I groaned, and he grinned at the desperation in my voice, completely tuned into me as always. In perfect sync, he kissed me again, hard, his tongue sliding into my mouth at the same time that his fingers finally thrust into me.

It almost felt like floating as he held me there, one arm around my waist, the other hand buried inside me and his mouth hot and wanting against mine. I could squirm and wriggle against his hold, but I wasn't going anywhere and I really didn't want to. I was exactly where I wanted to be.

With his fingers working their magic and his kiss stealing my breath, it didn't take long before my orgasm washed over me, leaving me feeling even more weightless than before. His kiss lightened but didn't stop as I gradually drifted back down to earth.

"That was amazing."

Though the words were exactly what was in my head, I hadn't spoken them. I opened my eyes to find Jackson smiling down at me, a look of awestruck affection on his face.

"You think *that* was amazing?" I teased him, taking a shaky step back on my still-wobbly legs. "Just wait."

~Jackson~

Being in the shower with Holly that way felt intimate in a different way than being with her in my room the night before. Although it was sexual, it felt like more than that, sensual and tender as well, and I had to admit that I felt more relaxed that way. Although my stiff-as-a-board dick would attest that the whole situation turned me on, it didn't feel like getting to the orgasm was the only point. The pleasure of the journey mattered just as much.

I couldn't be happier that she'd suggested it.

After I made her come, she took the body wash in her own hands and began to rub me down while my eyes closed in pure bliss. Her delicate hands caressed my chest, my back, my legs, and even my feet. There wasn't any place that didn't feel better with her touching it, but when she gripped my aching dick firmly in her soapy hand, I nearly came right then and there.

"This can't be comfortable," she teased me, stroking me slowly with just the right amount of pressure. "Let me help you."

I nodded, my mouth apparently unable to form any words, and I expected her to increase the pace of her stroking, to make me come with her hand just as she had the night before. It wouldn't take very much at all to finish me off.

She didn't do that, though. She let me go instead and, as I watched through half-closed eyes, she dropped down to her knees.

"Holly?"

I didn't know if I could handle what she seemed to have in mind, my arousal already so strong I could barely contain it, but she had no such reservations. Looking up at me, she gave me a wink before she brought her lips to my dick.

"Oh, fuck." I inhaled sharply, the words just a gasp of air as she took me into her warm, wet mouth. Somehow, my imagination had let me down again because it felt even better than I anticipated, and as her tongue caressed the bottom of my shaft, I felt like I just might die of pleasure. If such a thing were possible, that was going to be when it happened.

She must have known how close I was because she kept her movements slow and light, her tongue dancing over me as she took me in a little deeper, slowly sucking as she pulled all the way back. I lost all sense of time or place as she continued, and though I never wanted it to end, I knew it would, and soon. There was no way I could hold back for much longer.

Something almost like a whimper came out of me, a sound I was pretty certain I'd never made before, and Holly seemed instinctively to know what it meant. With one confident swoop, she suddenly took me in far deeper than before, my dick disappearing into her mouth as I felt the tip hit the back of her throat, and that was it. I couldn't wait anymore and my orgasm hit me hard, leaving me gasping for air as I pumped into her eager mouth.

"Good God," I managed to mutter as she gently released my dick, and Holly grinned up at me, licking her lips in a way that made me weak all over again.

"You took the words right out of my mouth," she teased, getting back to her feet and giving me a soft kiss. "I've been wanting to do that for quite a while, Jackson."

As reality began to sink back in, I couldn't help feeling a little worried through my smile as she rinsed herself off again. What we'd just done was about as close to actually having sex as we could get. We were so close to her goal, and I still felt a long away from getting her on the same page as me. What if I couldn't? What if this really was all she wanted from me?

How would I ever get over her if she decided to walk away?

~Holly~

I had no doubt about how much Jackson enjoyed his first blow job, but I also didn't miss the change in his mood just after. Somehow, I'd become tuned into his expressions and his body language in a way I didn't remember ever being with anyone else before.

Even so, although I noticed it, I wasn't exactly sure what the shift meant. Did he regret what just happened? Or maybe he just felt a bit vulnerable after taking such a big step with me?

Wanting so badly to erase any discomfort he felt, I switched the water off and placed my hand on his cheek gently, drawing his eyes back to me. "You know, the shower's not the only good thing in here. The bathtub's pretty great too. How'd you like to take a bath with me?"

He immediately caught my meaning, how I meant it as an invitation to cuddle and be close to each other in a non-sexual way, and his face relaxed into a smile, sending warmth spreading through me.

That smile was going to be my downfall, but maybe the fall wouldn't be so bad if Jackson was there to cushion my landing.

I filled the deep soaker tub while Jackson found some bubble bath among the hotel's many toiletries, and soon, we were snuggled up to-gether in the large tub, me leaning back against him as his arms circled my waist. Between the warm water and the hardness of his muscled, fit body beneath me, I felt I could melt right into him.

We talked for a little while about the day we'd had, focusing solely on the present as we'd already agreed, and before long, we lapsed into a comfortable silence. My eyes closed as I relaxed in the warmth of his embrace.

"Do you mind if I ask you something?" Jackson's voice asked from behind me, soft and low in my ear.

"Go ahead," I murmured in reply. I couldn't remember the last time I felt so comfortable.

"You've done this kind of thing with several different men, right?"

My eyes opened again as I frowned. Did he mean the bath, or what exactly was he talking about?

When I didn't answer straight away, he jumped in again. "I mean, I don't need a number or anything, and I wasn't implying anything, I just wondered..."

"Jackson." I cut him off by turning around and placing a light kiss on his lips, letting the kiss linger for a moment before turning again and snuggling back into him. "It's fine. I wasn't sure what you meant, but if you're talking about sex and other intimate things, then yes. I've been with several different men."

Off the top of my head, I didn't have a number handy. I could probably count if I really thought about it, but I didn't want to be thinking about other men right then. Why was Jackson?

"I was just wondering..." he repeated, sounding more nervous than before. "Is this different in any way? When it's you and me?"

The uncertainty in his voice nearly broke my heart. If anyone else had asked, I would have thought they were fishing for a compliment, but clearly, he didn't mean it that way. He'd never been with anyone else, so he really didn't know.

I thought about turning back to look at him, but it would be easier for me to explain it without being distracted by those sweet blue eyes of his, so I stayed where I was.

"It's very different. For starters, it's never quite the same with anyone. I suppose that's why people like to do it with more than one person. Or most people do, at least."

I meant that as a joke, teasing him as usual, but he didn't make any reply. If anything, his arms tensed around me, just a little. Perhaps the time wasn't right for joking, so I quickly moved on.

"More than that, there's a big difference when it's someone you know well compared to someone you know superficially, and I think we've done a pretty good job of moving past the superficial this week."

I could feel him nodding behind me in agreement but he stayed silent, waiting for me to continue as I searched for the right words. I had never had to explain this to anyone before or even really to myself, and I didn't want to get it wrong when he seemed so invested in my response.

"When you and I are together, it's physically amazing, of course." I wanted to make sure he knew that rather than just guessing at it. "But it's not just about how my body feels. Knowing that I can make you feel good too is just as important and satisfying."

He shifted beneath me as if steeling himself for his next question. "And what about the other men that you knew well? I don't need a direct comparison or anything, but I just wondered if it's different from them?"

Again, I could hear that nervousness in his voice that told me he really didn't know the answer, and once again, I searched my heart for the right words.

"It is different. Again, it's never the same with anyone because each person is different and so is each relationship. But if you want to know what makes being with you different for me? I guess it's that I feel safe with you. I know you respect me and trust me, I know how important it is to you that I enjoy everything we do, and that just makes the whole thing better."

As the words came out, I realized just how much truth there was to them. Even with the other men I'd been in relationships with, a part of me often felt that the sex had to be amazing to make up for the other things about myself that weren't quite good enough. With Jackson, it was almost the opposite. He already accepted me just as I was, and because he hadn't done any of the sexual side of things before, he had no expectations of me.

Instead of feeling I had to perform for him, it felt like more of a mutual adventure. It was exciting, but it was also comfortable in a way I didn't think I'd ever really experienced before.

That applied to everything about our relationship, not just when we were being physical. It felt different with him every time we were together, no matter what we did, and Gemma's words from the other day came back to me. *You're different with him. From the outside, it's hard to miss.*

Maybe she had it right. Maybe I was different because he was different. Because we were different together.

I opened my mouth to tell him so, but he spoke first before I had a chance. "I think I understand. I feel safe with you too, Holly."

Those words, so obviously true, melted my heart. He wouldn't be there with me, trying all those new things, if he didn't trust me.

"In fact, I feel so safe that I was wondering if we could try one more thing tonight."

Immediately, my heart beat slightly faster. Was he actually going to suggest that we have sex? He had said he wouldn't until I was ready to say I loved him. Did he know just how close I felt?

"What would you like to try?" I managed to ask, even though my throat had gone dry. The thought of him inside me, of seeing those blue eyes of his looking at me as he moved within me, had my whole body on fire.

The idea of him saying he loved me as he did it was almost more than I could bear.

Just like always, he kept me guessing. "Let's go to the bedroom, and I'll show you."

~Jackson~

Holly's words weren't quite a declaration of love, but I felt more hopeful after that conversation than I had before. She felt different with me than she did with anyone else, and though she didn't come right out and say it, I could feel in her tone that it was a good kind of different. She hadn't said the word 'better', but I'd heard it in her unspoken language anyway.

We were getting close to her acknowledging how she felt, and so, I had one last thing I wanted to do with her, one way to show her how much I wanted her to feel safe and treasured with me, just like she'd said.

Wordlessly, we both dried off in the big, fluffy hotel towels before going into the bedroom, both of us still completely naked. Holly's eyes darted to me curiously as we got to the bed, trying to figure out what I had in mind. She genuinely didn't appear to have any idea, which surprised me. As far as I could see, there was only really one thing we hadn't done yet.

Her body still felt warm from the bath as I pulled her to me, and my hands caressed her naked back while hers went to my chest. I'd been able to keep my arousal in check while we were in the tub, but it came roaring back with her touch, my dick hardening immediately at the contact with her soft body. Her fingers danced across my skin, sending shockwaves right through me, little electrical currents that travelled the whole length of my body before settling into my pulsing dick.

However, before I could get too worked up, I pulled back. What I had in mind had nothing to do with me; it was all about her.

"Lie down on the bed," I requested, my voice low and thick with desire. For the first time, I really had a chance to see her in all her naked beauty. Previously, she'd kept at least some piece of clothing on, and in the shower, I'd been a little distracted. Lying on the bed, her make-up washed away and her hair still damp, she had never looked more beautiful to me.

"Are you going to join me?" she teased when I stood there a moment too long, admiring her.

I definitely planned to. On my hands and knees, I crawled over to her and gave her a gentle kiss on the lips before moving down her body. The swell of her breasts was the most perfect thing I'd ever seen and I couldn't help stopping at them, letting my tongue flick across the puckered nipples, loving the way she sighed as I did.

Gradually, I moved lower, to her stomach, dipping my tongue into her belly button and nipping at the toned muscles surrounding it. As I moved down to the soft triangle of hair below, Holly inhaled deeply, finally seeming to realize what my intentions were.

"You don't have to do this if you don't want to," she told me, raising her head to look down at me. "Not all men like it."

I simply raised my eyebrows back at her. "How will I know if I like it unless I try?"

With a smile, she accepted that answer and laid her head back down on the bed. Goosebumps raised on her skin as I slipped my hands between her legs, opening them gently.

Again, I hadn't had a chance to have a proper look at her before then. Although my fingers had been inside her a couple of times, I'd never been eye-level with her, and the view captivated me. Gently, I spread her lips apart to take a better look, taking in the pinkness of her skin and her intoxicating smell. Just the idea of getting my mouth on her and bringing her pleasure through it had me salivating.

Trying to remember everything I'd read on the subject, I moved closer, running my tongue lightly between her folds of skin. Holly shivered in response and I repeated the action, with more force that time. As I connected with her clit, she groaned, her hips moving towards me all on their own.

With nowhere else I needed to be, I took my time exploring her. I wanted to know every inch of her. I wanted to know the spots that made her sigh and the ones that drove her crazy. I wanted to understand exactly how she worked so that I couldn't ever fail to satisfy her.

"Please, Jackson," she groaned from above me as I made her body jolt another time, her muscles tense with anticipation. "Stop teasing me."

That wasn't my intention, but I didn't mind if she thought I had that kind of control. As long as she was enjoying herself, I was satisfied, but if she wanted me to step it up, I would. Moving lower, I ran my tongue around the rim of her entrance a couple of times, smiling as she moaned and squirmed until I finally thrust it fully inside.

Above me, I heard her gasp, but the sound was overwhelmed by the taste and feel of her. Although I'd felt her from the inside with my fingers before, it felt different with my mouth, and I couldn't help wondering exactly how it would feel when my dick was inside her.

'When'. I almost laughed as I realized what I'd just thought: I was no longer thinking 'if'. I'd pretty much admitted defeat, but at that moment, I couldn't bring myself to care. My attention remained entirely on her, continuing to lick and kiss and suck her, alternating between her clit and her hole until I felt her starting to tense.

"Fuck, Jackson," I heard her cry out just before she came, just before her body contracted and warmth flooded my tongue as she released. Eagerly, I lapped it all up, not wanting to miss any part of her sweetness.

If I died right there and that turned out to be my last meal on earth, I couldn't have asked for anything better.

As her body stilled, I kissed my way back up, over her stomach and her breasts, ending with a soft kiss on her cheek. Holly's eyes were still closed, a sweet smile lingering on her face.

I'd never seen anything more beautiful.

As I lay down beside her, my arm across her body, her hand drifted down to my hard dick. "Do you want me to return the favour?" she asked breathlessly.

Although the idea of her lips on me again sounded incredible, I had to decline. Nothing could top what we'd just done for me and I wanted to bask in it for a little while longer. "Not right now. Let's just go to sleep, just like this."

Completely naked, I meant, our bodies next to each other. I wanted to spend the whole night just like that.

"Are you sure? You know I'd be happy to."

I leaned over to kiss her lips gently. "I'm sure. I'm good, Holly. That was a perfect end to a perfect day."

The words made her smile. "It really has been perfect. There's something I'd like to tell you, Jackson."

Something in her voice told me that whatever she wanted to say, it was serious. No trace of her usual teasing tone could be heard.

While I wanted to know what she had to say, I didn't want to spoil the moment either. "Can it wait until morning?" I suggested. "I just want to savour this a little longer."

Her face softened as she smiled again. "Of course. I'm not going anywhere."

"Me neither," I assured her.

We fell asleep just like that, not even bothering to get beneath the covers. Despite it being only a few days before Christmas, the heat in the room and our combined body heat made it more than comfortable.

The next morning, before the morning sun even began to stream in through the window, my phone buzzed with an incoming text and my eyes flew open, turning to Holly immediately to see if it had woken her too. Luckily, it hadn't, so I got up, separating myself from her as gently as I could so I could grab it before it went off again.

Stepping into the living room so I wouldn't disturb her, I unlocked the phone.

Are you up?

The text came from my mother, and I frowned down at the screen. Why would she be contacting me so early in the day? Or at all, really?

Yes, I wrote back. *Are you okay?*

It took a while for her next message to come through, but I could see her typing so I waited, and when it arrived, my stomach dropped.

I'm at the hospital. Can you come?

The hospital? What on earth happened? I told her to send me the details and I'd be on my way.

My clothes were still in the bathroom from the previous evening so I retrieved them and redressed quickly before finding a pen and paper in the hotel desk. Although I didn't want to wake Holly, I didn't want her to think I just vanished either, so I left a note explaining my disappearance and told her I'd see her at Macy's later with Gemma and Cole.

Placing the note on the bed beside her, I covered her with a blanket, taking one last look at her sleeping form to commit the moment to memory before I headed out the door.

Chapter Thirteen

A Missed Opportunity

~Holly~

The dream began very pleasantly. Jackson and I were moving into our new house, the one he'd been waiting to buy, and he couldn't have been more excited. A permanent smile rested on his face as he hauled boxes in through the front door and his dimples showed clearly, though it took me a moment to realize that meant his beard was gone. I was busy too, directing the movers where to put the furniture to fit all the designs I'd already laid out for us.

Although the day was long and we had a lot to do, I didn't feel tired at all. Somehow, Jackson made the whole experience fun.

When the moving truck left, we sat down on the couch among all the boxes and he put his arm around me, telling me how all his dreams had come true.

Leaning into his solid warmth, inhaling his familiar and comforting scent, I closed my eyes for a few seconds to enjoy the perfect moment. However, when I opened them, the scene around me had completely changed. Although I was still surrounded by boxes, I was back in my first flat in London instead. Instead of Jackson beside me, Paul was there, down on one knee, asking me to marry him all over again.

Shaking my head, I took a step back, a sense of loss washing over me. "No. You changed your mind. You're marrying someone else. Where's Jackson?"

I didn't want to be there at all.

Paul laughed as he snapped the ring box closed and shoved it back in his pocket. "Did you really think he was going to stay?" he sneered at me as he stood up, his face twisting into a cruel smile. "He sees what you are just as clearly as I do. You're a liar and a fake. You can blame me all you want, make me the villain in your story, but if you'd told me the truth up front, we never would have got to this point. You're just as much to blame as I am."

The words were nothing I hadn't thought a hundred times before, but they stung as much as if it were the first time I heard them.

"It's different with Jackson," I managed to whisper in my own defense. "I haven't lied to him. He knows everything and he said he wouldn't leave."

Paul raised his eyebrows at me before looking around the empty flat. All the boxes had suddenly disappeared, the room completely barren other than the two of us. "Then where is he now, Holly?"

I looked around too, hoping he might suddenly appear, but no one else was there. When I turned back to Paul, he'd disappeared as well. All alone, a wave of emptiness washed over me as the little voice in my head whispered, 'I told you so.'

My eyes shot open, and though I could see immediately that I wasn't in the empty flat, it took a moment for me to place the contents of the room surrounding me. Finally, I recognized the room at the Plaza and I took a deep breath, waiting for my heart rate to return to normal.

It was just a dream, and it didn't take a genius to figure out why my brain had come up with it. My insecurities were obviously playing tricks on my subconscious.

I'd been so close to telling Jackson how I felt the night before. If he hadn't asked me to wait, I would have actually said the words: I would have told him I was falling for him, and that he meant more to me in the short time we'd been together than any man ever had before.

And yet, even though I'd been willing to take the risk, a tiny part of me was still afraid that after I did, after I let myself fully believe that we might actually have a future, he would change his mind. I couldn't help it. No matter how perfect he had been, that voice in the back of my head wouldn't stop whispering that I wasn't good enough for him and never could be.

At least the way my dream ended didn't match with reality, since I wasn't all alone. A smile crept across my face as the rest of the night before came back to me, all the steamy fun in the shower and the absolutely incredible oral orgasm Jackson had given me right there in that bed. If I wasn't so completely convinced of his honesty, I would truly have to question whether he had lied about his inexperience. Nobody should be able to be that gifted on their first try.

Anticipation built as I turned my head to see him, eager for that first glimpse of his handsome face, but to my surprise, the other pillow was empty. Almost at the same time, I realized that I had a blanket covering me, which I hadn't before. Jackson must have already got up. The idea of him covering me with the blanket made me smile again as I could almost feel the tenderness in his strong hands as he did it.

The sun shone through the window stronger than I would have expected it to, meaning it must be later than I thought. I must have been having a very good sleep, at least until the nightmare woke me.

Still wanting my fix of Jackson's sweet smile, I threw the blanket off me and over the empty side of the bed as I got up, not bothering to put any clothes on as I walked briskly out into the living room. Maybe he'd already ordered breakfast for us? That was just the kind of thoughtful thing he'd do, and I felt almost entirely certain I'd find him there with a pot of tea and a tray full of food.

However, the living room was empty too, and the bathroom door also stood open, letting me know he wasn't in there either.

Against my will, my heart began to beat faster as the awful feeling I'd woken up with returned, that feeling of complete abandonment. Closing my eyes, I took a deep breath, trying my best to push it down. Jumping to conclusions didn't do anyone any good. He'd probably gone out to get us breakfast or something and had thought I wouldn't wake up until he got back. A quick peek into the bathroom showed me that his clothes were gone, so I picked up my own and carried them back into the bedroom before throwing the closet door open and picking out my outfit for the day.

We were going to Macy's just after lunch with Gemma, Cole and Noah, and I knew that Gemma would want photos taken, so I chose a soft pink cashmere jumper with a cowl neck. It came down over my hips, clinging to my waist and accentuating my curves. Paired with tight black leather pants, I felt pretty certain it would drive Jackson crazy, and the thought made me smile as I went through the rest of my routine, getting my hair and make-up just right.

By the time I finished, though, there was still no sign of him and I had started to worry again. How far could he have gone? My eyes drifted around the room, wondering if I'd missed something. The bed was still made since we'd slept on top of it, with just the blanket that he must have put on me spread out across it. Nothing else was out of place; the bedside tables were empty, nothing on the desk or the dresser other than my phone.

As my eyes landed on my phone, I almost slapped my forehead in frustration. Of course! He must have sent me a message to say where he was going. Nearly laughing with relief, I grabbed it from the dresser and unlocked it to check, but my relief proved short-lived. The only message waiting for me came from Gemma, asking if I wanted them to pick me up on their way to Macy's later.

I sent her a quick text back. *Sure, that would be great. You haven't heard anything from Jackson, have you?*

The worry inside me was getting strong. What if something had happened to him? I didn't want to even imagine it, but I still didn't understand why he would have left without saying anything.

She wrote back just as quickly. *Only that he'll meet us there.*

Did he tell you that today? I had kind of assumed he and I would go to the department store together, though we hadn't specifically said so.

Yeah, he sent me a message early this morning. Why?

Early that morning, he'd been in touch with Gemma but not with me? My confusion was growing by the second, but I wrote Gemma back to tell her not to worry and I'd see her later before sending a text to Jackson himself. With my fingers shaking, I tried to keep my tone casual and not betray all the worries and worst-case scenarios that were flying around my head.

Sorry I missed you this morning. Is everything okay?

I stared at the phone off and on for the next fifteen minutes before I saw the typing bubble pop up, and relief flowed through me. At least he was alright, but that confused me more than ever. Where had he gone and why? Why didn't he send me a message?

His response didn't make things any clearer. *I'll fill you in later, still sorting things out. Hopefully, I can still make it to Macy's, but don't wait for me if I'm not there. I'm not supposed to be using my phone so I'll have to switch it off now. See you soon, I hope.*

More than ever, it seemed like I'd missed something. I double checked that I hadn't accidentally deleted a text or email on my phone and that he hadn't left anything for me in the living room or even the bathroom, but I couldn't see anything out of the ordinary.

The emptiness of the room began to feel oppressive so I went down to the lobby instead and got a late breakfast in the restaurant, striking up a conversation with some other guests while I waited for Gemma and Cole to come and collect me.

Although Jackson had said he would be turning his phone off, I couldn't help checking mine every few minutes, just in case something had changed. However, the screen remained resolutely blank, just like the growing empty feeling inside me.

~Jackson~

My mom didn't give me any details about what happened or why she was at the hospital when she sent me her text. She just sent the address and instructions on where to find her when I got there, so I jumped in a taxi outside the Plaza and headed up to the hospital in the Bronx, not far from the botanical gardens. It would take at least half an hour to get there, so after sending Gemma a text to say how much I was looking forward to that afternoon, I settled back into my seat and let my thoughts wander as we made our way through the congested early rush-hour streets.

A smile crossed my face as I thought back to everything Holly and I had done the day before: the brunch, the store windows, the Rockettes, the gardens, and especially back at her hotel. It really had been an incredible day, one I knew I would never forget.

During my reminiscing, though, I remembered that Holly had wanted to tell me something just before we fell asleep. I had planned to ask her about it over breakfast, but obviously, that wouldn't happen. I'd have to remember to ask her the next time we were alone together, which hopefully would be later that afternoon after the Macy's visit.

As soon as my mind strayed to thoughts of being alone with her, my stomach fluttered as I imagined what the night might bring. Would that night be the night we actually had sex? I didn't know if I could resist her much longer and I knew it would be incredible, but a big part of me still wanted to wait until she said the words I was so desperate to hear. What were the odds that would also happen that day? It didn't seem very likely, which meant that Holly would win our challenge, to both my chagrin and delight.

At the hospital, I went to the desk and gave them the information my mother had passed on to me, and the receptionist asked me to wait there. A couple of minutes later, I was taken aback when a uniformed police officer approached me.

"Mr Hanmer?"

She wore a rather grim expression and my stomach immediately dropped. Why were there police involved? What was going on? "Yes, that's me. Jackson Hanmer."

"Come with me."

I followed her through a maze of hallways until we arrived at a small examining room where my mother sat on a chair against the wall, speaking to someone I assumed must be a doctor. Her arms were folded across her chest and when she turned to look at me as I walked in, I could see that her eye was swollen and bruised, with cuts across her cheek and near her lips.

The look of vulnerability in her eyes made her look younger than I'd seen her in a long time.

"Mom? What's going on?"

Immediately, she turned away, but not before I thought I caught what looked like embarrassment flash across her face. "It's fine, Jackson. They just didn't want to release me unless I had someone who could look after me for a little while."

"Look after you?" I repeated, trying to make sense of the scene in front of me. Why did she need looking after? "What happened?"

"Mrs Hanmer, is it okay if I have a word with your son?" the police officer asked, and my mom nodded, still not looking at me.

Feeling even more confused than I had before I got there, I followed the officer back out of the room to a quiet corner of a nearby waiting room.

"I'm guessing by the look on your face that this is all a surprise to you," she said sympathetically as we took a seat. She was probably about ten years older than me and had a kind smile, which I appreciated. "Unfortunately, this is the third time in two months your mother has shown up at the hospital to be treated for this kind of injury. The doctors suspect domestic abuse but she refuses to talk to anyone about it. Today, the injuries were serious enough that she could file for assault, which is why I was called, but she's not interested in talking to me either. Since you know her best, would you have a word with her?"

There was so much to process in what she'd just said, I barely knew where to start. Domestic abuse? Someone had hit my mom to give her those injuries? And the third time in two months... at that hospital? Did that mean she'd been living in the city that long? When I saw her the day before, she made it sound like she'd just moved in.

The most unbelievable part of all had to be the idea that I knew her best. The bloodied woman in that room was practically a stranger to me in so many ways.

"She's got a possible concussion," the officer continued, unaware of all my internal questions. "That means she should stay under observation, but she doesn't want to stay here. The doctors are insisting she have someone to watch her for the next few hours, at the very least. If you can agree to that, we'll send her home with you, but if you could talk to her about her injuries first and potentially pressing charges, I would appreciate it."

I nodded, trying to look more confident than I felt. "I'll do my best."

She led me back to the room where the doctor confirmed that my mom could be discharged when the police were finished with her, and they all left the room, leaving me alone with my mother for the first time in several years.

"I know what you're going to say," she told me preemptively as I took a seat across from her. "But it's not what you think. It was an accident."

"Was it the man you were going out with last night when I saw you?" I asked, pretty much ignoring everything she'd just said. Maybe his treatment of her had been part of the reason she hadn't introduced me to him.

Her lips tightened as she ignored my question too. "I just want to go home. I'm sorry if you had plans, they seem to think I need a babysitter, but once you sign me out, you can go on your way."

"I'm not leaving you alone, Mom," I told her flat-out. "If you want me to sign you out, then I'm staying with you. We can go to your apartment if you want or we can go to mine, but I'm staying with you as long as the doctor says you need me. And I really think you should talk to the police before we go."

"There's nothing to talk about," she insisted.

"Then just explain that to the officer. Tell her exactly what happened and how it was an accident, and they won't bother you about it again. I can stay with you or I can leave you with her, it's up to you. As soon as you're done, we'll go."

She must have decided that it would be quicker to agree with me because she gave in. "Fine. You can stay if you want to."

After calling the officer back in, I sat to the side and listened as my mom spun a rather implausible story about tripping over some trash in the street and running face first into a lamppost. Halfway through, I pulled out my phone to check the time and saw that I had missed a text from Holly a few minutes earlier. She asked if everything was okay, and I hoped she hadn't been worrying when she read in my note that I was going to the hospital. I should have sent her an update earlier, I just got too caught up in everything.

As quickly as I could, I tapped out a reply to Holly and switched my phone off. It was after eleven o'clock already, later than I'd hoped, but at least they finished talking shortly afterwards and after completing a bit of paperwork, we were finally back out on the street.

"Where do you want to go?" I asked my mom, flipping through the brochure the nurse had given me on the way out with details of what to watch for in my mom for signs of trouble. My stomach sank as I read that I should keep watch over her for at least twelve hours. It had been almost four hours since she first contacted me, but that still left eight hours to go.

Damn it. It looked like Macy's was definitely out, and seeing Holly at all that day seemed unlikely.

"We'll go to my place," my mom replied as we climbed into the cab. "Then you're free to leave whenever you want."

I couldn't help rolling my eyes as I got in next to her. It appeared she wasn't going to be any better at letting me take care of her than she had ever been at taking care of me. It looked like it would be a very long day.

~Holly~

Gemma messaged me to say they were pulling up outside the hotel, so I said goodbye to the new friends I'd made in the restaurant with hugs all around. I'd always been good at talking to strangers and charming people in the short term; Jackson and I had that much in common. The long term was where I usually fell flat.

The Stamers' driver hopped out to open the door for me as I approached, and I couldn't help laughing as I climbed into the black SUV and got my first look at the three of them. Cole was wearing a suit, as usual. I wondered if he even slept in one, I'd so rarely seen him in anything else. Meanwhile, Gemma wore another loud and bright Christmas jumper, and baby Noah was dressed in the most adorable little elf costume I had ever seen.

Though babies still made me slightly uncomfortable, I couldn't stop the squeal that came out at the sight of him. "Oh my God, Gem, he's so cute I can hardly stand it!"

"I know!" she squeaked back as Cole rolled his eyes, but I didn't miss the way the corners of his mouth twitched or the look of pure affection on his face as he looked at his son. "Jackson bought it for him, isn't it the sweetest thing?"

Of *course* Jackson bought it for him. That didn't even surprise me.

"Have you heard from him?" I asked, wondering if she knew any more than I did about where he'd gone.

"Not since that text early this morning. Why?"

"He says not to wait for him, that he might be late," I explained, showing her the text I'd received.

"Oh, no." Gemma looked genuinely disappointed as her eyes scanned the words. "That's a shame, he was so excited for this. What is he sorting out?"

I shrugged, trying not to show how much not knowing the answer to that was affecting me. "I'm not sure. He said it like I should know, but I don't."

Her brow furrowed as she joined in my confusion. "That doesn't sound like him. What happened?"

I filled her in with as few details about the night before as possible, but even the mention of Jackson staying over at the hotel with me had her grinning ear-to-ear. When I got to the part about him vanishing that morning, though, her smile disappeared.

"There has to be something we're missing. Maybe a text didn't come through?"

It relieved me to know she also felt his behaviour was out of character for him. "Maybe, but he turned his phone off after he sent me this and I don't want to bother him if he's in the middle of something important."

As we'd been talking, Cole had been tapping away on his phone and at that moment, it buzzed loudly, the sound filling the back of the vehicle. "Jackson?" he asked into the phone as he put it up to his ear. "Where are you?"

Gemma and I both turned to look at him in surprise, and I could hear Jackson's voice on the other end but not well enough to make out anything he said.

Cole didn't have any such trouble, replying directly into the phone. "Okay, let me know if you need anything." He hung up and turned to us with a smirk. "We could have spent the rest of the ride debating what he meant or what you were missing, but I figured this would be more effective."

"How did you reach him?" I asked curiously.

"Since his phone was off, I paged him to call me."

As tempted as I might be to make a sarcastic comment about Cole's need for control - who even gave their employees a pager anymore? - I was too curious to know what he'd found out to waste my time on that. "What did he say?"

"He's with his mom," Cole told us. "He won't be joining us, unfortunately."

"His mom?" Gemma repeated in surprise. "I don't think I've ever heard him mention her before."

"For good reason," Cole replied, his expression darkening. "But it's not my place to say anything. You can ask him yourself if you want to."

Maybe I would have to take back what I just thought about Cole's controlling nature; that was surprisingly restrained of him.

A second later, my phone buzzed with a text from Jackson.

I'm so sorry, Holly, I forgot my phone was off. I'm at my mom's apartment now and need to stay with her the rest of the day. I'll explain everything to you later but I'm sorry I'm missing the Macy's visit. I hope I can see you tomorrow.

"We're here," Gemma announced before I had a chance to send him any kind of reply. A quick glance out the car window confirmed our arrival outside the doors of a massive department store with window displays that rivalled any of the ones Jackson and I had looked at the day before. I would have loved to spend some time looking at them, but Cole ushered us all inside and into the lift, up to the floor where Santaland was waiting.

A man in a suit rushed over to greet Cole, fawning over him in that way that people often do with the super-rich, before we were invited inside. As promised, we had the whole place to ourselves, starting with a maze of decorated scenes to walk through, meant to keep people entertained while they were waiting for their turn for photos with Father Christmas.

Gemma and I had fun examining each of the scenes from a design standpoint as well as judging their Christmas spirit while Cole rather adorably kept trying to interest Noah in various animals or Christmas characters even though, as Gemma had predicted, the three-month-old couldn't really care less.

Although I did my best to enjoy myself, my thoughts were still partly with Jackson. I could imagine his big, enthusiastic grin as we walked through and how much fun he would have had with all of it. What was going on with his mom? When we ran into her the night before, she hadn't appeared to be in any hurry to get in touch with him again. Why did he drop everything to spend the day with her?

Finally, we reached the end of the maze and we were welcomed into a small room where Santa himself was waiting to take photos with us. I got in the first few and then stepped back to let Gemma and Cole have their own family photos taken. They made a beautiful family, I thought as I watched them. There was so much love in their eyes as they looked at each other and at their son.

That's what I want.

The thought hit me out of the blue, but with such certainty that it nearly knocked me over. Just over a week earlier, I walked down the aisle at Gemma and Cole's wedding, convinced that I was better off alone, but after spending the intervening time with Jackson, my thoughts had taken a complete 180-degree turn.

The first part of my dream came back to me, about Jackson and I moving into our new house together. It had felt so perfect, but more than that, it felt real. It felt possible. If I really wanted that, nothing stood in my way other than my own stubbornness. Jackson had already offered it to me, and I had no reason to doubt him beyond my own insecurities.

Maybe it was too fast to be thinking that way about a man I'd only really spent a week with, but the proof that it could work was right in front of me as I looked at Gemma and Cole. They'd only been together a short time before they got engaged, and they spent most of that time pretending that they didn't really have feelings for each other. A year later, they looked so blissfully happy it would almost make me sick if I weren't so happy for them.

So what, exactly, was I holding out for?

Although I was still confused about why Jackson hadn't come with us that day, suddenly, I found myself feeling a little bit grateful for the fact that he hadn't. I might not have seen the truth so clearly if he'd been there.

Being with him made every experience better. I wanted to hear his laugh and feel his arm around me and most of all see that look in his eyes when he looked at me.

I'd almost been ready to tell him how I felt the night before, but standing all alone in Macy's watching my best friend live out her happy-ever-after, I felt more than ready. I felt certain.

As soon as they were done with their photos, I cornered Cole. "Do you know the address to the building where Jackson grew up?"

Though he looked taken aback by my determined tone, he answered me as confidently as usual. "I think I remember it. Why?"

"Can you drop me off there?"

Gemma's eyes sparkled in anticipation, sensing that something was up. "What's going on, Holly?"

I grinned back at her, unable to hide my own excitement. "It's time that Jackson and I had a talk."

Chapter Fourteen

CROSSED WIRES

~Jackson~

Apparently, I wasn't as subtle as I hoped when I checked my phone again.

"If you're so anxious to talk to that girl, you should just go," my mom suggested. She'd tried to kick me out about ten times already despite me telling her each time that I wouldn't be going anywhere until I felt certain she'd be alright.

"I'm not anxious," I lied. "And who said anything about Holly?"

Of course, I *had* been looking for a text from her. After Cole paged me, I realized that I owed Holly an update and so I'd sent her a short message. I could see she'd read it but she didn't reply, and I'd started to get a little worried. Was she annoyed with me for ditching her? I couldn't really explain the whole story over text, but maybe I could excuse myself for a minute and give her a call? They were probably at Macy's, though, and I didn't want to interrupt their good time. Waiting seemed to be my best option.

Sitting there with my mother couldn't have felt much more bizarre. The layout of her apartment was nearly identical to the one that we'd lived in when I was growing up, but the rooms were sparsely furnished and when I had gone to make us some lunch, the kitchen had hardly any food.

"Do you need more money?" I asked her bluntly, looking at the empty fridge. "I can give you more. You should have told me if it wasn't enough."

She shook her head, her lips tight. "I don't need anything else from you."

She repeated that gesture in the living room where the two of us sat on mismatched armchairs facing a TV with a purple line down one side of the screen, shaking her head at my attempt to downplay how much I wanted to hear from Holly. "You've never been much good at hiding your emotions, Jackson. It's obvious you're crazy about her."

That made me smile in spite of everything. She had that right, even if it surprised me that she could see it. Her next words, however, wiped the smile right back off my face again.

"So, what's wrong with her?"

My brow furrowed. "What do you mean by that?"

She gave me a faint smile that had no joy in it. "You always pick the ones who are slightly broken, the ones you have to fix. What's this one's story?"

Where on earth did that come from? She'd never said anything like that to me before, and I honestly didn't think she'd ever paid enough attention to my girlfriends to notice any kind of pattern. Not that there *was* a pattern, I hastened to add in my head.

Before I could figure out how to answer her, she kept talking. "That's probably why they never stay, you know."

Those simple words hit me like a punch to the gut. If my mom, of all people, set out to say the most hurtful thing she could to me, it would have been hard to come up with something worse than that, and I lashed back out at her before I could stop myself. "Well, you're the authority on not staying, so why don't you enlighten me about exactly what I'm doing wrong?"

She flinched at my words, and for a second, I almost regretted saying them, but a moment later, her jaw set again and she carried on. "It makes you feel good to be the one who can solve everyone's problems. Someone in my support group explained it to me."

"Support group?" I repeated in confusion. When had she joined a support group, and for what? I felt completely lost in the conversation.

My mother simply nodded, not elaborating on any details about the group. "We had a psychologist come in and talk to us one day. He told us all about people who need to be needed. It's called a saviour complex. As soon he was done, I thought: well, that's Jackson."

My eyes closed for a second as I tried to take in what she said. "You think I have a saviour complex?"

Once again, she nodded. "Even as a kid, you were always trying to fix everything. Everything you did had to be perfect. Do you know how exhausting that can be?"

I kept repeating her words back to her, but I couldn't help it. Nothing was making any sense to me. "Me trying to be a good son was 'exhausting' for you?"

She scoffed as she looked away. "You weren't just trying to be a good kid; you were trying to be perfect, and it just made me feel worse. Do you know what it feels like to constantly feel like you're letting someone down? I knew I wasn't cut out to be a mother, but you kept insisting I was a great one. Every time I came home, you were so excited to see me and acted like I could do no wrong, which only made me feel more guilty. The expectations were suffocating."

She was honestly blaming her disappearances on me? Because I'd tried to make her feel a part of our family?

"But it's not just me. What about that girl who broke your heart at prom?" she continued, as oblivious to my inner turmoil as she'd always been. "You had the perfect night planned, right? You did everything just right, so why do you think she went with your friend instead?"

His money and status probably had a lot to do with it, but I didn't think that was what she meant. I had no idea where she was going with this, but clearly, she'd been thinking about it for a while, so I prompted her to continue. "Why do you think she did?"

She answered in a tone that suggested it couldn't be more obvious. "Because he didn't expect perfection from her. You were so obsessed with making things perfect that you forgot to think about who she was and what she really wanted."

Somewhere deep in my subconscious, I had to admit there might be a tiny bit of truth in that. I'd never thought about it in quite those terms before, but her stumbling across one small nugget of truth didn't change just how much this whole conversation surprised and stung me.

"You always need to be the hero," she continued, on a roll and eager to get it all off her chest. "Layla's told me about some of the other women you've been in relationships with, how you tried to fit them into your image of what a perfect girlfriend should be. That's why I would bet any money that this British woman's got something about her that needs fixing. The problem is that people don't want to be fixed, Jackson. They just want to be accepted."

She talked about me with my sister? Did Layla actually agree with her? Where was all of this coming from?

"So, you want me to just 'accept' the fact that your new boyfriend is beating you?" I blurted out, unable to take another word quietly. What gave her the right to lecture me about my relationships when hers was so clearly dysfunctional?

I expected her to deny it again, but instead, she looked me straight in the eye. "He's got a temper, but he doesn't mean to hurt me. He's trying to stop. He cares enough about me to want to try, and yes, I accept that, because he doesn't expect me to be anything other than what I am either."

I really tried to wrap my head around that logic, but I couldn't do it. No matter how frustrated I was about what she'd just said to me, it didn't change the fact that she was wrong.

"Mom, you deserve better than that. There are plenty of men in this world who would treat you properly, men like Brian."

She raised her eyes to the ceiling, looking just as frustrated with me as I was with her. "There you go again, trying to solve my problems for me. I don't need you to fix it, Jackson. Have we ever had a conversation where you weren't trying to be the responsible one and make everything better?"

"Because I care about you," I almost shouted at her. How was our lack of a relationship my fault? I really didn't understand. "Maybe if you cared about me even a little bit, you would know how that feels."

"You don't even know me," she shot back. "You care about the version of me you've created in your head, the one who's just a step away from being fixed. The one that you can save. Well, I don't need to be saved or fixed, Jackson, and neither does this woman that you're with now. You're going to drive her away just like you always do if you don't back off and give her the space to just be herself."

As I thought back over the last week with Holly, an awful feeling of realization washed over me. Maybe my mother actually had a point, at least where Holly was concerned. I had tried to create the perfect dates, the perfect conditions for her to realize that *I* was perfect for her.

Had it all been too much? I hadn't been trying to make Holly be anything other than herself, at least not consciously, but maybe it came across that way to her?

Snippets of conversations we'd had flashed across my mind.

You've built it up in your head so much that you have to find the perfect woman for you that you're missing out on the other things you could be experiencing and enjoying, she told me when I told her I was a virgin.

You're a really good man, she said to me on the carriage ride in Central Park. *It means that you deserve someone just as good in return. I'm not like you, Jackson. I'm a mess.*

And then just yesterday over brunch: *How can you be so perfect? Is there some kind of class that teaches you what to say?*

Did she feel I expected perfection from her? Did she feel exhausted and suffocated like my mother did?

Through the fog of my swirling thoughts, my phone rang, cutting through the tension in the room and I grabbed it from my pocket, grateful for the distraction. However, when I saw the name on the screen, my stomach lurched uncomfortably.

I tried to make my voice sound as normal as possible when I answered. "Hi, Holly. I'm really sorry but this isn't a great time. Can I call you later?"

"Oh." Her exclamation sounded both surprised and disappointed. "Actually, I'm just outside the building. I thought you might like some company, but if it's not a good time, I can go."

Outside? She actually came there to see me? I couldn't understand how or why, but given all the other surprises of the day, it counted as one of the milder ones.

Glancing at my mother and the clock, I tried to decide what to do. Though my mother seemed fine with no signs of a concussion, I'd never forgive myself if I left and something happened. However, given the conversation we'd just had, I could hardly invite Holly up to join us, pretending we were some kind of happy family. I'd have to stay on my own for a while longer, no matter how awkward and uncomfortable it was.

"I'll come down," I offered, not wanting to send her away without seeing her when she'd obviously made an effort to get there. At least I could explain the situation to her. "Just wait there."

After hanging up, I explained to my mom that I was going out for a few minutes, and I made her give me her key so that I could get back in. I wouldn't put it past her at that point to lock me out. Still feeling completely off balance from the conversation I'd just had, I headed downstairs to see Holly.

~Holly~

Standing outside Jackson's old apartment building, I was a bundle of nervous energy. Back at the department store, it had seemed so simple to go there and tell him that I wanted to be with him, but when I called him to tell him I'd come, he didn't sound quite as happy to hear from me as I'd hoped. I put it down to the stress of dealing with... well, whatever he was dealing with, which I still didn't fully understand.

My eyes swept over the street while I waited for Jackson to come down to see me. A few people hurried along the sidewalks on either side, but no one lingered outside other than me. A bitter wind blew that day, and I shivered against it despite my warm winter coat.

Although it was still afternoon, the sky was already almost completely dark, while lights from all the different apartments bathed the street in a gentle glow. It must have been close to the shortest day of the year, I thought idly, though I couldn't even say what day it was anymore. Being on holiday, and especially spending nearly every waking moment with Jackson or thinking about him when we were apart, had warped my sense of time.

Gemma and Cole had offered to stay and wait in the car while I called up to Jackson in case he wasn't there or he was too busy, but I'd sent them away. I didn't want an audience and I had been hoping that he would ask me in anyway. After our phone call, I didn't feel quite as sure that he would, but that would be okay. I didn't want to impose. Once I said what I'd come there to say, I could always take a taxi back to the hotel if I had to.

Finally, the door opened and he appeared, wearing a scarf to protect against the chilly wind, his hands shoved in his pockets. He smiled at me as he approached but something new lingered in his eyes, a wariness that hadn't been there before.

What had he been through that day? My heart immediately went out to him.

"Thank you for coming," he said as he stopped a few feet away from me on the pavement. A couple of stray pieces of trash blew down the street, whipping around his feet. "How did you know where to find me?"

"Cole said you were with your mother," I explained. "And when we saw her here yesterday, she said she was living here, so I figured it was a good guess. Cole remembered the address from when you were younger."

He smiled, but once again, it didn't quite reach his eyes. "You didn't have to go to so much effort Holly, but I appreciate it, really. I wish I could invite you in but I'm afraid things are a little strained right now."

That was obvious from the look on his face. "What happened?" I asked gently.

In short, clipped sentences, so unlike his natural exuberance, Jackson explained the text he had received that morning, what had happened at the hospital and why he was staying with his mother. Finally, the expression in his eyes made sense to me. I couldn't imagine what he was feeling, knowing his mother was in an abusive relationship like that and he couldn't do anything about it. I wished there was something I could do to help them both, but I didn't know where to begin either.

"I hope my note didn't worry you too much," he concluded. "I meant to text you again from the hospital, but things got a bit hectic."

"Note?" I couldn't help repeating the word curiously, and his brow furrowed.

"The one I left on the bed?" he prompted, and I almost groaned in frustration. I must have covered it up with the blanket when I woke up, and I felt like such an idiot. I should have known he wouldn't have left without saying anything.

I didn't want him to know that I'd ever doubted him, so I played along. "Oh, that note. Right. No, I was only worried that you were okay."

If he thought my response sounded odd, he didn't show it. However, his face remained uncharacteristically tight and my gut instinct told me the time wasn't right to say what I'd come to say to him. As a businesswoman, I knew how important timing was in making someone an offer, and I could usually read a room pretty well.

Even so, I was more convinced than ever that I did want to say it to him eventually. Everything he'd just told me proved exactly what kind of man he was. His mother had never put him first, and yet he gave up his time to look after her. I knew how much he had wanted to go to Macy's and how much he was enjoying our time together, but he put all of that aside to be there when she needed him.

It just went to show that he wouldn't walk away, no matter how difficult things were, and despite my disappointment that I couldn't tell him how I felt right that second, it still left me feeling pretty good overall.

What was the worst that could happen if I waited another day?

"Are you sure you don't want me to stay?" I asked as unobtrusively as I could. I didn't want to stick my nose in where it wasn't wanted, but I also wanted him to know I would be there for him if he needed me. "I play a mean hand of poker if we need to kill some time."

I was rewarded with another small smile for that joke, but the sparkle in his eyes was still missing. I hadn't realized exactly what a difference it made to his face until it wasn't there. "Thank you, but no, that's okay. In fact..."

He trailed off, swallowing hard as if preparing to say something difficult.

"Gemma and Cole are heading up to Isabel's tomorrow, right?"

I blinked in surprise, taken aback by the sudden change of subject. "Yes, that's right."

We'd just been talking about it in the car on the way over there. They were heading north of the city to Cole's sister's house to spend some time with his family before Christmas, returning on Christmas Eve. They had invited me to join them but I told them I'd rather stay in the city. I didn't add 'with Jackson' to my statement, but I knew they understood it anyway.

That was another thing I'd planned on telling Jackson, just in case he hadn't already figured it out.

However, the next words out of his mouth took me completely by surprise. "I think you should go with them."

My stomach dropped as he looked away, not meeting my eye, and my mind began to race. Why would he say that? Was he trying to get rid of me? The wind blew some stray strands of hair across my face as I tried to figure out how to respond, and my hand shook as I tucked them back behind my ear.

"What about you?" I finally asked.

He looked back up at the building for a second before turning back to me with a slightly pained expression. "I've got some things I need to take care of. It won't be for long, just a few days."

"I understand that, but maybe I could help?"

His lips tightened. "I don't think so. And besides, things between us this week have been pretty... intense. A little break might be good for both of us."

A break?

Suddenly, my lungs felt empty, like all the air in them had been sucked out and carried away by the strong wind.

I came there to tell him I was ready to make our relationship official, to move it to another level, and he was talking about a break?

What had changed since we were last together?

What had I done wrong?

"Holly?" Jackson's voice cut through the fog of my thoughts and I realized he must expect me to say something.

Somehow, I managed to form a reply. "Sure, if that's what you want."

The words sounded tinny in my ears as I tried to smile at him. For a moment, I was right back in the little room at my engagement party with Paul, handing my ring back to him, all while his words from my nightmare echoed in my head. *Did you really think he was going to stay?*

"Gemma will be thrilled," I managed to add, trying to keep myself calm and focused on the present.

That made Jackson smile a bit more genuinely. "She will, and I'll still see you for Christmas when you get back. In the meantime, we can both think things over without any pressure."

Pressure?

Was this because of what happened the night before? Was he backing off because of how far we had gone together?

I really didn't understand what was happening other than that he didn't want to see me for the next few days. That little voice in my head that I'd managed to silence earlier starting sneering at me again. *This is just an excuse, you know. A few days will turn into a few more, and then you'll be going home and never seeing him again. This is the beginning of the end.*

Why had I ever let myself think this time would be any different? I knew it would happen, I *knew* it, and I'd still let myself believe. How much of an idiot could I be?

"Holly, are you okay?" Jackson said my name again and I looked up to see him looking down at me in concern. It was only when I blinked that I realized there were tears in my eyes.

Firmly, I willed them back. I had already cried in front of him far too much the day before and I wouldn't do it again, no matter how much it hurt.

"I'm fine. I don't want to keep you from your mom, so you should go. I guess I'll see you on Christmas Eve."

Before he could say anything else, I turned and walked away.

Chapter Fifteen

REALIZATION

~Jackson~

It took every ounce of strength I had in me not to run down the street after Holly and beg her to stay. I knew she must be confused about why I sent her away, and the look on her face nearly killed me, but I honestly thought it would be better that I didn't tell her the exact reason.

If my mom was right and my expectations were making Holly feel boxed in and pressured, she might not be comfortable telling me that she wanted some time to think things over. She would insist that everything was fine, that we could continue as we were, but it seemed to me that the only way she'd be able to sort out what she really felt for me was if she didn't have me constantly breathing down her neck about it.

In an ideal scenario, a few days apart would prove to her that we were better together, which was my sincere and fervent belief.

But maybe it wouldn't. Maybe she really did feel suffocated, as my mom had said, and so with a few days' distance and Gemma to talk things over with, she might decide she didn't want to continue our relationship at all.

It would hurt me, almost more than I could bear to think about, but at least I would know that I hadn't forced her into anything she wasn't comfortable with. She knew what I was offering her, so all she had to do was decide whether or not to take it.

If you love someone, set them free. Weren't people always saying that? So I did, hoping with every fibre of my being that she would come back to me and then I would know for sure what she really wanted.

When Holly had turned the corner of the street and I could no longer see her, I climbed wearily back up the steps to my mother's apartment, and she gave me a rather curious look as I walked back into the apartment alone.

"I thought for sure you'd bring her up here or else you'd decide to go with her. You could never resist being the gentleman."

I could have asked her what was wrong with trying to be a gentleman, but all of a sudden, I felt exhausted and sad and not in the mood to argue or even talk to her anymore. I suggested that we simply watch TV instead and thankfully, she agreed.

Finally, enough time had passed that I could safely leave her alone. Although the chilly wind still blew as I left the building, I decided to walk home anyway. I could use the time to think, and my thoughts were all over the place as I walked through the dark, cold streets, thinking back over all the relationships I'd had and trying to decide how much of what my mother said was valid.

Did I really try to fix people? I did try to help, but I had never thought of that as a bad thing. Even in my non-romantic relationships, I was a helper, like how I supported Cole through his particularly rough patch after his fiancée left him. I thought about calling him and asking him if he had felt I forced my help on him, but I could almost hear his voice in my ear telling me not to be an idiot, so I didn't bother to make the call.

I really didn't think I wanted to 'fix' Holly or make her something other than what she was, but maybe intentions and actions were two different things. Maybe she felt that I did?

The more I thought about it, the more convinced I became that a bit of time apart for her to think things over could only be a good thing. I just had to figure out how to get through the days without her.

In the morning, the urge to send her a text almost overwhelmed me. I could at least wish her a good trip, couldn't I? However, after a long internal debate, I convinced myself it would be better not to. I was trying not to crowd her, and there wouldn't be any point in sending her away just to shower her with texts the whole time. How could she have space to think if I kept encroaching on it?

Even though it was Saturday, I went into the office to try to distract myself. Staring at my office wall was slightly better than staring at my apartment wall, but not by much, and after a few hours, I went back home again. The whole world around me felt less colourful without Holly's smile or her teasing banter. It would only be for a few days, I tried to tell myself, so why did it feel like the end of the world?

The evening of the third day, two days before Holly was meant to return, my phone rang and for a moment, my heart leapt, hoping she'd decided to reach out to me. Disappointment flashed through me as I saw it wasn't Holly's number, but the feeling was only momentary. For the first time in three days, I smiled voluntarily as I answered the phone.

"Hi, Layla! This is a nice surprise."

My sister and I were in touch pretty regularly by text or email but phone calls were less common, simply because we were both usually pretty busy. We were planning to speak on Christmas Day, only a few days away, so her call that evening was unexpected.

"I hope it's a nicer surprise than the one you had the other day," she replied, which confused me for a moment until I realized what she must be referring to.

"You talked to Mom?"

"Yeah. She told me about running into you and how you helped her out at the hospital."

My mother's words immediately came back to me about how she and Layla had talked about my past relationships. Maybe I'd have a chance to find out exactly what my sister thought and if she truly agreed with everything my mom had said.

"Did she tell you why she was in the hospital?" I asked curiously. I didn't know how close they were. I was surprised that they had been talking at all, really, not just about me.

"She did, and she told me about your conversation afterwards." It didn't look like I would have to figure out how to bring it up. Layla seemed to want to dive right in, and her next words took me completely by surprise. "You know she's full of shit, right?"

I hadn't expected that response at all and I blinked blankly at my apartment walls. "What do you mean?"

"All this saviour complex bullshit," Layla elaborated. "She's been spouting off to me about it for a little while, trying to find any excuse to make herself feel better about what she did to us as kids. I've learned it's just easier not to argue with her about it, but I didn't think she'd say it directly to you. Now, I'm worried that you actually believed her, because you're such a good guy, you can't imagine that anyone else could be so selfish."

Once again, I found myself in a conversation that had me completely off balance, so I tried to go back to the beginning. "How long have you been in touch with her for?"

"About a year. She reached out, surprisingly, saying she wanted to have a closer relationship with me now, blah, blah, blah. Really, all she wants is someone she can call and complain to about everyone that's ever done her wrong in her life. She still can't take responsibility for a single damn thing, Jackson. Nothing's changed. I let her talk and don't take any of it to heart. I don't really care if she wants to play the victim, it doesn't matter to me, but if she's going to try to make you feel bad for being the best person that I've ever known? That's where I'm drawing the line."

Tears sprang to my eyes at my sister's protective tone, making me glad we weren't on video so she couldn't see how emotional I'd gotten. "I'm not perfect, Layla," I argued. I wished people would stop saying I was. "Maybe she had a point."

"No, she fucking didn't!" my sister shouted, and I winced as I held the phone further from my ear. "If you think that for even a second, I am getting on a plane to come and knock some sense into you, do you hear me?"

Despite myself, I had to chuckle at the image of my little sister trying to beat me up. "I hear you," I assured her. It was hard not to. "But it did get me thinking, especially about this woman that I'm kind of seeing right now..."

Immediately, Layla's tone turned softer. "Mom mentioned her too. Tell me about her."

As best I could, I explained to Layla the basics of my relationship with Holly, what I loved about her and, without going into too many details, the stumbling blocks in Holly's past that were holding her back from trusting me completely.

Layla was silent for a moment after I finished speaking. "So, let me get this straight," she said slowly, putting thought into each word. "She's afraid of getting into something that could be pulled out from under her."

"Right," I agreed. "It's happened to her too often before."

"And you agreed to try out a relationship with her up until Christmas?"

"Yes," I agreed again.

"And then, before that time was up, you asked for a break and sent her away?"

As soon the words were out of her mouth, I could suddenly see it completely clearly, along with the look on Holly's face when I had suggested it.

"Oh, fuck, no," I breathed out, more to myself than to her. What had I done? Why didn't I see what it would sound like to her? I got so caught up in my mom's mind games that I lost sight of the bigger picture.

Layla sounded relieved that I'd put it together for myself. "I love you, big brother, but yeah. Fuck, no. You gotta go fix that, now, and whatever crap Mom told you, erase it from your brain. If this woman is the one for you, she's gonna love you just as you are. You don't need to change a damn thing, okay?"

"Okay," I agreed, already standing up and looking for my keys. "Layla, I have to go."

"Yes, you do! I want updates! Good luck, Jackson."

"Thank you," I told her sincerely. "Seriously. I owe you big time."

With only my keys and my wallet, I ran out the door towards Grand Central station. There should still be time for me to catch a train that night and be at Isabel's door before they all went to bed.

I just had to hope that I wasn't too late.

~Holly~

Gemma was surprised but pleased when I got in touch to tell her that I would go with them to Isabel's house after all.

"You're going to love it, Hols," she promised me. "I've been looking forward to it for months. Isabel goes all out for the holidays. Easter was incredible and I think I'm still full from Thanksgiving. I can't wait to see what she does for Christmas."

I did my best to sound cheerful. "It sounds great. I'll get packed up and meet you down in the lobby when you guys get here."

When they collected me in the SUV with their driver the next morning, Noah was asleep and Cole had his laptop out to do some work, so Gemma and I sat together in the back seat.

"What happened with Jackson last night?" she asked curiously, speaking quietly so that Cole wouldn't overhear us.

Sticking to the basic facts, I told her that he had been looking after his mother so I couldn't go in but that we'd had a brief talk and he'd suggested I go with her and Cole so that he'd have time to do what he needed to do, and so that we could have a little break from each other.

"A break?" Gemma repeated, sounding confused as her eyebrows drew together. "Why do you need a break?"

I tried to shrug as if the question hadn't been haunting me all night. "I guess just spending every day together was a lot."

She shook her head. "I don't buy that for a second. Did something happen?"

"If it did, I don't think I was there for it," I joked weakly. The truth was that it wasn't really a joke. I felt like I had missed something yet again, just like I'd missed the note he left for me, which the housekeeping staff had helpfully left for me on the dresser. They must have found it when they made my bed. Reading it when I got back to the hotel the night before, the handwritten and heartfelt words made me feel even worse.

What had changed since he wrote that note? I simply didn't understand.

It took nearly three hours to reach Isabel's house, and my mouth dropped open as we approached. Although we weren't all that far out of the city, the farm had real snow on the ground. The white columned house on the acreage looked like something out of a magazine, decked out in lights and garland with a massive, fresh wreath on the front door. Inside was even more beautiful, the smell of the fresh Douglas fir Christmas tree filling the air along with the scent of freshly baked cookies and the sound of children laughing as they ran in to greet their Uncle Cole and Auntie Gemma.

The perfect family scene was something I had never really experienced before, and I decided then and there that I would do my best to enjoy it, no matter how upset I was about the whole situation with Jackson.

I'd have to move on eventually, so I might as well start that day.

The next couple of days were like living in a Christmas film. We took the kids on a sleigh ride and made gingerbread houses, went ice skating and sang carols, badly, and the grown-ups relaxed in the evening with rum and eggnog around the fireplace. Gemma and Cole were cuddled up together under a blanket and from the way her mouth kept twitching, I had a good guess where his hands were. Isabel and her husband seemed to be having just as hard a time keeping their hands off each other.

I definitely felt like the odd one out. As I sipped my drink and watched the flames dancing, I couldn't help wondering what Jackson was doing. Was he thinking about me, or had he truly closed the door on us already, just as I was afraid he had?

On the afternoon of the third day, I needed a moment to escape all the perfection, and I went out onto the front porch, watching the light snowfall that had started earlier that day. It really was beautiful, but all I could think was that I wished Jackson were there to see it with me. My fingers twitched in my gloves, wanting to pull out my phone and send him a message or even a photo, but I resisted, just as I'd been doing the whole time. He wanted a break, so I wasn't going to force myself in where I wasn't wanted.

The door opened behind me and I turned to see Gemma coming out, holding two mugs of hot chocolate. "Here," she said, handing one to me. "Chocolate makes everything better, right?"

I took it from her with the best smile I could muster. "I don't think it's going to be quite enough this time, but thank you anyway."

We both took a sip from our mugs, looking out over the landscape for a moment before Gemma turned to me. "I've tried my best to stay out of this Holly, I really have, but I can see that you're miserable and I don't understand what happened. You guys are so perfect for each other."

"*He's* perfect," I corrected her. "I'm just me. I think that's what happened."

She shook her head at me. "That's ridiculous. Come on, Hols, explain it to me. I know you and I know him. Maybe I can help figure out what's going on."

Hesitantly, I began to tell her about it, and once I started, I couldn't stop. I told her everything, even the truth about what happened with

Paul after all that time. Partway through, we moved to a bench on the porch where there were fuzzy blankets, wrapping ourselves up so we could keep warm as we kept talking.

When I'd finally finished, Gemma pulled me into a long, warm hug. She didn't say anything, but the action meant more to me than any words could. "I don't know what brought on this break nonsense," she admitted. "But one thing is clear to me: if you don't want him to change his mind, then don't let him. Go and fight for him, Holly. Show him that you're not going anywhere either."

"But what if he doesn't want me?" I asked, wincing at just how whiny I sounded. "It might be too late."

"And it might not," she countered firmly. "But sitting here with me, you'll never know for sure."

"You think I should go right now?"

Gemma nodded. "I can take you to the train station and you could be at Grand Central Station in a few hours. Just say the word, Holly. Is that what you want?"

What *did* I want? As I thought back over the last two weeks, all the time I'd spent with Jackson and the time I'd spent without him, I had to admit I really didn't have any doubt.

"I want him," I blurted out. "I want *us*."

Gemma's face lit up. "Yes! Then go grab your bags!"

Less than an hour later, she waved from the platform as I boarded the train back to New York. She'd given me Jackson's address so I could go straight to his apartment when I arrived. I still had my room at the Plaza, but if all went well, I wouldn't be going back there that night.

That gave me the rest of the train ride to figure out exactly what to say when I saw him again, and how to convince him that, at last, I was all in.

Chapter Sixteen

Grand Central Station

Watching the seconds tick by on the big clock atop the Grand Central information booth, it felt like time was moving in slow motion. Only one train leaving that night would get me where I needed to go and it was due to arrive in ten minutes. I kept one eye on the clock and one eye on the departure board, waiting for the platform number to be posted.

While I waited, I pulled my phone out of my pocket more than once, making sure I hadn't missed anything from Holly. I hadn't heard from her at all since our conversation on the street in front of my mother's apartment building, though after what my sister said, I understood why. It still didn't stop me from hoping she would reach out to me anyway.

Briefly, I toyed with the idea of letting her know about my plans, but in the end, I decided not to. The romantic in me couldn't resist the idea of turning up at her door unexpectedly and sweeping her off her feet. I'd apologize for my mistake, she'd tell me how much she missed me, and we'd kiss out in the snow before going up to the guest room at Isabel's mansion together, just like in the climax of nearly every romantic movie ever made.

At least, I really hoped it would go that way.

Finally, the platform number flashed on the screen and I joined the crowd of people making their way there, jostling with families and people with bags of gifts going home for the holidays. Nobody seemed to be in quite as much of a hurry as I was, so I took a deep breath and forced myself to move at the same pace as everyone else rather than taking my impatience out on any of the innocent travelers.

The train pulled up right as I got to the platform and I headed down to the far end where it would be less busy. Normally, I wouldn't mind being surrounded by happy families and excited kids, but that evening, I wanted some quiet. I wanted time to work out exactly what I would say to Holly when I saw her. Now that I knew just how badly I'd screwed up, I wanted to find the perfect words to not only apologize but to let her know that I was ready to take as much of her as she was willing to give me.

I was ready to admit defeat. I would take that first bite of the candy cane if I had to, I just needed her to know exactly what she meant to me. I didn't want to spend another minute of the holidays without her.

After the train came to a full stop, I stepped to the side of the door as it opened, waiting for the people to get off. When it seemed everyone had, I crossed the threshold into the train and turned the corner, only to walk smack into a late straggler struggling with her bags as she rushed down the aisle towards the door, her head down.

"Holly?"

I could hardly believe my eyes as I took in her beautiful face and blonde hair in front of me. Why would she be there, on that train? Was I thinking about her so much I'd started hallucinating? But as she looked up at me in equal disbelief, I knew it had to be true. My mind wasn't playing tricks on me; she was actually there.

"What are you doing here?" I asked, reaching down to grab the bags in her hand as she struggled to catch her balance.

"I was coming to see you." Her eyes were soft and not at all angry as she looked up at me, and my heart soared with hope. "What are *you* doing here?"

"I was on my way to see you," I replied, mimicking her answer, and her laugh made me laugh too. All the tension and sadness of the past three days seemed to melt away in the warmth of her smile.

"We're a fine pair," she teased me. "What if you'd chosen a different carriage? We'd have completely missed each other."

I shook my head in response, a wide grin across my face. The coincidence was almost impossible but to me it could only mean one thing: "It must be fate."

"Must be," she murmured back. Something new shone in her eyes as she looked at me that made my heart beat faster, but before I could ask her exactly what it meant, we were interrupted by a voice behind us.

"Can we get by?"

I turned to see a young couple with their own bags, looking at the seats beyond us impatiently, reminding me that we were still standing in the aisle of the train, blocking everyone else's way. I apologized to them and, still holding Holly's bags, stepped back onto the platform with her following close behind me.

"Why were you coming to see me?" she asked, her pink cheeks making her look even more beautiful than usual. "I thought you wanted a break from me."

Oh, God. I suspected she thought that, but to hear her say the words out loud nearly killed me. I needed to set her straight immediately.

"Actually, I thought *you* needed a break from *me*," I corrected her. "I didn't want to be away from you at all, I just got worried that…"

Someone bumped into me, cutting me off as they headed for the train, and Holly smiled again, her eyes bright as she looked around the crowded platform. "This isn't really the best place to talk, is it?"

"It really isn't," I agreed. There must be somewhere better we could go, and as I glanced around the station, the perfect idea came to me. "I know somewhere we could speak in private. Come with me."

My hands were full with the bags so I couldn't hold onto her, but Holly walked right beside me as I brought us back to the main terminal and down the stairs to the lower level with its vaulted, arched ceilings.

Groups of people walked by, going in and out of the restaurants or just passing time, and Holly looked around curiously. "This isn't any quieter than it was upstairs," she pointed out.

"Just wait," I promised before leading her to one corner of the domed archway. "Stand right here and face the wall."

Confusion crossed her face, but she did as I requested, putting her trust in me in a way that made my heart swell as I walked away to the opposite corner and faced the wall there.

"Holly?" I asked quietly, ignoring all the other conversations going on around us. "Can you hear me?"

"I can," her sweet voice came back, filled with amusement. When I glanced over at her, she was looking at me through the crowd of people, grinning, before turning back to the wall to speak to me again. "This isn't exactly what I thought you meant by somewhere private."

"I thought you might find it interesting," I said into the wall, which carried the sound up and over the arch to her. The whispering wall was a feature of the building that not everyone knew about but I had always found fascinating. Though none of the people passing between us could hear me, standing where she was, Holly caught every word. "And if I'm being honest, it's a little bit selfish on my part. It's easier for me to apologize when I don't have to look in your eyes and remember that I hurt you. I didn't mean to imply for even a second that I had changed my mind about us, and I'm so sorry that that's how it sounded. When I suggested you go, I thought you might want some time away from me, to clear your head without any pressure from me, so you could decide how you felt about us."

"My head is never more clear than when I'm with you," she replied, and once again, my heart felt lighter than it had in days, if not years. "But to tell you the truth, I'm glad that we had this time apart."

"You are?" My breath caught in my throat as I began to wonder if I had jumped to conclusions about what had brought her back to the city. Had the time away proven my mother right? Had she given up on us after all?

"I wanted to talk to you about our challenge." Those words made me glance over at her again, hoping for some clue where she might be going with this, but she still faced the wall, one hand resting on it as she leaned in closer. If I could possibly be jealous of a wall, I was, wishing it were my chest she was leaning onto instead.

"I wanted to talk to you about that too," I told her, wanting to lay all my cards on the table. "I'm done, Holly. You win."

Her warm laughter echoed over to me along the wall. "Will you let me finish?"

"Sorry," I apologized, wincing at the wall in front of me. *Shut up, Jackson*. I was supposed to be making things right with her, not making them worse. "Go ahead."

The sound carried so well between us that I could even hear her intake of breath before she spoke again. "Well, before you stole my thunder, I was going to say that *you* win, Jackson. I'm taking the bite."

My heart kicked into a gear I didn't even know it had, beating faster than it ever had before. Did that really mean what I hoped it did? I didn't want to jump to any conclusions but I couldn't stop the hope rising inside me.

"What are you saying?" I asked breathlessly.

"I'm saying..."

The pause she took there nearly brought me to my knees. Whether she did it because she felt nervous or merely for dramatic effect, I couldn't say, but I had never needed someone to finish a sentence so badly in my life.

"I love you."

My heart seemed to stop beating entirely as my whole body froze. I stared blankly at the wall, trying to determine if that really just happened or if it had been a trick of the acoustics, making me hear only what I wanted to hear.

"What?" I managed to whisper, my fingers brushing against the wall as if it were her face. "Can you say that again?"

"I love you."

That time, the words didn't come from the wall. They came from directly behind me, and I spun around to see Holly standing there with tears in her eyes. It reminded me of the last time I saw her, but the reason for the tears couldn't be more different.

They were tears of happiness, matching my own.

"I love you too, Holly," I managed to say before she threw her arms around me. The bags slipped from my hands onto the floor as my arms wrapped around her, and my lips met hers halfway in a kiss that was desperate and joyous and needy all at once.

She loves me. The words etched themselves into my brain and my heart as our bodies pressed together. It felt like we could never get close enough.

I wouldn't have ever wanted the kiss to end, but a few whistles and catcalls from the other travelers quickly reminded us that we were still very much in public. As I pulled back from her, our eyes met and we both laughed, both at being caught in the kiss and in relief that finally, more than a year after this had all started between us, we were on the same page.

"So, I said it," she reminded me, biting her lip as she fought against her grin. "Which means you won."

"But I already told you that you won," I teased her in reply, loving the way her eyes sparkled in response. "How about we go back to my apartment right now so you can claim your prize?"

"I think that's the best idea you've ever had." We laughed again as I picked her bags up off the floor, and with her arm linked through mine, both of us grinning ear to ear, we headed for the exit.

~Holly~

Jackson's lips brushed against mine softly as we sat in the back of the taxi on the way to his flat. It seemed impossible to keep our hands off each other, mostly because we didn't really want to, not after that incredible kiss back at the train station, and not with the anticipation of what lay ahead of us when we finally got to his place. However, we were trying not to get too carried away until we could be in private, so for the time being, those light, teasing kisses would have to do.

Nothing about our reunion had gone to plan, but I couldn't be happier with the way it had worked out. As soon as we bumped into each other on the train, I knew that we were going to be okay. The distant look in his eyes from the other night had completely vanished. When I looked at him, I saw only the admiration and the affection for me that he'd always shown, and I knew right then that he was mine. All I had to do was give myself to him too.

That didn't mean the words came easily. I still had to fight against every painful memory and insecurity I ever had, but knowing the reward that waited for me if I got them out made the effort worthwhile, especially once Jackson told me that he forfeited our challenge. He was ready to give himself to me fully even if I didn't love him the way he wanted, just to prove to me how much he wanted me.

I could have drawn it out or made him feel bad for sending me away, but what would be the point? He made a mistake and he acknowledged it. Hell, it wasn't like I hadn't made mistakes of my own during the previous two weeks, and he never held them against me. When he took us to the whispering arch, speaking to me privately from across the room in the most adorable way I could think of, I knew the truth in my heart.

I love him.

I was completely in love with that sweet, charming, handsome, giving and forgiving man, and I didn't want to waste another minute not being with him.

Maybe it wouldn't work out. Maybe something would happen to tear us apart someday, but it no longer seemed a good enough reason for us not to be together *that* day, and the next one, and for as long as he would have me.

I didn't want to wait any longer to be happy.

At last, we made it to his building and we tumbled out of the taxi, still holding onto each other. Jackson had to let me go to grab my bags, but we didn't even make it to the front door before he was kissing me again, harder than he had in the cab.

A moment later, he groaned against my lips in frustration. "I really need my hands free."

"Then let's go upstairs," I teased him. "What are you waiting for?"

He glanced down at the bags in his hands. "My keys are in my pocket. Can you grab them?"

He made it too easy for me. Reaching down, I brushed the front of his trousers before dipping my hand into his pocket. It didn't take much to find the hard outline of his cock through the fabric and run my fingers along the edge of it, pretending to be searching for the keys.

"Fuck, Holly," he groaned with his eyes closed. "Wrong pocket."

I couldn't help laughing, and he followed suit, though his laugh sounded considerably tighter with repressed need than it had a moment earlier. I reached across to the other pocket next, teasing him just a little more before pulling the keys out and letting us in the front door.

The lift was empty when it arrived and as soon as we were inside, he dropped the bags and his hands were on me. His hard, strong body pressed me against the wall as his lips claimed mine and my hands roamed across his broad back. One hand tangled in my hair as he pulled my head back, forcing my mouth open naturally so his tongue could slide inside.

This was a very different Jackson from the first night we had gone up to my hotel room together. He had been so uncertain then, but through our gradual initiation into the pleasures of being together, his confidence had grown, and my declaration of love that evening seemed to have knocked down any resistance he still had to being with me. The hard proof of his arousal grinded into me as his tongue swirled around mine, tasting and owning me in a possessive and incredibly sexy way.

I didn't think I had ever been as turned on as I was right then. My knickers were soaked and my whole body ached for him. The knowledge that his beautiful cock would finally be inside me that night was the biggest aphrodisiac I could think of.

"Fuck," he muttered again, the curse word sounding strange from him since he swore so rarely. "I didn't press the button yet."

He moved away from me to press it and we both laughed again at the oversight, but the laughter only lasted a second before our mouths and bodies were fused back together again.

Soon, the doors opened and we were practically running down the hall, the anticipation killing us both. My hands fumbled with the keys, my fingers shaking so much I could barely hold them steady, but at last, I got the door open and we stumbled inside. My bags didn't make it two feet past the door as he dropped them and picked me up instead, my legs wrapping around his waist as he easily lifted me from the floor and carried me towards his bedroom.

His strong arms supported me as he crawled onto the bed with me still attached to him, my head hitting the pillows as he laid me down.

He pulled back from me just far enough to look into my eyes. "I want to do everything we've already done all over again," he whispered almost desperately. "But I don't know if I can wait that long."

"I don't want you to wait," I promised, reaching up to kiss him hard before falling back to the pillow again. "I need you inside me, Jackson. Right now."

With another groan, he stood back up, removing his clothes as quickly as possible. I did the same, shuffling out of my trousers and knickers, then wriggling my top off before reaching behind me to undo the snaps of my bra.

"Do we need a condom?" he asked as he pulled his boxers down. His cock was so hard and ready and the idea of feeling him inside me so overpowering, I might have said no even if we did need one. As it was, though, I was on birth control and tested regularly, and I knew I had absolutely nothing to worry about from him.

Still, I couldn't help teasing him just a little. "Do you have any? How old are they?"

He gave me a sweet, sheepish look. "Actually, I bought some a couple of weeks ago. The morning after the wedding."

He always had been sure about us, hadn't he? The thought of him making a special trip to the shop just for that had my thighs clenching yet again.

"Well, you wasted your money. I want to feel *all* of you."

His cock jumped at my words, and he crawled back onto the bed with me, the look in his eyes so intense that it felt like it would burn a brand on my heart. *His* brand, marking me as his, in that moment and for always.

"I love you, Holly," he reminded me, rubbing his cock through the wetness between my legs before pushing into me in one single, exquisitely satisfying thrust.

~Jackson~

"Jackson!" Holly moaned out my name as I entered her and the sound of it multiplied the intense sensations I already felt so much that it honestly amazed me I didn't just come right there and then.

For a moment, I couldn't move or speak or do anything other than take in the amazing feeling of her warm and wet centre wrapped around my throbbing dick, embracing it and cocooning it as if it had always been meant to be there.

She fit me perfectly, in every way. She truly was my dream woman.

As much as I wanted to stay in that moment forever, eventually, instinct took over and my hips began to move almost of their own accord. With long, languid movements, I pulled back out of her and pushed in again, both of us sighing in pure pleasure. I couldn't really imagine what it felt like for her, but for me, every single nerve ending in my body was at its most sensitive but none more than the ones along the length of my dick, sliding into the welcoming depths of her body.

I pushed into her again, feeling like I burrowed deeper each time until no distinction remained between us, no more boundary of where I ended and she began. We were simply one.

Holly's hands caressed my chest and shoulders as I propped myself up on my arms, the rotation of my hips starting to come faster.

"Oh, God, that's perfect," she whimpered, and I couldn't have said it better myself.

I knew I couldn't hold back much longer so I reached one hand between us, finding her clit with my fingers as my dick continued to sink into her, over and over again, and almost immediately, her legs began to tremble.

"Yes, Jackson, oh.... yes..." I could see the moment her orgasm peaked, and that was all I could take too. Her body clenched around me and I let go, releasing deep inside her, and as the intense pleasure washed over me, I dropped onto my elbows, my arms shaking too much to hold me up any longer.

Wave after wave of satisfaction passed through me, stronger than anything I'd ever felt before, and finally, after all those years of waiting, I knew exactly what I'd been missing.

I didn't regret the wait, not for a second. Waiting for that night, and for Holly, had been completely worth it. It was everything I could have imagined and more.

Holly must have been aboard the same train of thought because she looked up at me, her lips forming a smile as her voice came out breathlessly. "Well, I guess you're not a virgin anymore."

"I guess not," I agreed with a smile, bending down to kiss her lips gently. I was still inside her and I honestly didn't know if I ever wanted to leave. It felt too good right where I was.

"And you're okay with that?" she asked, her voice betraying that hint of vulnerability that always made my heart melt. Did she really have to ask?

"I've never been happier, Holly," I promised her truthfully. "I wanted you to be my first, and that was perfect. Absolutely incredible."

"It was incredible for me too," she told me, and I could see the truth of that in her eyes.

"But I'm sure I can do better," I teased her, and instantly, she smiled again, on the same page as me as usual. "I think we're going to need to do a lot of training though."

"That can probably be arranged," she agreed, her hands roaming across my chest again, and my dick already began to twitch back to life inside her. "How about we start right now?"

"You read my mind."

Our kisses began softly before turning harder and more demanding. By the time we finally fell asleep, I'd come three times in total and Holly a handful more than that. Luckily for us both, we had nowhere to be and nothing to do the next day. The whole city still waited to be explored, but at that moment, all the adventure we needed was right there in my bed.

Chapter Seventeen

CHRISTMAS EVE DAY

~Holly~

Waking up the next morning to Jackson's warm, naked body beside me felt like waking up *to* a dream. Nothing I could have dreamt up would be better than that reality. A quick glance at the clock on the bedside table told me it was nearly noon, but he was still asleep despite the hour. I supposed that after being up half the night enjoying each other, it shouldn't come as a big surprise that we both needed a little extra sleep.

As soon as the memories of the previous night came back to me, so did the fluttering in my stomach and the aching desire for him. He had completely satisfied me, far more than any man ever had before, and yet, I wanted him even more afterwards. Jackson was like some kind of drug, becoming more addictive with each taste. I didn't know if I could ever get enough.

A satisfied smile took over my face as more memories flooded in. He was such an eager student, ready to try anything. I felt almost entirely certain he was compiling a list somewhere in the back of his brain of all my reactions so he would know which things I enjoyed, which were just okay, and which ones drove me absolutely wild. It seemed that where he was concerned, most things fit into the latter category.

Maybe I could return the favour and drive *him* a little crazy that morning. Slipping from his embrace, I slid down his body to where his soft cock rested sleepily against his leg. With a little help from me, it wouldn't stay soft for very long.

I'd given him a blow job in the shower a few days earlier, but it hardly counted. He'd already been more than halfway gone by the time I got my lips on him. That morning, I could start from scratch, as it were, and really draw it out. I could make him beg me for release, and the thought nearly had me salivating.

A few feather-light flicks of my tongue across his head were all it took for Jackson to start to squirm. His body shifted beneath me as I took the tip of him softly into my mouth, letting my tongue swirl around the ridge at the base of his head.

"Holly?" The word was half-question and half-moan from somewhere above me.

"Down here," I replied cheerily before sucking on him hard for just a moment and letting him go.

"I figured that out," was his sarcastic reply, but I could hear the excitement in his voice.

Now that he was conscious, his anticipation kicked in. He began to harden and lengthen almost before my eyes as I ran my tongue up and down his shaft, slowly and firmly. As I moved lower, gently sucking one of his balls into my mouth, a sharp intake of breath came from the head of the bed.

"Is that okay?" I asked, not entirely sure what the gasp meant. Most of my previous partners liked it, but I didn't want to assume anything. We were still figuring each other out.

His reply sounded rather choked. "Yeah. I just... wasn't expecting it."

Having confirmed I was on the right track, I resumed my task, licking and sucking on his tender sack as my fingers lightly trailed along his cock, feeling it twitch beneath my touch. Each little moan and groan from him sounded like the highest praise, the best sounds I had ever heard.

I continued to explore his body in a way I'd never really done with a lover before, exactly as he'd done with me. I wanted to know everything he liked, especially since he might not even know it himself. My job was to help him figure it out, and my pleasure too. Licking and sucking on the sweet spot just beneath his balls? A definite yes. Pressure on his anus? Not so much. Scraping my teeth along his inner thighs? Back to yes.

When I'd teased him enough, I turned my full attention back to his cock which by that point already glistened with a few drops of precum. I licked them up greedily before taking him all the way into my mouth.

"Oh, fuck," Jackson muttered, making me smile around his cock. He had no idea what he was in for. I was just getting warmed up.

Using my hands and my mouth, varying the rhythm and pressure, I brought him right to the brink a couple of times, backing off each time just before the orgasm hit. His leg muscles tensed and his hands threaded through my hair but he let me have full control, setting my own pace, until finally he couldn't take it anymore.

"Please, Holly," he begged. "I can't... I need to..."

That was what I'd been waiting to hear. Gripping his base firmly in one hand, I ran my thumb across his shaft while taking as much of him in as I could, his head hitting the back of my throat while my tongue stroked him each time, until, with one last utterance of my name, he came hard and fast into my mouth.

When his pulsing had stopped, I laid his cock back down, kissing it gently before returning to the welcoming embrace of his arms. "I could get used to that," he murmured, kissing my forehead tenderly.

Eventually, we had to get up and get some food, but Jackson insisted that we remain naked, and I couldn't really complain when the view I got was so enticing. "No clothes at all today," he said when he made the request. "Tomorrow, we can go back to real life. Today is just us."

That sounded perfect to me.

After lunch, we returned to the bedroom. Another long and unhurried round of lovemaking followed, and while we were wrapped up in each other's arms afterwards, I finally remembered that I still had some unanswered questions.

"What exactly happened with your mom?" I asked, my fingers tracing his eyebrows as we lay facing each other. "And why did you think I needed a break from you?"

He grimaced at the reminder. "She said some things that made me doubt myself. She said I always have to be perfect, that I try to make the people around me perfect too, and that it's overwhelming for them. She used the word 'suffocating' and said that you probably felt the same way. I got worried that you were just too kind to tell me, so I thought if we had a few days apart, it would give you a chance to see how you felt when you had some breathing room."

Suffocating? How could anyone say that about the sweet, supportive man in front of me? And especially his mother, when, from what he'd told me, he only started trying to be perfect to make her want to stay with them in the first place.

Anger towards the woman I'd barely met flowed through me but I forced myself to keep my reply calm and focused on Jackson. I had to make sure he knew just how untrue her words were.

"That's exactly the opposite of how I feel. You don't try to make me perfect, Jackson. You've accepted me for exactly who I was, right from the start. If anything, it's harder to breathe when I'm *not* with you. You give me the space to be myself and it's not restraining in any way. It's actually incredibly freeing."

His face relaxed into a sweet smile. "My sister said you'd say that. She said if you were the right woman for me, you'd love me for me, even if I try too hard sometimes."

"Is there any member of your family you haven't discussed me with?" I couldn't help teasing him, and his blush made me laugh. I ran my fingers along his reddened cheeks and down into his beard, reminding me of something else I'd been meaning to ask him about. "You know, I like the beard, but I miss seeing your dimples too."

His eyebrows raised in surprise and dismay. "If you don't like it, it's gone, Holly. I can shave it off right now."

I laughed again as he started to get out of bed, pulling him back down and wrapping my arms back around him. The walls of his room seemed to echo with our laughter, there was so much of it when we were together.

When he was securely back in my arms, I asked him to elaborate. "Why did you decide to grow it in the first place?"

Jackson shrugged, looking a little sheepish. "Mostly for work. I thought it made me look a bit older and more serious. People always see me as the joker and Cole as the serious one, so I thought it might give me a bit of extra authority."

I could see that, but he'd missed one important thing. "The twinkle in your eye gives you away though," I pointed out with a smile. "But it's not a bad thing to be light-hearted. I could never love a man who took himself too seriously."

"Then I'll never be serious again," he promised, rolling over on top of me as he began kissing me again. "Except when it comes to making you happy."

Our lazy day together finally gave way to night, and almost before I knew it, I woke up again in Jackson's bed the next morning: Christmas Eve day. That time, though, the other side of the bed was empty when I awoke.

Just as I was about to go and see where he was, Jackson entered the room, carrying a tray with hot breakfast and a cup of tea, and wearing a Santa hat. To my disappointment, he also had other clothes on too, but I still grinned happily at the sight of him as he placed the food down in front of me.

"Good morning." He gave me a gentle kiss that still managed to set my pulse racing.

"Good morning yourself," I murmured back. "This looks amazing. Is every day going to be like this?"

"*Yesterday* was amazing," he contradicted me. "Today is going to be a bit different. We're actually going to leave the apartment for one thing, so after you've eaten, we'll get ready to go. I hope you're ready, Holly, because I'm going to give you a Christmas Eve you'll never forget."

~Jackson~

I was grateful that Holly slept in a little bit that morning. It gave me a chance to not only make her breakfast but to make a few plans as well. Ideas had been coming to me the day before about what we might do together for her first Christmas in New York – the first of many, I hoped – and the time had come to start putting things into action.

Cole answered the phone with a curse when I called. "Do you have any fucking idea what time it is?" he groaned.

"Time for me to cash in every favour I've ever done you," I answered him just as bluntly. "I'm going all out tonight, and I need your help."

He muttered something I couldn't quite make out before a new voice sounded in my ear.

"Jackson? What's going on? Is everything okay?"

"Hey, Gemma. Everything's fine. As I was trying to explain to your grouchy husband, I've got something special I want to do for Holly tonight, but I need some help."

As I expected, she told him off for not being more helpful over his continued protests that it was too early to do anything. Finally, she asked me what I needed and we got to work on the planning.

Once Holly and I had eaten our breakfast and she had gotten dressed, we headed out into the city with my bags of gifts. Cole had sent one of the company drivers for the day so we wouldn't have to worry about getting taxis to ferry us between places.

"This won't take long," I promised her. "I've just got to deliver a few presents and the rest of the day is for us."

"It's fine," she assured me with her teasing smile. "I love seeing you all excited about this."

She gave my Santa hat a tug as we both laughed. It felt like I hadn't stopped smiling ever since Grand Central Station. We stopped at my office first where I handed out gifts to my team and introduced Holly to everyone. They already knew her by reputation since she and Gemma were in charge of redesigning all the new hotels that my team acquired, but with my arm around her waist, I made it obvious that her connection to Stamer Hotels had nothing to do with why she was with me that day.

From there, we went to a couple of hotels I was currently in the processing of trying to buy. I figured a personal appearance from the potential new owners, bearing gifts, could only make a good impression on the staff.

"You're so good at this," Holly said to me as we climbed back in the car after the last of those stops. "I don't know how anyone can resist you when you set out to win them over."

"You tried your hardest," I pointed out, giving her a wink to let her know I meant it as a joke.

Thankfully, she laughed. "I really did," she murmured, giving me a kiss. "But you were irresistible."

One last gift remained in the car and one last stop for us to make. As we got closer to my mother's building, the tension that Holly had managed to erase over the past day and a half started to creep back into my body, and Holly immediately noticed.

"Can I ask you something? I don't mean it to sound judgy at all, I'm just curious."

She could hardly have made me more curious. "Of course. You can ask me anything, Holly."

"Why do you still try so hard with your mum? I mean, from where I stood, when we ran into her the other night, it felt like she blew you off. And after the things she said to you the other day... well, I just don't really understand why you're taking her a present."

The question didn't offend me at all. Cole had asked me the same thing often enough, why I didn't simply cut her out of my life and be done with it, but in my mind, the answer was fairly simple.

"Because she tries too," I explained. "It's not as often or as hard or in the way I would want her to, but she does try. She always came back. No matter how many times she left us or for how long, she always came back eventually. If she didn't care about us at all, she would have vanished forever, but she never did. I think deep down she does want a connection with us, she just doesn't know how to do it. And honestly, that makes me sad for her rather than angry. I just want her to know the door is always open if she ever figures it out. I don't give up on people, Holly."

I added the last sentence to let her know that it didn't just apply to my mom. I meant it for her too; now that she was a part of my life, I wasn't changing my mind about her, ever.

Holly shook her head, but the look on her face was one of appreciation. "You really are a good man, Jackson Hanmer."

"Not too good, I hope," I teased her, leaning in for a quick kiss. "Because I would like to be very bad with you later."

I buzzed up to my mom's apartment when we arrived and she came to meet us at the door, looking surprised to see me and more surprised to see Holly.

"You mentioned the other day that you were going to ask to see me on Christmas," I reminded her, even though she had never actually gone ahead and asked. "I'm afraid I've already got plans with Holly, so I wanted to give you this now, and wish you a Merry Christmas."

"Thank you." My mom still looked surprised as she took the gift from my hands, and she stood there just looking at me, waiting for the other shoe to drop.

"Merry Christmas, Darla," Holly added, putting her arm through mine supportively. I could hear the slight sharpness in her tone, as if she were attempting to remind my mom that she hadn't returned the sentiment yet.

She still didn't do it, looking over at Holly instead. "When are you going back to England, then?"

Immediately, I stiffened. Holly and I hadn't actually discussed that yet, but we would obviously need to talk about it over the coming days. Although she knew I wanted to be with her and I knew she felt the same, logistically, we still had to work some things out.

To my surprise, though, Holly answered right away. "I go back just after New Year's but I'm sure I'll be back again soon. Maybe Jackson and I can see you again then."

I couldn't have hoped for a better response. Not only was she thinking about us being together, but she referred to us as a unit: 'Jackson and I.' That sounded perfect to me.

After exchanging a few more words, Holly and I got back in the car and I turned to her as soon as we were settled. "I'm sorry she put you on the spot like that. I know we haven't talked about what comes next yet."

"We haven't," Holly agreed. "But I've been thinking about it."

I couldn't hold back my smile of delight. "What have you been thinking?"

"I'll tell you tomorrow," she promised, laughing as I groaned in frustration. "I need something to give you for Christmas, right? I haven't had any time to go find you a gift."

"You spending the day with me is all I need," I told her honestly, but if she wanted to give me some clues about what she imagined for our future, I certainly wouldn't object.

The rest of the day passed in a whirlwind as I tried to fit in all the New York highlights that we hadn't got to yet. We went up the Empire State Building to see the view. We went to the Museum of Modern Art where I knew Holly would be fascinated by the design elements, and I wasn't wrong. We took a private boat out into the harbour to see the Statue of Liberty and the view of the Manhattan skyline.

Then, after a romantic, candlelit dinner, I led Holly to a nearby building and we took the lift up to the very top. When we stepped outside onto the roof, Holly's jaw dropped open as she caught sight of the helicopter waiting there. "Are we really going in that?"

"Would you like to?"

Her giddy smile was all the response I needed and we were soon buckled in and soaring above the city, seeing all the Christmas lights and the trees dotted around the usual city lights.

"Some little kid is going to think we're Father Christmas, flying around the city on Christmas Eve," Holly laughed.

Following the tour, the helicopter dropped us off on top of a different building in Midtown. From there, we walked back to the place everything had started for us, just two weeks earlier: the Christmas tree outside Rockefeller Centre.

The whole plaza was filled with people but I led us straight to a special table that had been set up on a red carpet. Decorated with twinkling lights, red roses and a bottle of champagne, it sat behind a velvet rope that was lifted for us as we approached.

"Are you serious?" Holly gasped as she looked around. "Did you do all this? Jackson, this is too much."

"Nothing is too much for you," I reminded her. "And look over there."

I pointed to the skating rink below us where a team of ice skaters had just come out in matching Santa dresses. A large crowd gathered to watch them as they went through an elaborate choreographed routine of snaking patterns and synchronized moves. Holly was fascinated, her eyes never leaving the ice.

At the very end, another skater came onto the ice and handed out some cards to the others, who began to lift them up in turn until the letters spelled out:

Holly, turn around.

Chapter Eighteen

The Very Best Way

~Holly~

My head was spinning from all of the amazing surprises Jackson kept pulling out of his hat. The whole day had been unbelievable, each thing we did better than the one before, but even so, it never crossed my mind that the ice skating performance was just for me until the skaters held up the message with my name, telling me to turn around.

My heart beat faster as I willed my body to slowly turn. It couldn't be what it felt like, could it? That would be too fast, too soon. As much as I loved Jackson, I could feel my panic rising at the idea of him kneeling there with a ring, and Paul's proposal flashed before my eyes again. That had been after we'd been dating for a year, and it had still been too soon. It still hadn't been enough time for him to figure out the reasons he didn't want to be with me after all. How could Jackson be so certain so quickly?

Given all of those thoughts swirling around my head, when I turned and saw him standing there behind me, holding a single red rose and a key in the palm of his hand rather than a ring, relief flooded through my body.

Relief... and maybe just a tiny bit of disappointment.

Which was crazy, wasn't it? I didn't actually *want* him to propose. At least, I hadn't thought I did until the disappointment showed up all on its own, taking me by surprise.

"Holly, you already know that I love you." He spoke loud enough that the people around us could hear him, and a quick glance told me that we had quite an audience. Heat rushed to my cheeks with the knowledge that all of this was about as public as it could get.

No chance of taking it back. Was that why he'd gone to so much trouble? Just to make sure I really wouldn't have any doubts?

"I wanted to give you something to make it official," he continued. "This key is for my apartment, but also for my heart, and my life. All of it is yours, as much as you want of it, for now and for always."

Along with several 'awwww' sounds from the gathered crowd, I heard a rather familiar squeal and looked over to see Gemma, Cole and Noah standing amongst the crowd of onlookers. Gemma immediately clapped her hand over her mouth and motioned for me to look back at Jackson rather than paying attention to her.

Why were they there? Where had they come from?

I looked back at Jackson who still had his eyes on me, smiling sweetly. He bounced the key in his hand for a moment before holding it out and offering it to me. "What do you say, Holly? Can I trust you with my heart?"

Could *he* trust *me?*

A veil lifted from my eyes as I pondered those words. It had been so easy for me to get caught up in all my past hurts that I forgot this was just as big a step for him as for me. He had every reason to be nervous but he wasn't letting it hold him back, and as I looked at the amazing man in front of me, I knew the answer without a doubt.

"I'll take good care of it," I promised, reaching out to take the key from his hand to the delight of the crowd. As soon as our hands connected, he took hold of me, pulling me close to him and giving me a sweet, lingering kiss that made all the rest of the world fade away until all that remained was me and him.

"You looked a bit shocked when you turned around," he whispered in my ear after his lips left mine. "Were you expecting something else?"

He must have known what it would look like. "It crossed my mind but I wasn't *expecting* it."

"Would you have freaked out if it had been what you thought it might be?" he murmured, still holding me tight.

"Possibly," I had to admit. Now that my initial knee-jerk adrenaline spike had faded, I felt a lot calmer, but who could say if I would have panicked in the moment if he really had been down on one knee.

"Are you disappointed?" he continued, and I blushed at the fact that he could read me so well. No one had ever paid so much attention to my feelings before.

"Of course not," I lied, refusing to acknowledge even to myself that I felt unsatisfied in any way with how things turned out. "I love the key, it's perfect."

"I'm a bit sorry to hear you say that." His eyes twinkling mischievously, he pulled back from me completely and took a couple of steps back. "Because I did have one more question."

The world seemed to go into slow motion as he reached into his pocket, pulled out a ring box, and dropped to one knee in front of me. My hand flew to my mouth in disbelief as the crowd around us began to applaud.

That sneaky, scheming, wonderful man. He knew exactly how I would feel and exactly what to do to make me confront my fears and doubts head on.

I might not have been ready for the question two minutes earlier, but after acknowledging the disappointment I felt when he didn't ask it, I was ready for it then.

Jackson looked up at me, his eyes shining with what could only be called love. "Holly, no one is perfect, but you're perfect for me. You check off everything on my list and so many other things I never even knew I wanted. I know this is fast, but I also know how I feel and what I want. I want to marry you and spend the rest of our lives having days like today, and days like yesterday, and any kind of days, as long as we're together."

My eyes finally left his face to glance down at the beautiful, sparkling ring in the box. Exquisite and almost mesmerizing as it reflected the lights from the nearby tree, its shine paled next to the sparkle in his eyes.

"Holly Chapman," he concluded simply when I looked back up at him. "Will you marry me?"

It felt like the whole world held its breath as the crowd waited for my reply, but all I could see was the incredible man in front of me, who in two weeks had somehow made me go from thinking I would never find the kind of love that Gemma had, and thinking that I was perfectly fine with that, to wanting it more than I'd ever wanted anything before.

And there he knelt, offering it all to me. All I had to say was...

"Yes."

The word burst from my lips with far more force than I expected, and the crowd laughed and cheered as Jackson grinned up at me.

In a second, he was back on his feet and pulling me into another kiss, deeper and more desperate than the one he'd just given me. My arms wrapped around his neck as he pulled my hips flush against him. I didn't care how many people were watching us. At that moment, all I cared about was him.

"Alright, that'll do." Cole's dry reprimand pulled us back to reality and we both turned to see him, Gemma and Noah standing right beside us. "I think the people have seen enough."

Despite his words and tone, I could see a gleam of happiness in his eyes, and he gave me a small nod of acknowledgement before turning to Jackson and offering his congratulations as Gemma wrapped me up in a big hug, or at least as big a hug as she could give me with her baby boy between us.

"Let's go back to our place," she suggested, her eyes bright with unshed tears of joy. "We'll take the champagne and go. We need to celebrate!"

Jackson grinned from ear to ear as he plucked the champagne off the table himself. "Thanks for the offer, but I think we'd prefer to celebrate alone tonight. We'll see you tomorrow."

It had always been the plan for the four of us to have Christmas lunch together, so we agreed a time and said goodnight to them. The crowd around us had mostly dissipated but a few people still cheered and clapped as Jackson and I walked back towards the street. I waved and smiled and thanked them, recognizing once again just how very public he had made the whole thing.

Everybody knew about it. There was no way to pretend it never happened.

"You are unbelievable," I told him as we climbed into a taxi to head back to his apartment.

"In a good way?" he teased as his lips brushed against mine.

"In the very best way," I assured him before kissing my new fiancé as hard as I could.

Christmas Day was perfect. We had a lazy morning in bed before heading to Gemma and Cole's where we watched them help Noah open all his presents from 'Uncle Jackson', even though the baby couldn't have been less interested in the whole proceeding. Once he'd gone down for his nap, we had a relaxed, wonderful meal and eventually, talk turned to the future and where Jackson and I would be living.

He looked over at me curiously. "You said you'd been thinking about it. I don't know if our engagement changes anything you'd been thinking?"

"It does a little, but I think the basic idea could still work."

"Which is?" He wasn't the only one waiting eagerly for my response; Gemma and Cole leaned forward too.

"I think you should move to London and live with me." Disappointment immediately flashed in Gemma's eyes as surprise flickered in Jackson's. He obviously hadn't been anticipating that, but I hadn't finished yet. "At least for a year. That will give us enough time to buy the house here and fix it up just as we want it."

Understanding spread across his face as his surprise melted into a tender smile. "Are you sure? We can look at other houses..."

I shook my head firmly. "That one is your dream. You're already giving me everything I could dream of, so I know it will be perfect."

As he leaned over to kiss me, Cole sighed. "I was going to offer everyone dessert, but after that, I don't know if I can take anything too sweet."

Gemma gave him a playful smack across the arm, and he smirked at her before whispering something in her ear. From the way her cheeks reddened, I suspected it had nothing to do with me and Jackson.

Jackson and I spent the next week almost entirely in his apartment, making plans and making love. He closed the deal on the house in just a few days and got to work on hiring contractors, telling me the design would be entirely up to me. He would be able to work from London easily enough but there were still a lot of arrangements to make to set everything up. We also spent more time with Gemma and Cole, who were both genuinely pleased that we would eventually be coming back to New York even though Gemma moaned that a year was far too long to wait.

Finally, New Year's Eve arrived, our last night in the city for a while, and we had promised to babysit Noah so that Gemma and Cole could attend an important party for business leaders in the city. As we played with Noah, I really let myself imagine me and Jackson with a baby of our own for the first time, and, surprisingly, it didn't seem all that scary.

Once we'd put him down to bed, I turned to Jackson with a happy smile. "So, what did you have in mind for the rest of the night? We could watch the New Year's Eve special from Times Square on TV, although it's a bit strange that it's taking place just a few blocks away."

"We could," he agreed. "Or we could have some fun instead."

The gleam in his eyes took me by surprise. What exactly was he suggesting? In our friends' flat?

The expression on my face made him laugh. "We've got the baby monitor," he reminded me. "So it doesn't matter if we stay here or if we go to another room in the apartment. Like, I don't know... Cole's secret sex dungeon, perhaps?"

My mouth dropped open as I burst into laughter. "Gemma told me you didn't know about that!"

"Of course I know about it," he scoffed, laughing along with me. "I'm not an idiot. One locked door in the whole apartment combined with the things they say to each other when they think I can't hear them and it wasn't hard to put it all together. And even better than just knowing about it..."

He gave me a sexy grin that had my whole body thrumming in anticipation.

"I have a way in."

~Jackson~

Holly's shock at my suggestion and the fact that I knew how to break into Gemma and Cole's secret room delighted me. I didn't think she'd ever been more surprised at anything I'd said.

"And here I thought you were just an innocent, wholesome virgin," she teased me, stepping closer to me, close enough that our bodies were nearly touching but not quite. Even at that distance, I could feel the heat coming off her.

"I never claimed to be innocent. You're the one who keeps calling me good, but I certainly hope I've proven in the last week that I'm not entirely wholesome and no longer a virgin."

Her blue eyes smouldered at those words and at the memories they evoked, all the different ways we'd made love in many different places around my apartment. I had a lot of time to make up for and a lot of positions to try, and luckily for me, Holly was happy to engage in a little experimentation.

One thing we hadn't tried, though, was any kind of kink. I wasn't entirely sure if it would be our thing, but I figured we wouldn't know until we gave it a shot. Based on the things I'd overheard between Cole and Gemma in the last year, I had a feeling that their locked room would be the best place to figure it out

I also reasoned that after all the babysitting I'd done over the last few months, they could hardly complain if we made use of the facilities for one night. I suspected if I just asked, Cole would have no problem with it, but for some reason, the idea of it being a secret made it all a little more exciting. Our friends would never have to know.

Taking Holly by the hand, I grabbed the baby monitor and made my way down the hallway to the locked door with the fingerprint scanner.

"How are you going to get us in?" Holly asked curiously as she looked down at the scanner.

From my pocket, I produced a small business card case. With Holly watching, I opened it to reveal not cards, but a row of fake silicon fingerprints, and I peeled one off and placed it over my own finger before placing my finger on the scanner.

Sure enough, the light turned green and the door clicked open.

"You've got Cole's fingerprint?" she gasped, looking even more surprised than before. "Have you got some kind of secret life as a spy that I don't know about?"

That idea made me laugh. "Of course not. What I do have is Stamer Hotels' IT security department, a boss who is often unavailable, and a reputation as a trustworthy guy who would never abuse his position. All

I had to do was tell them that Cole had asked me to make a few copies of his fingerprint for when he forgot his phone and needed me to get him some information and they were happy enough to make them for me."

"I am truly shocked." Holly tried to look disapproving, but there was too much of a smile in her eyes for me to buy it. In the next moment, she confessed as much. "I'm a little bit impressed too. This side of you is pretty sexy."

My dick had already been half-hard most of the night as I imagined the things we might get up to, and now that we were there with her calling me sexy and looking at me with that gleam in her eye, it quickly grew even harder. I gave her a quick kiss, just teasing her with my tongue against her lips before I pulled her into the room with me and closed the door behind us.

The sight that greeted us was a little overwhelming. Although I knew about the room, I'd never seen it for myself, and it all looked more intense than I'd been expecting. Along with the bed, there were benches and an X-shaped cross with restraints built into it. One wall held different instruments to cause different sensations and a large closet took up most of another wall, though I couldn't begin to guess what might be inside.

After we both looked around silently for a minute, I turned to Holly with a rather sheepish grin. "I have no clue where to start.

Luckily for me, she seemed to have a better idea as she took the baby monitor from me and placed it down on one of the benches before turning around to face me with an inviting smile. "I guess the first thing we need to do is decide which of us is the dominant one."

I had given that some thought earlier. Although I loved the thought of having full access to her body, she never denied it to me anyway. Overall, the idea of letting her tell me what to do was far more stimulating for me. I could only hope that she agreed.

"I'd like you to be in charge, if that's okay."

Her teeth scraped across her lower lip as she grinned. "I was hoping you'd say that."

The sight of her lip in her teeth combined with her words sent a wave of desire through me. I took a step towards her, wanting to comb those lips with my own teeth, but Holly held out a hand to stop me.

"Hold on. Did I say you could move?"

It looked like she had already gotten into character, and I loved that she wanted to explore and try things out with me. "I'm sorry," I apologized, bending my head to her in a show of contrition.

"Sorry, what?" she teased me as I looked back up.

That was a good question. What should I call her? I'd read a few things in different books, but I felt a little silly using any of them so I stuck to something basic. "Sorry, ma'am?"

The smile in her eyes told me she approved. "That's better. Now, take off your clothes."

It amazed me how comfortable everything felt with her. Only a few weeks earlier, I'd never been naked with a woman, but that night, I stripped with no hesitation at all. When I was fully nude, Holly circled around me, inspecting my body. She gave my ass a playful slap before coming back to the front of me and grabbing hold of my dick at the base.

"Fuck," I muttered as blood rushed to the spot.

Holly shook her head at me. "I didn't say you could speak, either. I think you need a bit more training."

Her tone of voice, teasing but commanding at the same time, only made the throbbing in my dick worse, and I nodded eagerly. "Yes, ma'am."

With a nod, she released me and went over to the closet while I watched curiously, not sure what she might be looking for. Throwing the doors open, she was greeted with a variety of different outfits and accessories, most of which I couldn't even begin to guess their purpose. Sticking to basics, Holly pulled out a scarf and walked back over to me. "I don't think they'll miss just one of these," she said with a wink before tying it around my mouth like a gag.

The reminder that we were doing all of this in someone else's home only turned me on more, for reasons I couldn't articulate. I rarely broke any rules at all, but Holly brought out my adventurous side. Once the scarf was secure and Holly confirmed it felt okay for me, she ordered me to lie down on the bed. Leather restraints were secured to the side of the bed with velcro cuffs and she wrapped them around my ankles and wrists, leaving me lying star-fished and completely exposed. In spite of all of that, I felt completely safe, trusting the woman in front of me entirely.

"Just shake your head if you want me to stop at any time," she told me as she began to take off her own clothes. I nodded my agreement, my eyes glued to her body as she revealed it to me. Although it was no longer a new sight, it still amazed me each time I saw it, her curves and her smoothness beckoning to me like a siren.

Once she was fully naked, she went over to the wall and took a look at all the different instruments hanging there. My dick jumped in anticipation as I followed her gaze, trying to guess what she might choose. I was surprised and maybe even a little disappointed when she chose two rather tame-looking items: a feather duster and a wooden spoon, but the look in her eyes when she turned back to me quickly erased any disappointment I might be feeling. She definitely had something in mind.

She walked back over to the bed with a mischievous gleam in her eye. "Well, Jackson, you've really surprised me tonight."

Crawling onto the bed between my legs, she began to run the feather duster across my feet, making me squirm at the tickling sensation.

"I had you pegged for a good boy from the day we met," she continued, starting to move the feathers up my leg. "But you're actually a little bit naughty, aren't you?"

Since I didn't know if she wanted me to respond, I didn't, concentrating on the feel of the feathers instead, and suddenly, she brought the wooden spoon down on my thigh, not too hard but enough that it left a sting.

"Answer my question," she instructed, moving the feather duster to the spot she'd just hit with the spoon. The contrast of the feather light caress with the sting from the spoon felt intense, and my dick twitched again.

I nodded my response that time, agreeing with her that I could definitely be a bit naughty, and she smiled.

"Good. I don't want you to be *too* good."

With those words, she bent down and licked her way from the base of my shaft to the glistening tip. Her tongue felt electric and I shivered with pleasure as my arms pulled against the restraints instinctively. There was hardly any give in them.

I was completely at her mercy.

After teasing me for a few minutes, kissing and licking the whole length of my dick, she sat back up and continued her exploration of my body with the duster, alternated with light smacks from the spoon whenever I didn't respond to her quickly enough. Being disciplined that way by Holly felt both dirty and sweet at the same time.

Sometimes, I didn't answer her on purpose just to get the smack, while other times, I honestly got so lost in the sensations that I forgot to reply. Her tongue swirled around my nipples, wetting the skin before she blew on them, making them even more sensitive, twirling the feathers around them before bringing the spoon down and making my back arch with both pain and pleasure.

With almost every move she made, I moaned against my gag, squirming at every touch. She was amazing at this. I wouldn't have done nearly as well, and when she reached up and scratched her nails against my scalp through my hair, I nearly saw stars.

At last, she'd teased me enough, and she bent down to give me a kiss. "You've been such a good boy. Now, you can have your reward."

Giving me a wink, she turned around and slid her legs beneath my thighs as she lowered herself onto my aching dick. The pleasure as she took me in deeply was even stronger than usual after all the build up, and I cried out her name even though it came out as muffled nonsense against the gag.

Restrained as I was, I couldn't do anything but let my orgasm build as she rode me in reverse, her beautiful ass on full display. Watching her from that angle, seeing my dick disappear into her warm pussy with each bounce, had to be the sexiest thing I had ever seen. Her own moans of pleasure as she rubbed her clit, her hand occasionally straying to my balls too, only added to the experience, and it wasn't long before I couldn't take any more. The wave of my orgasm reached its crest and I called out her name behind the gag as I came deep inside her, feeling her pulse around me at almost the exact same time.

Though I hadn't done a single thing, I still felt out of breath as Holly gently climbed off me and turned around to remove my gag.

"Well, that was fun."

"It really was," I agreed when I could speak again. "Maybe we need one of these rooms in our new house."

"I don't know about that," she laughed. "This is a bit much, but I can certainly tie you up anytime you like. After all, you belong to me now, Jackson."

I really did, and I couldn't be happier about it.

We got dressed again and made sure everything in the room was clean and placed back where we found it. The wooden spoon, we could wash, but the feather duster and the scarf we took with us. Maybe it would confuse our friends if they found them missing, but with multiples of those items, not to mention all the other things in there, I figured they'd probably never notice they were gone.

With everything back in place, we returned to the living room and spent the rest of the night as perfectly respectable babysitters. Cole and Gemma returned shortly after one in the morning and we all wished each other a happy new year and said our goodbyes. Holly and I were flying to London the next day, so it would be a while before we were all together again, but I knew that we would be. We had a lifetime of memories to be made, all four of us.

When the last slightly tearful goodbye had been said, Holly and I stepped into the elevator while Cole and Gemma waved from the other side. Just as the doors began to close, Cole gave me his familiar smirk.

"Just so you know, Jackson, there's a sensor on the door to that room that alerts me when it's been opened. Just in case you were planning on trying to sneak in again."

The doors closed on my stunned face. Holly and I turned to each other with our mouths hanging open in shocked silence for a moment before we both dissolved into laughter.

Chapter Nineteen

HAPPY EVER AFTER

~The following December~

~Holly~

As I looked in the mirror one last time to make sure everything was in place, I could see Gemma giving me a slightly dewy-eyed look, and I quickly turned around.

"Don't you start!" I warned her. "I already know I'm going to be a mess when we get out there, I don't need to lose it before we even begin."

Gemma quickly blinked her tears away. "I'm sorry, Hols. I'll try. It's just amazing, when you think about it, you know? Only two years ago, we were both single and planning our work Christmas party. Now, I've already been married for a year and after today, you will be too, all because we happened to choose that particular hotel on that particular night to have our party. It's just funny how life turns out, isn't it?"

All of that was true. That one night had completely changed both our lives, in ways we couldn't have begun to imagine at the time.

I also had trouble believing it had been a whole year since her wedding already, a year since I'd walked down that aisle in New York and saw Jackson waiting at the end and thought how incredible it would be if he were actually waiting there for me. At the time, I thought that fantasy would never come true, and yet, there we were in London with all our friends and family waiting in the next room to watch that exact thing happen.

As someone knocked on the door, I looked up at the clock with a frown. It shouldn't be time for us to go yet. Hopefully, nothing had gone wrong.

Gemma went over and opened the door to reveal her husband on the other side.

"Jackson sent me to make sure everything's okay," he explained, managing to sound both amused and put out at the same time. "I think he's just taking advantage of being the one in charge for a change."

That sounded about right. Jackson would never miss out on a chance to tease his best friend, and he would certainly remember how Cole sent him to check on Gemma at their wedding. I remembered it too, especially the way the sight of Jackson after a year apart nearly knocked me off my feet. How had we ever gone a year without seeing each other? When he had to travel for business for even a week, it felt far too long.

Jackson had adapted so well to living in London that we would really miss it when we moved to New York the following week. The whole city seemed different when I had him to explore it with. He'd insisted that I take him to all my favourite spots, and when we'd gone through them all, we discovered so many new ones together. Every day with him was an adventure, I never knew what idea he was going to come up with next, and he still hadn't lost any of his enthusiasm and love for life that had drawn me to him in the first place.

Even though I would miss the life we'd built for ourselves in London, I was excited to go to New York too. Our house there should be ready and waiting for us; the contractors had sent us pictures as they worked on it but we hadn't seen it in person yet. Even though we had taken a couple of trips to New York during the year to visit Gemma and Cole and to see Jackson's family, we had stayed away from the house, wanting to wait for the grand reveal at the end. Jackson trusted my vision for it completely, just as I trusted him enough to leave my whole life behind.

First, though, we needed to get married.

After Gemma sent Cole away, she threw open the door to where the rest of my bridal party was getting ready and they all rushed in, full of excitement. Unlike Gemma and Cole's wedding which had only me and Jackson as attendants, mine was a big family affair. Both my sisters were bridesmaids as well as Jackson's sister, Layla, who had become one of my closest friends over the last year. Meanwhile, Jackson had all three of my brothers and his own brother, besides his best man, Cole.

When I first brought Jackson to meet my family, I held his hand tightly as we walked up to the door of my parents' council flat. We could already hear arguing inside as we approached and my heart sank. I didn't know who was arguing or why; with my family it could honestly be anything, and I was tempted to turn right around and run back home before Jackson could be disillusioned.

However, Jackson gave me a gentle kiss and promised me everything would be alright. He kept his word, as always, and in less than ten minutes, he managed to thoroughly charm them all. With my parents, he was polite and respectful but not too formal. He got in the middle of my brothers' argument over football by admitting he knew nothing about football in the first place, and got them all laughing and joking with each other as they tried to explain it all to him. He complimented my sister's shoes as if he knew they were the one thing she splurged on, and he was on the floor with the kids playing some complicated game about dragons and dinosaurs before I even knew what was happening.

"He's nothing like your other boyfriends," my sister snorted to me as we watched him running around pretending to breathe fire on the shrieking kids. "I was beginning to think you only went for the stuck-up assholes."

That certainly used to be my type, but not anymore.

Jackson's mom had even flown over for the wedding, along with her new boyfriend who seemed like a big step up from the last one. We'd only met him twice before, but he seemed eager to build a relationship with us and Jackson was hopeful. I had sent Gemma out into the church a few minutes earlier to make sure she had actually shown up that day, as I knew how hurt Jackson would be if she didn't. Luckily, she was there, so I didn't need to get my hands dirty while in my wedding dress. I still didn't have any kind of warm and fuzzy feelings about her, but I respected the way that Jackson kept including her in his life, no matter what.

Finally, we got the official call to go, and we all gathered in the church entrance. One of my nieces was our flower girl while little Noah was the ring bearer, looking absolutely adorable in his suit. He wasn't really able to walk and carry the rings at the same time, so the rings were placed in my niece's basket and she held Noah's hand to take him up the aisle to his dad who was already waiting there.

All my bridesmaids took their turns, followed by Gemma who gave me one last hug before leaving me alone with my dad.

"Are you ready?" he asked, his voice a little gruff with emotion. He wasn't usually the sentimental type, but weddings could bring it out of anyone. "You've got a really good one there, Holly."

He didn't need to tell me that. I'd known it from the very start.

~Jackson~

My heart couldn't have felt any fuller as I stood at the front of the church, watching Holly's bridal party come in. I'd wanted this since pretty much the moment I first laid eyes on Holly, and I could hardly believe it was finally happening.

Everyone in the crowd oohed and aahed over the adorable flower girl and ring bearer, and Cole stepped over to give his son a hug and praise him for a job well done before handing him to Isabel to watch for the ceremony until he was needed again.

Holly's sisters came in, followed by Layla, who gave me a big, exaggerated wink as she took her place on the other side of the altar. Gemma walked in next, the emerald green that Holly had chosen for the bridesmaid dresses suiting her perfectly, and I couldn't help noticing the way that Cole's eyes softened at the sight of her, even though he'd already seen her in that dress earlier that day.

At last, the bridal march started and Holly entered, and my breath caught in my throat as I got my first look at her.

Her dress fit her like a glove, following each of her curves in a way that made my hands itch with the need to touch her. Her bouquet was made up of white flowers with sprigs of holly dotted throughout it, matching not only the green dresses of the bridesmaids but, of course, her name too. Her sleek blonde hair was hanging down as usual and her make-up was beautiful, but honestly, all I could really see were her eyes, fixed on me and shining with love.

I shook hands with her father before taking Holly's hand in mine and giving her a kiss on the cheek. "I told you I'd see you at the altar," I whispered in her ear, and her eyes sparkled as I pulled away.

"You did," she agreed, biting her lip to hold back her smile. "Looks like you win, Jackson."

I certainly felt like I had.

The minister began speaking before I could respond and soon, we got to the vows. Holly had insisted that she go first because she said I was certain to make her cry and she wanted to be able to get hers out without blubbering.

"No one is perfect," she started, giving me a teasing wink.

Those were the words I'd used in my proposal and I knew that she knew it. I loved that she remembered that, and that it meant as much to her as it did to me.

"For a long time, I thought there was something wrong with me. I thought the reason my relationships didn't work out was because I wasn't the kind of woman that men like you wanted to marry. But every day, in the way you love and accept me, you've shown me how that was never the problem. The problem was simply that I hadn't met the right man yet. Now that I have, my heart is yours, completely and forever. I love you, Jackson, and I can't wait for every single crazy adventure you're going to come up with for us. You are perfect for me."

I could see now why she had insisted on going first. My eyes were filled with tears of joy and I wasn't sure how I was going to get my own words out, until Cole leaned over and offered me his handkerchief.

"You look like you could use this more than me," he smirked and the whole crowd laughed. That was just what I needed to get myself collected, and I gave my eyes an exaggerated dab, making our loved ones laugh even more before handing it back to him.

"I thought I was ready for a relationship years before we met," I told Holly, focusing back on her. "I wanted it more than anything, or at least, I thought I did. I know now that I wasn't truly ready. There was no one I wanted to give all of myself to until you walked into my life. And although you fit every criteria on the list I made for my perfect woman, it's all the things I never even knew I wanted that really made me fall in love with you. Every day I'm with you is the best day of my life, and my heart is yours, completely and forever."

I hadn't planned to say that last bit, but I loved it so much when she said it, I had to steal it from her. I could tell by the smile on her face that she knew it too.

"I love you, Holly. You're perfect for me too."

The rest of the ceremony was over in half a second, it felt like, and when the minister told me I could kiss Holly, I wrapped my arms around her in that amazing dress of hers and sealed all my promises to her with the most heartfelt, passionate kiss we'd ever had.

I had everything I'd ever wanted and the best part was, we were still at the beginning.

~Three years later~

~Holly~

"This was not a good idea," Gemma complained as we both settled onto the bench in Central Park. "The nearest toilet is too far away and I can't seem to go five minutes without needing one."

"I could always bring you a chamber pot," Cole teased her as he adjusted her coat and scarf to make sure she was comfortable. "You could just go into the trees for privacy."

I would have teased her too if I wasn't in almost exactly the same boat. Gemma was eight and a half months pregnant and I was only two weeks behind, and I also felt like my bladder had shrunk to the size of a pea.

"You can both take it easy," Jackson promised as he set our nearly 18-month-old daughter Olivia down on the ground so that she could chase after Noah. "We've got the kids covered."

"You better," I warned him. "It's your fault we're in this mess, both of you."

They looked far too pleased about that when I hadn't meant it as a compliment.

"Noah, stay away from that dog," Cole called out, his brow furrowing as he looked over at his son on the grass. He grimaced before turning back to Gemma with an apologetic look. "Sorry, I'll be right back."

He jogged away after them, looking out of place amongst all the real joggers in his suit and tie. He and Jackson had both been at the office that day while Gemma and I worked from her apartment, but Jackson had insisted on them both coming home early and all of us going for an outing in the park since the weather had gifted us with a beautiful, sunny, December day.

"I really hope this little one can wait just a few more weeks," Gemma told me as she rubbed her hand across her swollen stomach. "I would love to have a Christmas baby."

"For that kid's sake, I hope not," I laughed. "You would make her have a Christmas-themed party every single year for her entire life!"

Gemma opened her mouth to protest but quickly closed it again, all but admitting that I was completely right. She turned to Jackson instead. "And you're still not going to tell me whether you're having a boy or a girl? It makes shopping for presents so much more difficult when I don't know."

Jackson offered her an apologetic shrug before turning to me. "Holly wants it to be a surprise, and her word is final."

"Way to throw me under the bus!" I protested, and we all laughed again.

We did know that we were having another girl, and I knew that Gemma would be delighted at us both having daughters at the same time, but I liked it being something that was just between me and Jackson for a little longer.

"We've all got our secrets," I reminded her. "Don't make me bring up your sex dungeon again."

Gemma just shook her head at me. "You lost all rights to tease me about that when you helped yourselves to it that night," she replied with a laugh. "Cole still laughs about that, by the way. The look on your face, Jackson, when you realized he knew…"

We all laughed at the memory, which seemed like a lifetime ago sometimes. So much had changed since then, and yet, so much was still the same. Jackson was still the best man I'd ever met, and I loved him even more than I did when I married him, though it hardly seemed possible.

There was no doubt in my mind we were all exactly where we were supposed to be.

~Jackson~

I was still laughing over the reminder of that New Year's Eve when Cole called out to me. "Jackson, a little help here?"

I looked over to see him holding Olivia, whose lower lip quivered unhappily. I quickly excused myself from Holly and Gemma and ran over to see what the problem was.

"What's going on, Livy?" I asked as I scooped my daughter from Cole's arms. She wasn't the kind of kid who cried for no reason. She was tough, just like her mom.

"Noah," she managed to whimper. "Hand."

Cole and I both turned to four-year-old Noah who was looking at the ground rather than us. "What happened, buddy?" Cole asked him gently, kneeling down to his level. Cole the father was so different to Cole the CEO that I sometimes felt they were two different men entirely.

"She just wants to hold my hand all the time," Noah muttered to the ground. "But I don't want to."

Cole glanced back up at me and we both smiled. "It's tough to be a ladies' man sometimes," he told his son wryly. "But you can tell her no nicely so you don't hurt her feelings, okay?"

Noah nodded, glancing up at his dad finally to make sure he wasn't in too much trouble. When he saw the smile on Cole's face, he relaxed.

I gave Olivia a kiss on the cheek as I tried to explain it to her too. "When Noah says no, it doesn't mean he doesn't like you. He just wants to play on his own sometimes, alright?"

She nodded too, her lip straightening out, so I placed her back on the ground and the two of them ran off again, playing together a moment later like nothing had happened.

We stood together in silence for a moment, watching them, until Cole turned to me. "Are you ready for twice as many kids in just a few weeks?"

"I don't think it matters if I'm ready," I pointed out. "They're coming whether we're ready or not."

Cole nodded. "I suppose you're right. I just hope that Noah's not too disappointed when he's the only boy. He's already finding it hard with just one little girl chasing after him."

My mouth fell open as I turned to him. "How do you know we're not having a boy?"

"Please," he scoffed, trying to hide his smug smile. "You're so easy to read, Jackson. You've never been able to keep anything from me."

That wasn't true. He had never known that Holly was the first and only woman I'd ever slept with, but if he wanted to think he knew everything about me, that was fine. I'd let him think that. It was hardly worth arguing about, not when everything in my life was about as perfect as it could possibly get.

~Cole~

It was far too satisfying to see the look on Jackson's face when he realized his big secret wasn't actually a secret at all. I hadn't told Gemma since I didn't want to ruin Holly's big reveal, but I couldn't resist the chance to let Jackson know that I knew.

"I haven't told anyone else," I clarified out loud for his sake. "And I won't."

"I won't tell Holly that you know either," he agreed. "Just keep your mouth shut."

I simply raised my eyebrows at him before changing the subject.

"My assistant took another three calls today at work about Holly, offering to buy out the Anchor contract from us."

Jackson beamed with pride, as I knew he would. That was exactly why I'd told him.

Holly's designs for their New York townhouse had been featured in one of the top interior design magazines last month and there had been people banging down my door ever since, trying to get me to release her and Gemma from the exclusive contract they'd signed with us. Of course our wives had no intention of walking away from the contract, but I found it satisfying to know the rest of the world appreciated their talents just as much as we did.

They were two of the most gifted creative professionals I'd ever come across, in addition to being beautiful and loving partners.

Although I'd always had wealth and privilege in my life, it wasn't until I had Gemma too that I truly appreciated just how lucky I was.

After letting the kids play a little longer, we returned to our wives who were now both desperate for a restroom, and we walked the few blocks back to Jackson and Holly's house. It impressed me every time I walked in. As much as I loved my apartment with Gemma and all the ways she had made it our own, even I had to acknowledge that their house was something special.

The only thing it really lacked was a room like the one we had at our place.

As soon as the thought crossed my mind, I walked over to my wife who had just come back from the restroom, looking a lot more comfortable.

"I picked up some more of that massage oil you like," I murmured in her ear. "We could put it to use later tonight if you want."

Desire flared in her green eyes as she looked back at me. "Do you even have to ask?"

I didn't. Gemma's sex drive only seemed to increase when she was pregnant, to my delight.

"Until later, then," I told her, smirking just a little at the look of frustration on her face. She was going to be thinking about it for the rest of the night, I was sure of that.

~Gemma~

As much as I always enjoyed spending time with Holly, Jackson and Olivia in their beautiful home, I was almost desperate to get home by the time we finally said our goodbyes. Cole had been teasing me all night ever since he mentioned the massage oil. Every time I looked at him he would rub his hand across the back of his neck or slide it down his thigh.

To anyone else, it wouldn't look like anything unusual, but I knew exactly what it meant. He was enjoying getting me all worked up at the thought of his hands on me, just as he always did.

And I couldn't really complain when I loved it so much.

As soon as we stepped out of the lift into our flat, Cole gave me a quick, hard kiss. "I'll put Noah to bed," he offered, his dark eyes gleaming with anticipation. "You go take a bath and relax."

That sounded like heaven so I quickly agreed. I left the bathroom door open as I sank down into the warm water so I could hear Cole and Noah talking as they went through Noah's bedtime routine. Cole was such an amazing father: patient and supportive and caring, all the things my own father had never been to me. I let my hand drift down to my stomach and imagined the little girl growing inside who had no idea how lucky she was going to be.

After Noah's story and a few dozen more questions that he always seemed to come up with to avoid going to bed, I heard the bedroom door close before Cole appeared in the bathroom doorway. "How are things going in here?" he asked, his eyes wandering over my naked, wet body.

Even as big as I was at the moment, he never made me feel anything less than perfect and wanted.

When I told him I'd finished, he helped me out of the bath and dried me off gently before wrapping me in the towel and leading me towards our private room. After Holly called it a sex dungeon, I thought of it that way too, although I never called it that out loud. It made it sound much kinkier than it actually was, at least in my mind.

Once we were inside, he led me to the specially designed queening chair he'd had made. It was a comfortable chair with a backrest to support me, especially when I was as pregnant as I was then, and the seat had a large opening in it.

After I was comfortably settled, Cole pulled out the massage oil and got to work, rubbing my feet first before working his way across my whole body. I groaned and moaned shamelessly as his fingers eased the aching tension in my body. Only after he'd finished worshipping every inch of me did he give me a deep, hungry kiss and then he disappeared from my view. Although I couldn't see him, I knew where he was: positioning himself beneath my chair where I was exposed and ready for him.

I moaned again as his tongue made contact with my clit. His hands reached around the chair to hold onto my legs as he pulled himself up, thrusting his tongue into me deeply.

"Cole," I cried out as he worked his magic, licking and sucking and kissing every inch he could reach between my legs until I was trembling with my need for release. No matter how many times he did it, it always felt just as exciting as the first.

"Come for me, Gorgeous," he ordered from beneath me. "Come all over my face."

Fuck. My body reacted instantly to his words as it always did, the orgasm gripping me hard as my body contracted in pleasure.

Cole's tongue didn't let up, continuing to lap at me even after my shuddering had stopped. When he stood before me a moment later, his satisfied smile was all it took to get me turned on again.

I could never get enough of him, and after all those years, I knew for certain that I never would.

~Jackson~

A couple of weeks later, Holly and I sat on the couch of our beautiful home, each with a cup of tea as we watched Olivia toddle around under the Christmas tree, playing with the bows on the presents and trying to pick them up, even though some of the boxes were bigger than she was.

"Careful, Livy," I called out for about the twentieth time as she tried to wrap her tiny arms around another large gift.

"Open?" she asked, her bright blue eyes, so like her mother's, looking up at me in hopeful optimism.

"Not yet," I told her with a smile. "Tomorrow."

I looked over at Holly, expecting her to be smiling too, but instead she grimaced while rubbing her stomach. It wasn't the first time she'd done so that afternoon.

"Everything okay?" I asked, trying not to worry. I knew that when I got worried, it only stressed her out and she didn't need any extra stress.

"Just a twinge," she assured me. "Nothing serious."

We talked a bit more about our plans for the next day. We'd be having a quiet morning at home, just the three of us, before going over to Gemma and Cole's for a big Christmas lunch. No matter how much Cole and I tried to convince our British wives that the big meal should be at supper time, they insisted on having the turkey in the middle of the day instead.

Holly's hand continued to massage her stomach until I couldn't help asking again, "Are you sure you're okay?"

"There's some tension," she admitted. "It must just be Braxton Hicks though. I'm not due for a couple more weeks."

I knew that, but I also didn't think we needed to take any risks. "Why don't we go to the hospital anyway and just have them take a look?"

Holly groaned. "On Christmas Eve? That's no fun."

I batted my eyelashes at her to make her laugh. "For me? Please?"

Holly rolled her eyes at my theatrics. "You're worse than Liv is, but if you really want to, we can go."

I quickly called over to the hospital to let them know we were coming. Cole had insisted on making all the arrangements for the birth, just as he had done for Olivia's birth, and just as he had for Gemma, whose due date had already passed. For once, I didn't fight him when he offered to help. When it came to Holly and my girls, I could swallow my pride.

As we piled into the taxi, Holly's face scrunched up in discomfort again. "Okay, this might actually be happening. That was a pretty big one."

Excitement rushed through me even as I held her hand sympathetically. Were we really about to meet our new daughter? That would be the most amazing Christmas present ever.

At the hospital, we were quickly shown to our private birthing suite, and it wasn't long before the doctor confirmed that my beautiful wife was, in fact, in labour. The doctor warned us it might still be a while before excusing herself, saying she had another patient to check on. After getting Holly settled and comfortable, I asked if she needed anything.

"I'm okay for now, but Liv is probably hungry."

"I'll take her to get some food and for a bit of a walk," I offered. "But call me right away if anything changes, okay?"

She promised she would and I picked up our little girl and headed out into the hallway, where I bumped almost straight into Cole and Noah.

"What are you doing here?" The words came out of both our mouths almost simultaneously.

"Gemma's down there," Cole explained, pointing to an open door just down the hall. "Looks like it's happening tonight. Holly?"

"Right behind me," I told him, pointing to the open door I'd just left. Cole took a step to the right until he could see her and gave her a wave.

"Is Gem really here?" Holly called out in excitement. "Can I see her?"

Cole and I exchanged glances. "Is that allowed?" I whispered. The doctor had just told Holly she should stay in bed.

Cole smirked at me. "With the amount I give this hospital? It's allowed if I say it's allowed."

Though I rolled my eyes, I knew he wasn't exaggerating. His foundation, the one he had originally set up just to put me through college, was one of the largest donors in the city to a lot of good causes, including the hospital. They would bend over backwards to do whatever he asked.

Sure enough, by the time Liv and I returned from getting supper, Holly had been moved into the same room as Gemma and they were chatting away happily as the nurses came and went.

They'd even set up a small play area in the corner for Noah where his nanny was playing with him, so I sent Liv off to play too while I went to sit next to Holly.

"Are we taking bets on which baby's coming first?" Cole asked, earning him a dirty look from both women.

"I think you'd be better off taking bets on which of you is going to get told off worst for getting us into this mess in the first place," Gemma countered, giving her husband a teasing glare.

Cole found Miracle on 34th Street on TV and we laughed about the kids' visit to see Santa earlier that week. Liv had been absolutely terrified, but as soon as we left, she wanted to go right back and see him again.

Soon, Gemma's contractions grew more intense, and Holly's followed not long afterwards. Noah's nanny took him and Liv down the hall to another room where they could rest while Cole and I did our best to make our wives as comfortable as possible.

"Remind me why I ever thought it was a good idea to do this again?" Holly asked as she squeezed my hand so hard that I thought I might need a doctor myself before long.

"Because you love me and our family?" I suggested gently, kissing her forehead. "You're doing amazing, Holly. I'm so proud of you."

It took some time, a bit of screaming and quite a few tears, including some from me, but finally there were two beautiful, perfect little girls in the room with us. Cole and Gemma cuddled their daughter while I watched in awe as Holly held ours, her tiny little sleeping face one of the most beautiful things I had ever seen in my life.

I had to say 'one of' because her mother still took the top spot, always and forever.

Having been born on December 24th, we decided to name our daughter Noelle, while Gemma and Cole settled on Eve.

"What time is it?" Gemma asked suddenly, making us all laugh.

"Are we keeping you from something?" her husband smirked at her.

"I mean: is it Christmas yet?"

That was a good question, actually. I'd lost track of time, and apparently Cole had too. He pulled out his phone to check. "Just after midnight," he confirmed. "Merry Christmas everyone."

"Merry Christmas," I murmured back before giving both Holly and our new daughter a kiss as I said it to them too.

There could hardly be a more perfect way to start our Christmas Day. Looking around the room, surrounded by people I loved, I wasn't sure I had ever been happier than at that moment.

Sometimes, people found love when they weren't looking, but sometimes, it turned out to be exactly where they looked for it.

~~THE END~~

IF YOU ENJOYED THIS...

The romance continues in the next book in the series, Tinsel Temptation, following Holly and Jackson's daughter, Olivia, and Cole and Gemma's son, Noah.

Turn the page for a preview from the first chapter!

TINSEL TEMPTATION

~Olivia~

The day I'd been waiting for had finally arrived. As my roommate came bounding into our shared dorm room with a Santa hat on her head, I knew what she was going to say before the words were out of her mouth.

"Liv, your hot dad is here!"

Alright, I didn't expect her to say *exactly* that. "Please, Tessa, I just ate. I don't want to think about my dad like that."

Her lips pressed into a pretend pout as she flopped down on my bed despite her bed being only six feet away. "You can ignore the facts if you want to, but I swear he's going to be mobbed by half the dorm if you don't get down there soon. The sharks with daddy issues are already circling."

Luckily, I'd been packed for hours already. I'd been counting down to that day for months, ever since my mom told me we were going to spend Christmas with the Stamers up at Aunt Isabel's farm.

Technically, Isabel wasn't my aunt, but 'my dad's best friend's sister' sounded more complicated than it needed to be. Basically, my dad, Jackson, was best friends with the man I called Uncle Cole, while their two wives - my mom, Holly, and Cole's wife, Gemma - were also best friends. Because they were all so close, our two families had grown up together. Gemma and Cole also had two kids close in age to my sister and I. In fact, my sister, Noelle, had been born on the very same day as Eve Stamer, and they had always been best friends too.

The prospect of spending time with all of them excited me, but one person in particular stood out as the one I *really* couldn't wait to see. The one who made my stomach flutter whenever he crossed my mind: Noah Stamer.

Two and a half years older than me, Noah was absolutely perfect in my eyes, and I'd been in love with him for as long as I could remember. From the first moment I realized that I could pick the person I got to marry, I wanted to pick Noah.

It took a little while longer for me to realize that he got to have some say in the matter too.

We were very close as kids; not quite siblings, but closer than friends. Even as we got older, we still had fun together, but I suspected that deep down, he still saw me as the little girl who used to chase after him and force him to play with me and my dolls. Meanwhile, I'd begun to think about him in very different ways.

That distance between us only got worse when he went to college. The few things we had in common seemed to disappear as he got a whole new set of friends and new interests. When he came home to visit, I would try to talk to him, but everything I had to say sounded childish, even to me. I didn't know how to connect with him anymore, and when I suggested that we keep in touch by text, he blew me off. He did it nicely, to be fair, but it stung all the same.

For two years, I'd suffered, but that year, things were different. Having started at college too, halfway through my first year, I had my own stories about campus parties and midterms and everything else that made up college life. Finally, we were on a level playing field again and I couldn't wait to hang out with him that Christmas. It would be the first time we'd seen each other since the summer, and I simply knew that the time had come for us to make a real connection.

Whether he realized it yet or not, Noah was finally going to notice me.

Giving Tessa a big hug and wishing her a merry Christmas, I ran down the stairs to where my dad waited. Tessa had been exaggerating a little bit about the girls circling, but not by much. Quite a few kept glancing over at him, pretending not to be, and if I wanted to be completely honest and objective, I could see why.

Although he was approaching fifty, my dad was still in great shape. His slightly curly brown hair had a sprinkling of grey but his warm eyes and his kind smile made him look younger than his age. Dressed in a well-cut winter coat with a scarf around his neck, he looked like he'd stepped off the pages of a gentleman's magazine, and if he weren't my dad, I would have to agree he *was* kinda hot.

He also looked completely oblivious to the attention he was receiving. My dad only had eyes for my mom; they were ridiculously in love even after more than twenty years together, which, as a teenager, kind of grossed me out. I found their public displays of affection embarrassing, but with a few more years behind me, I had to admit they were pretty sweet together.

If I could find someone who looked at me the way my dad looked at my mom, I would be pretty damn lucky, and if Noah Stamer ever looked at me that way, I could die a happy woman.

"You ready to go, Livy?" My dad's face lit up as he saw me and he reached out to take the bag from my hand.

"I can't wait." That was the truth, though he didn't need to know exactly why.

He had come on his own to pick me up while my mom and Noelle travelled with Aunt Gemma, Uncle Cole and Eve up from the city. Noah would be driving himself and arriving a little later.

As we drove the few hours up to the farm, there was hardly a moment's silence. My dad wanted to know everything about my classes and my friends and I told him about all of it in detail. We had the same sense of humour and we'd always gotten along well. He'd always been the one I ran to when things went wrong. Though I loved my mom too, I couldn't really argue with anyone who said I was a total daddy's girl.

He asked about men and I could be honest with him there too: I'd been on some dates but I hadn't found anyone special yet. Tessa claimed my single status was because my standards were impossibly high, and maybe she had a point. After all, I wanted someone like Noah, but no one could compare to Noah besides Noah himself. He was truly one-of-a-kind.

So, although I went out with other guys and made out with some of them, it never turned into anything serious. I hadn't slept with any of them either, though I didn't share *that* particular piece of information with my dad. We had a 'don't ask, don't tell' policy when it came to my sex life and his, although at least he actually had one.

I was still waiting for the right moment to lose my virginity, a moment I hoped with all my might would happen in the next few days.

Finally, we pulled onto the snow-covered drive up to Isabel's gorgeous house, fully decked out for Christmas, as always. Fresh pine garlands draped between the columns of the porch, the outside trees were covered in lights and weather-proof decorations, and a large wreath hung on the front door. By the time we got out of the car, the porch had filled up with people waiting for us.

"There she is!" My mom's British accent rang out above the general cries of greeting and I quickly found myself swallowed up in hugs from her, Isabel, Gemma, Noelle, Eve and Isabel's daughter, Jennifer. Meanwhile, Cole hung back, watching the whole scene with a hint of bemusement as he said hello to my dad.

"Merry Christmas, Olivia," Cole said to me when I finally got myself disentangled from the others. "Are you ready to come work for me yet?"

We had a long-standing joke about how I would follow my dad into the hotel business and be Noah's right-hand-woman, just like my dad was Cole's second-in-command. To be honest, I didn't really care that much about hotels, but the idea of working with Noah definitely carried some appeal, so I hadn't completely ruled it out either.

"Not quite yet, Uncle Cole," I replied with a smile as we stepped inside. The pine scent was even stronger than it had been outside, coming from the gorgeous eight-foot tree that dominated the hall, and Christmas music played in the background, lending the whole scene an extra bit of festive ambiance. Isabel had gone all out. "I've only written my first exams, there's still a long way to go."

"A formality," he assured me as he headed towards the kitchen, the social centre of the house.

I hurried to keep up with him, my socks sliding on the polished hardwood floors as I kept my voice low so the others wouldn't hear. "Do you know when Noah's getting here?"

His lips tightened, which was about as much emotion as he ever displayed. "Actually, I just heard from him. He won't be arriving until tomorrow. I told him if he misses Christmas Eve, he'll break his mother's heart and I'll kick his ass, so let's hope he listens to that, at least."

Gemma might be disappointed, but she wasn't the only one; my heart sank too. I had to wait another whole day? That felt like a lifetime when I had been so ready for that night. Apparently, I wore my best underwear for nothing.

What could be so important to keep Noah at school an extra day? Hopefully, whatever had come up would be taken care of by early the next day and we could still have most of Christmas Eve together. As far as I was concerned, he couldn't arrive a moment too soon.

~Noah~

The sun shone brightly on Christmas Eve morning as I threw my bags in my car, ready for the drive up to my aunt's farm.

"Have a good time," Tate called out from the porch of the house we shared. "Though how you're going to go ten days without getting laid, I have no idea."

His exaggeration made me roll my eyes. "I have done it before, you know."

"What, when you were six?" he shot back with a laugh. His disbelief wasn't entirely unreasonable; since we'd moved into the house we shared, I certainly hadn't gone that long and neither had he.

"Last night should keep me satisfied for a while," I replied, laughing as his eyes lit up at the memory.

My dad had been pissed off at me when I delayed my trip home, but how could I refuse? Twins had been on the fuckit list Tate and I shared since we became friends and realized we were into the same kind of things, and while we were out the day before doing some last-minute shopping, we met an amazing pair of twins who were *very* willing to help us cross that particular item off our list. I couldn't pass up the opportunity.

The fuckit list – essentially a bucket list for all the kinky shit we wanted to do before we had to grow up and be professional – had been Tate's idea and he took it very seriously. He even had it written down, though that seemed dangerous to me. As the future CEO of Stamer Hotels, I didn't need all my college antics getting out in the open, but he swore the file was unhackable, and reluctantly, I let it go. My dad had taught me the value of discretion, one of many lessons I'd learned from him that I took very seriously.

Just like how I always used protection since my dad liked to remind me that I was the product of his own forgetfulness. He meant it as a joke and I took it that way; he and my mom loved me, I'd never had any doubt about that, and I knew they never regretted having me. However, I also knew he wasn't kidding: he really had forgotten just one time and ended up with a kid out of it, and I had no intention of letting that happen to me.

I couldn't imagine being tied to any one woman that way, at least not at that point in my life. Eventually, I would have to be, I supposed, if I wanted to have an heir to take over the family business, but that all seemed far in the future. Up to that point, I'd never met anyone who held my interest both in and out of the bedroom that way.

"You're sure you don't want to come?" I asked Tate as I moved around to the driver's side of the car. I'd already offered to bring him along, partly to keep me company on the drive and partly because I felt bad that he had no family of his own to go home to. Our home lives could hardly be more different. Where I grew up the adored and pampered eldest child of a wealthy, successful couple, his dad was in jail for killing his mom during a domestic violence episode that went too far. The story was horrible, and he'd only told me about it one night when he got drunk and lost his filter.

Nobody else would ever guess at that dark history from spending time with him. On the outside, he was cool, confident and laid-back, like the world had never been anything but kind to him. Still, I suspected his past was part of what drew him to the kind of lifestyle we'd both embraced: a need for physical pleasure to distract him from his emotional pain.

That, and the fact that it came with no strings and no attachments. Neither of us dated; we weren't interested in that.

"Nah, I'm good," Tate replied, turning me down once again. "I've got the whole house to myself so maybe I'll call one of the guys over and finally cross number twenty seven off the list. I've been dreaming about it lately."

Since he knew I'd kill him for doing that one without me, he obviously didn't mean it. "Keep dreaming. I'll see you after New Year's."

With a last wave goodbye, I got in the car and headed out of town, out onto the highway that would take me to the farm.

The lack of sex aside, the week actually promised to be a really good one. Both my mom and my aunt were crazy about Christmas and they always made sure we had a great time. My cousins would be there along with my sister, Eve, and the Hanmer girls too. We were all pretty close in age and I always enjoyed getting a chance to kick back with them. There would be lots of snow and we had an ongoing snowball war that had been in progress for at least ten years already. Each Christmas we were together, we simply picked up where we left off, with my team consisting of me, my cousin, Darryn, and Olivia Hanmer.

A smile spread across my face as soon as Olivia crossed my mind. Her fierce competitiveness had made her a natural pick for my team. Every year, she had a new strategy on how we were going to overcome our 'enemies', meaning our two sisters and my cousin, Jennifer. It didn't matter to her who they were: if they were in our way, they were going down.

Even as a little kid, Olivia had to be the best at everything, and she usually succeeded. A star volleyball player, she'd earned herself an athletic scholarship to Princeton, though she qualified for an academic one as well. She'd graduated from high school at the top of her class in the spring, somehow managing to be both class president and homecoming queen at the same time. With her long blonde hair and blue eyes, she looked like an angel until you tried to beat her at something and then she'd turn into your worst nightmare.

Once, Tate had caught a glimpse of a picture of her I kept on my phone and his eyes nearly popped out of his head. "Where the fuck have you been hiding her?"

I quickly turned the screen off so he couldn't get a closer look. From experience, I knew that the longer you looked, the more beautiful she seemed. "She's a friend of the family. Off-limits."

Though he groaned in disappointment, he accepted that answer. He knew I never had any problem sharing, so if I said no, it meant no. And the truth was that I didn't think of Olivia like that, like one of the girls I usually hooked up with. She inhabited a completely different part of my life and she knew nothing about my particular proclivities. On the rare occasions I did try to imagine a future where my kids and I were the ones coming up to Isabel's farm at Christmas, my wife usually bore a striking resemblance to Olivia.

However, it wouldn't be Olivia herself, because as much as she was off-limits to Tate, she wasn't an option for me either. Her dad had made that very clear to me.

Usually, Jackson was the friendliest, most easygoing guy I'd ever met, but at Olivia's graduation, he'd caught me staring at her a moment too long, and he laid down the law, his expression more severe than I'd ever seen it before. "I like you, Noah, but I love my daughter a lot more. You're not looking for anything serious right now and that's fine, but if you even think of messing around with Olivia on a whim, I will not only cut your balls off, I'll take Stamer Hotels down from the inside. I've worked there twenty-five years, you know I can do it. Are we clear?"

"Yes, sir." It would be hard not to be, since he hadn't left much to the imagination.

So, even though Olivia hinted at wanting to keep in touch once she went to college, I put her off. Subjecting myself to temptation would be pointless when the stakes were so high.

Still, I had to admit I was looking forward to seeing her that day. Maybe she even had a boyfriend that she'd brought home with her. That would probably be for the best, to help remind me that we were friends and nothing more. That was all a girl like her and a guy like me would ever be. Sweet and innocent, she deserved someone who would appreciate that.

She deserved someone very different than me.

I half-expected a big welcoming committee as I pulled up the drive to the farmhouse, but although the house looked as festive as ever, not a soul was in sight. After I parked and grabbed my bags from the back seat, one bag with my clothes and the other full of presents, I headed inside.

"Hello?" I called out as I walked through the front door. The scent of freshly-baked gingerbread wafted through the air, mingling with the pine of the Christmas tree, but the house was unusually quiet.

"Noah?" My dad was the one who responded, appearing from around the corner with a stern expression. He might be playing tough, but I knew him well enough to know that he was happy to see me. "It's about time."

"You already gave me the lecture," I reminded him as he came over to give me a hug. We were practically the same height; actually, I was pretty sure I was a tiny bit taller, though he'd never admit it.

"Hey, Noah! Glad you could make it." Jackson appeared next, a beer in his hand and he quickly joined us to give me a hug too. "How was the drive?"

"Fine," I assured him, glancing around to see who else might be nearby, but it appeared to be just the two of them. "Where is everyone?"

"They went out for a sleigh ride," he explained. "You just missed them. We volunteered to stay behind and keep an eye on the cookies."

"And the football game," my dad added with a smirk. "Come and join us."

"I will in a minute," I promised. "Let me just run this stuff upstairs. I'm in the green room?"

Aunt Isabel's guest rooms were all colour-coded, like a B&B, and the green room had been mine for years. Once my dad nodded in confirmation, I headed up there with my bags. Everything was clean and fresh as always, and the scattered memories of a dozen past Christmases flitted across my mind. Something about being there always made me feel like a kid again. Maybe it always would.

After putting everything away, I started to head back downstairs, but as I passed by the open door of the room next to mine, something caught my eye: a bit of black lace on top of the white dresser. Taking a quick look around to make sure no one else was there, I ducked into the room to take a closer look.

As I'd suspected from the hall, the fabric was a pair of rather seductive panties. I had seen enough of them in my time to be able to recognize them from a distance. Clothes folded like that on top of the dresser usually meant that Aunt Isabel had done laundry and left it there for whoever was staying in the room. That room usually stayed empty, and having only a single pair of panties cleaned was a little strange, but the thought crossed my mind that they might be my sister's and that quickly made me back out of the room again.

Shaking my head at myself, I headed down the stairs. In that house, nothing remotely kinky should be crossing my mind. The two parts of my life were completely separate and I wanted it to keep it that way.

Nothing good could come from mixing the two together, I knew that for sure.

~Olivia~

The sleigh ride had always been one of my favourite parts of Christmas at Isabel's farm. As we glided along the snowy path, my mom and Aunt Gemma were singing British Christmas pop songs, making us all laugh as they argued over the lyrics. The afternoon was beautifully sunny, not too cold but not warm enough that the snow was melting either, and it would be perfect weather to pick up our snowball fight as soon as Noah arrived.

Although I always enjoyed it, I had been tempted to skip the sleigh ride that day just in case Noah showed up while we were gone, but I couldn't think of a good excuse. My mom would want to know why I didn't want to go, and since I couldn't exactly tell her the truth, in the end, I didn't even try to get out of it.

However, as the horses came back around the front of the house, the silver Mercedes caught my eye, a car that hadn't been there before, and my heart leapt in anticipation. He'd arrived! That initial joy was quickly followed by a wish that I had brought a mirror to double check how I looked before I saw him. Was my hair messed up from the wind? Did my lips look dried out from the cold? I quickly wet them, running my tongue across them, top and bottom. I wanted to look perfect for the first time he saw me, because in my dreams, as soon as he saw me, he would wonder how he had never noticed me that way before.

In my head, the whole encounter had been all planned out, played over in my imagination a hundred times or more. Noah just needed to follow the script.

The men must have been waiting for us because they came out onto the porch as we pulled up outside the house and my heart skipped a beat as I caught sight of Noah at last. How could he possibly have gotten better-looking since I saw him last? He had a lot of his dad in him, the height and build and the dark hair and strong jawline. However, he had his mom's sparkling green eyes which somehow softened his look, making him less imposing than Cole and even more appealing, at least to me.

Those eyes suggested that a playful man lay beneath the hard exterior, and I desperately wanted to find out to what extent that was true.

"Noah!" Gemma cried out in excitement, hopping down from the sleigh to go hug her son. Eve went next and soon, he was surrounded. Meanwhile, I took my time, waiting until everyone else had left and lowering myself slowly from the back of the sleigh, hoping that if he happened to glance my way, he would get a nice view of my ass in the jeans I'd picked out especially for that day.

Everything I'd chosen to wear had been selected with one message in mind: Olivia Hanmer was all grown up.

It seemed to be working, because when I turned around, he had stepped free of the rest of the group and had his eyes fixed on me, a half-smile on his face. "Hey, Liv."

"Hey, yourself." I gave my best confident, flirty smile, the one I'd been practicing in the mirror, hoping I didn't have gingerbread dough on my teeth or anything. "You finally made it."

"Yeah. Sorry I'm late." He swallowed as his eyes scanned me, and I wished once again that I could see what I looked like. "I hope you didn't start the snowball fight without me."

"Of course not. I need to fill you in on this year's plan before we begin."

That made him laugh, his eyes twinkling as he did, which set my stomach fluttering. "I figured you would. Let's go talk strategy, then."

Doing my best to hide my giddy smile, I stepped past him and headed towards the front door. I could have sworn I felt his hand against my back through my bulky winter coat, just for a second, but it quickly disappeared.

Everyone else had already begun to assemble in the kitchen so we headed there too after I'd shed my coat and boots at the door, the melting snow leaving tiny puddles on the floor. Noah was accosted by his cousins as soon as we entered Isabel's huge kitchen, wanting to catch up with him, and I watched in frustration as he sat down with them around the island in the centre of the room. Sure, they were family, but I wanted him to choose to spend time with me first. Instead, my mom,

Gemma and Isabel drew me into their conversation, though my gaze continually drifted to Noah's back.

"Everything okay, Livy?" My dad had always been able to read me so I did my best to cover up how I felt with a smile as he walked over to me.

"Yeah, I'm just a little chilled. I think I'm going to go put another layer on."

"Good plan. I think you guys are all getting kicked out soon so the adults can gossip about you."

Leaving the busy kitchen behind, I headed upstairs to the blue room where I was staying that year. Usually, I stayed in the yellow room at the end of the hall but Noah always stayed in the green one, and since I wanted to be as close to him as possible, I'd requested the one next door to him instead. If Isabel thought my request was odd in any way, she didn't mention it.

My underwear on the dresser caught my eye as soon as I walked in, and I quickly swept them into the drawer. Isabel must have left them there; I had put them in the dryer that morning but forgot about them. The last thing I needed was for someone else to catch sight of them, like my dad, for one.

I didn't put them on just yet, figuring I would wait and see how the rest of the afternoon went first. I didn't want to waste them again and end up washing them over and over again, which might start to look suspicious. For the moment, I just needed some warmer pants to wear outside.

"There you are." Noah's deep voice from the doorway sent electricity all through my body as I jumped in surprise. "I thought we were making plans and you disappeared."

As he took a step into my room, my heart began to pound. I had imagined that moment so many times, the two of us alone together in a bedroom, any bedroom, and as he looked around the room curiously, I almost thought his eyes rested a moment on the spot where my panties had previously been sitting. That didn't make any sense, though; I must have imagined it.

"You don't usually stay in this room," he pointed out, his eyes moving back to me in all their startling greenness.

"No, I don't," I agreed, scrambling for a reason I could give him for the change besides the real one. "But it's got a perfect view over the creek where I think we should set up our stronghold this year."

I pointed to the window and, with a smile, he followed me over to it. "Show me."

The two words were simple but full of authority and they sent a shiver down my spine as I imagined him saying them to me in a completely different context. My stomach was going crazy as desire built up even lower, making me glad I hadn't put my best panties back on or they would definitely need to be washed again.

Fuck, I needed to concentrate.

That was a lot easier said than done as he leaned over my shoulder to peer out the window, his firm body giving off heat and his masculine scent flooding my senses.

"Th-there," I stuttered, pointing to the spot I'd chosen. "If they go anywhere between the trees and the house, we'll have a clear shot of them."

He took a deep breath in as he considered it, and I had to fight the urge to lean back against him. Did he feel the magnetism between us? He had to, didn't he? It couldn't all be in my head.

But to my disappointment, he took a step back. "That's a great idea. Let's go get Darryn and get started."

"Sure." I put on a bright smile to cover my true feelings. "I was just going to change my pants."

I could have sworn his pupils dilated a little before his eyes flicked back to the spot on my dresser where my panties had been. "What?"

I gestured down to my jeans. "These will get soaked out in the snow, I'm going to put on something warmer."

He nodded, swallowing again, as if the air were particularly dry. "Right. I'll meet you downstairs, then."

He left the room, closing the door behind him, and I quickly changed into the ski pants I had brought along for just that occasion. When I got back downstairs, everyone else had their winter gear on too; all the younger generation, at least. Our parents had opened some wine and were pretending to be too busy with dinner preparation to join us, but we all knew they just wanted an excuse to talk, as my dad had said.

We must have been outside for hours but it felt like mere minutes with me and Noah working together and laughing together as we tried to take down our opponents. Even when it got dark, we didn't stop, using the Christmas lights from the house as our only illumination. By the time Isabel called us all in to eat, I was exhausted in the best possible way.

Well, maybe the *second*-best possible way. Hopefully, I would be able to make the comparison for myself very soon.

As we peeled off our winter layers at the back door, Noah grinned at me. "We nearly had them surrounded out there. After all these years, I thought it might finally happen."

His smile filled my whole body with warmth. "There's still the rest of the week."

"The whole week," he repeated, his eyes seeming to fill with a heat of their own before he quickly looked away. "I'm going to change into something dry."

That was a good idea, so I followed him up the stairs, each of us going into our own rooms. That time, I *did* put my black lace panties back on. Why the hell not? I might as well think positive. I also put my skinny jeans back on with a form-fitting Christmas sweater my mom had picked out for me; a jumper, as she called it, still holding onto some of her British terms despite having lived in the USA for more than twenty years. After giving my hair a brush, I gave myself a nod of satisfaction in the mirror. Noah would *have* to notice me looking like that.

When I got back into the hall, Noah's door stood open, and a flash of disappointment ran through me that he hadn't waited for me to go back downstairs. It only lasted a second though, until I heard a drawer close and realized he must still be inside. Smoothing down my hair once more, I stepped into the open doorway, and my jaw nearly hit the floor.

He was standing there with his shirt off, a new one in his hands, about to pull it over his head.

It had been a few years since I'd seen him without a shirt on, not since the last beach vacation we all took together, and he had definitely filled out since then. With muscles like that, he must be using the gym on campus nearly every day. His chest and abs were fit and firm and *perfect*, and I very nearly literally began to drool.

Forcing my mouth shut, I knocked on the door so I wouldn't startle him. He looked up in surprise anyway before quickly pulling his shirt over his head. "That was quick."

I shrugged at him. "I already knew what I was going to wear. I'm very decisive."

He smiled again, almost to himself. "I bet you are."

Clearing his throat, he stepped towards me as my heart began to beat faster. His eyes were fixed on me as he drew closer, so close that I could feel his body heat once again. Along with the memory of that chest beneath his sweater, it had me aching in all the right places.

"Liv?"

He said my name softly, his face only inches from mine.

"Yeah?" I resisted the very strong urge to lick my lips even though they were incredibly dry. I didn't want to look *too* obvious.

"You're in the way."

I blinked at him in confusion for a second before I realized what he meant: I was completely blocking the door.

"Sorry," I mumbled, taking a step back, and he walked past me, throwing a smirk over his shoulder.

"Let's go, they'll all be waiting for us."

Right. Dinner. Family. That was what we were there for.

"I'm coming."

Those two words nearly made him trip over his feet, grabbing hold of the banister at the top of the staircase just before he fell down the stairs.

When he glanced back at me, his expression almost looked pained, but he didn't say anything. He simply stared at me for a moment before turning and continuing down the stairs.

MORE FROM THE AUTHOR

<u>Contemporary Romance – 18+</u>

Callahan Series
A Matter of Time
A Piece of Land
A Change of Heart
A Work of Art

Christmas in the City Series
Mistletoe Mistake
Candy Cane Challenge
Tinsel Temptation
Gingerbread Gamble
Stocking Standoff

Standalones
Leading Lady
A Set of Three
Charity Case
Hired Lover

<u>Contemporary Romance – New Adult/Clean</u>

It Figures duet
It Figures
Figuring It Out

<u>Historical Romance – 18+</u>

Lady in Waiting Series
Lady in Waiting
King in Training
Princess in Hiding

<u>Paranormal Romance – 18+</u>

Cold Lake Pack Series
The Curse and the Prophecy
The Spell and the Legacy
The Dream and the Destiny

Mismatched Mates Series
Mismatched Mates
Misguided Motives
Mistaken Meanings

Serena's Story
The Alpha's Second Chance
The Returned Mate
The Vampire's Consort

Sacrifice Series
Blood Donor
Life Giver

<u>Paranormal Romance – New Adult/Clean</u>

The Alpha's Prey

KEEP IN TOUCH

My Patreon account has daily updates from my works-in-progress, bonus chapters and more – join me there to comment and read along as my next books are being written: www.patreon.com/melodytyden

You can find and follow me on Facebook at: facebook.com/melodytyden

Join the Facebook group Melody's Romance Corner for fun games, interaction with the author and exclusive news and excerpts.

You can also sign up to my newsletter at www.melodytyden.com for all the latest news.